PO[illegible]ED ON THE MOOR

A British private detective mystery

RIC BRADY

THE BOOK FOLKS

Published by The Book Folks

London, 2025

This book is a work of fiction. Names, characters, businesses, organizations, places and events are either the product of the author's imagination or are used fictitiously. Any resemblance to actual persons, living or dead, events or locales is entirely coincidental. The spelling is British English.

ISBN 978-1-80462-336-7

www.thebookfolks.com

POISONED ON THE MOOR *is the seventh standalone mystery in The Yorkshire detective mystery series by Ric Brady. The full list of titles, in order of publication, is as follows:*

MURDER ON A YORKSHIRE MOOR
BUTCHER ON THE MOOR
MISSING ON ILKLEY MOOR
DETECTIVE ON THE MOOR
COLD CASE ON THE MOOR
SHOOTER ON THE MOOR
POISONED ON THE MOOR

More details can be found at the back of this book.

Chapter One

The dying sun cast streaks of peach, pink, and scarlet across the sky. Sarah Hardy studied the formations of the clouds, wondering if they foretold a 'shepherd's delight' for the following day or something else. Then the thought struck her – she wouldn't live long enough to find out.

It was late spring, and the evening was too warm to wear cardigans but not warm enough for summer dresses. She had plumped for both, a white-and-red striped dress she had bought a few summers ago.

Stepping out of the back entrance of Cragg Hall, her barn conversion up on Addingham Moorside, she joined her guests in her large back garden. They were all drinking glasses of the punch she had made that afternoon, which was a relief, as she feared nobody would touch it. She had also made some potato salad, which was in a big bowl that rested on the outdoor table, next to a bowl filled with fresh lettuces. Dessert was an apricot tart she had spent all morning preparing.

The energy levels of her guests had begun to drop, despite the booze and music. It was that moment at a dinner party when the guests had nearly had their fill of alcohol and were getting hungry and restless. Luckily, the sausages and burgers were sizzling on the gas barbecue near the far wall. The wind wafted the greasy smoke away from Sarah and her invitees and into the opposite field.

They had just suffered through several weeks of wind and rain when doing anything on the patio, let alone sitting out to eat, had not been an option. However, a few days beforehand, the weather forecast said the upcoming May Bank Holiday weekend would be mostly settled.

Sarah had invited eight friends and all of them had turned up, although Ralph and his wife Claire couldn't get a babysitter so they had already left. They had brought their one-year-old with them, which had changed the dynamic slightly, as little William was the only child in Sarah's circle of friends. She felt slightly sorry for Claire, who rarely left the house these days. Sarah was at least grateful that she would never have that problem.

She felt a pang of grief. What about the life she had felt destined to have? Those two blonde twins her imagination had concocted. When she had dreamt of her future, there they were – two faceless and formless children. Sarah knew it was silly to grieve imaginary twins, but she had always felt a maternal need to care for them. Well, those two children would forever remain faceless and formless. Fragments of her own mind that would soon too cease to exist.

She shook away her tragic thoughts and searched between the plates, bowls, and jugs on the outside table for her glass of punch. She found what she thought was hers and gulped some down. She slyly wiped away a stray tear before her guests noticed. She couldn't let them know their host was in the midst of a nervous breakdown. Her shoulder knocked into someone, and she spun round to see it was just Tom.

He interrupted his rugby conversation with Lee to ask if she was okay. Clearly, he had been watching her. He always did.

He wrapped his muscly arm around her waist and pulled her close to him. As their bodies touched, she remembered those two times she had been with him. His scent, which was almost hidden by his aftershave, made her feel hungry. She pressed her hip against his.

"Are you alright?" he asked, looking down into her eyes. His lips were close to hers.

She nodded and sipped her punch. Passion fruit and gin with a dash of honey. She had juiced everything herself that afternoon and now realised she had laced it with too much liquor; her senses were already numbed.

Tom's arm hung around her waist while he restarted his conversation with Lee, comparing the Leeds and Bradford rugby teams. A subject of which Sarah knew very little. She much preferred Australian football. Now that was a sport.

She drunkenly rested her hand on Tom's bulky shoulder. He was what she thought a man ought to be: tall, rugged, handsome, strong… Everything that her husband wasn't.

She then caught Mark glaring at her from his seat across the table. Mark had been talking business with Noura, a conversation which, by the look of her face, she hadn't followed. Mark must've broken off his monologue to stare at Sarah; his eyes full of spite.

Sarah got the message, stepped away from Tom and patted his back.

"It's time we eat. Hey, people!" she shouted at her guests.

Everyone looked round, some wearing amused looks.

"Let's go eat! Go help yourselves. Plates are over there, and Mark will serve the meat. Won't you, Mark?" She didn't look at Mark's expression, and, instead, watched her guests follow her instructions. As they congregated around the barbecue, Sarah slipped away from the table.

A gentle breeze rustled her dress as she ambled down the stone steps to the lower terrace of her sloping garden. Her guests remained on the upper level near the barbecue. She caught glimpses of them through the railings that surrounded the patio.

She crossed the lawn on the lower terrace until she came to the drystone wall at the end of her garden. She sat on the wall's coping stones and surveyed Cragg Hall above her.

She and Mark had bought the old barn conversion several years earlier. He was from this area and had always wanted to set down roots here, despite promising her that one day they would move to her home country. She should have realised long ago that it would never come to pass.

She turned away from her two-hundred-year-old house and her guests around the barbecue and faced the valley down the hill. She felt the wind in her long hair. The River Wharfe, which snaked between the buildings in Addingham and Ilkley, sparkled in the fading sun.

She had never wanted to die here. She always believed she would grow old in Sydney like her grandmother, full of piss and vinegar. Those plans of living out her twilight years in a Sydney suburb would be consigned to the same bin that contained her imaginary twins.

It's funny how life turned out, she thought, downing the last of her punch.

And with one last look of that Yorkshire valley, she closed her eyes and fell backwards, letting the wind blow through her hair.

She landed on her back in her garden and never opened her eyes again.

Chapter Two

Henry Ward was sitting in his luxe folding camping chair in his backyard, happy to be getting some fresh air and making the most of the lack of rain. He had recently bought the chair with the intention of using it when he went fly fishing. He wanted to have something comfortable to sit in while resting beside the riverbank, watching his fly bob up and down on the surface of the water. But considering he rarely went fishing these days, the chair had become his most-used piece of outdoor furniture.

The late evening sky didn't appear to threaten anything but another good day tomorrow, which made a change for West Yorkshire. The sun was faint yet quite warm, and a book on Britain's rare birds rested open on his lap.

He had been doing some research, as reports had come in about sightings of an Australian kookaburra in the area. The book had described the bird as a large kingfisher-type bird, with brown wings speckled with aqua-blue spots. Fewer than ten of them were known to live in the UK. All of them were presumed escapees from zoos or private collections. Some had been spotted down south in Surrey, while others had been seen in Scotland.

That was until a week ago, when a bird spotter in Thirsk heard the kookaburra's distinctive cry – which sounds like a cartoon character's manic laugh. That was only thirty miles away as the crow flies.

The buzz in Addingham's birdwatching committee, of which Henry was a semi-serious member, was that the kookaburra could pass through Addingham on its way south – in search of warmer climes.

That would be a find. Imagine a rare Australian bird catching fish in the River Wharfe.

He smiled at the thought of it, his eyes half-closed as he fought the urge to doze off. He was mildly aware of a honeybee buzzing around his potted lavender.

Tessa, his wire fox terrier, was curled up on the paving stone next to him, fast asleep. She occasionally whimpered as she hunted imaginary hares in the fields of her dreams.

Henry had no idea what time it was. Cracking open an eye, he guessed it was late evening, as he'd had his dinner around 5 p.m., and he must have been outside for a while now. He would sit there for a little bit longer, as the air was starting to cool. The faint smell of barbecued meet hung in the air, suggesting his neighbours on Main Street were making the most of the pleasant evening.

It was the start of the Early May Bank Holiday weekend, and Henry had no plans. That was not to say he hadn't been socially active the past month. He had made it down to Bristol to stay with his son's family for a weekend. Two colourful drawings his grandchildren had made now decorated his fridge door. One was of Henry and the other was of Tessa, but Henry had trouble working out which was which.

Next weekend, Henry was due to visit his estranged daughter Carol and her family in London. He had not seen her for eleven years, not since Henry's ex-wife, Pat, divorced him. Carol had taken her mother's side in the dispute, while Dean, Henry's son, had tried to ride both horses. But he too had mostly leant in his mother's direction.

It felt good to be back in touch with his family. Henry had been so ashamed of all he had put them through, what with his drinking, the divorce, and his forced retirement from the police after a corruption inquiry. He had pretty much imprisoned himself in his cottage as a consequence and had almost succeeded in becoming a hermit. If it hadn't been for his neighbour, Jean Whitehead, he would have become one of those strange old men who never left their homes.

He glanced over to the back of Jean's house. She was staying with her second son, Chris, in Cambridge for the weekend. He was a professor in a subject Jean had never mentioned, and Henry had often wondered why that was. Anyway, Jean had told Henry to keep an eye on her house. Which he would do. Not that there was much crime in Addingham. Well, occasionally the odd murder happened, which often necessitated Henry's involvement to catch the killer. It was more that Henry felt it necessary to involve himself. Much to the disappointment of the local police. But that had changed recently, as Detective Superintendent Samuel Murphy had asked Henry to help them investigate difficult cases in an unofficial capacity when the need arose. The local police force was struggling to meet the impossible demands they were under, and Murphy thought Henry could fill the gap.

But since Murphy had struck that deal with Henry, a few months ago, he hadn't given him a case worth his time. The most 'interesting' one he had been offered was a string of cash machine robberies from local banks and newsagents, which Henry declined. Henry had been a detective chief inspector who had led inquiries into murders and wouldn't waste his intellect looking into cash machine robberies.

Oh well, Henry thought. He tapped the open book on forensics on his lap and closed his eyes. Murphy would call him up at some point with a case worth his skills. Hopefully after a long, restful Bank Holiday weekend.

He could do a spot of fishing tomorrow, Henry realised, half asleep. Or, if he couldn't find the right gear from his cellar, why didn't he just move his comfortable camping chair to a secluded spot near the river and doze off there?

Not a bad idea, he told himself, enjoying the fresh breeze that carried the scent of lavender blow over him.

An irritating buzzing sound stirred him. It was at a lower frequency than the honeybee around his plants, and Henry realised it was his mobile phone in the kitchen.

He ignored it and kept his eyes closed. It was 7 p.m. on a Bank Holiday Saturday. Whatever it was could wait.

The phone's vibration stopped and then restarted immediately.

"Bloody crumbs," he said, hauling himself out of his chair.

He startled Tessa out of her dream as he stepped over her, and she grumbled in annoyance at not catching the hare she had been chasing.

Henry wandered into his kitchen, and his stomach dropped when he saw Detective Sergeant Ellie Hargreaves' name on his phone. Not only was she Murphy's minion, but she was also a foul-mouthed detective whose moods were as dark as her jet-black hair.

Henry took a breath, said goodbye to his lazy weekend, and answered. "DS Hargreaves. To what do I owe–"

"Shut it, Henry. There's no time for chit-chat."

This wasn't her normal greeting. Henry sensed something very bad had happened. "Are you alright?"

"Get up to Addingham Moorside. Cragg Hall, if you know it."

"Cragg what? Why? What's going on?"

"We've got one person confirmed dead, and three more in a critical condition."

"Jesus! What the bloody hell happened?"

"We've no idea. It could be extreme food poisoning, or someone spiked the punch."

"What do you mean…" Henry couldn't think. Too many questions assaulted his mind. "Someone's poisoned the punch?"

Hargreaves swore loudly. Henry heard her car's siren blaring in the background and guessed she was negotiating traffic on a country lane gummed-up with bank-holiday drivers.

"How long will you be?" he asked.

"Bloody next week at this rate." She blared her horn and swore again.

"Cragg what-was-it?"

"Cragg Hall on Addingham Moorside. Uniform are already there, plus four ambulances. Murphy wants you on the scene. You'll get there before me as I've not even got to Otley yet."

"Right," Henry said. If he set off now, he would be there in five minutes. "I'll see you soon."

"And Henry! If uniform ask, you're a consultant with the investigative team."

"Alright," Henry said, realising he would need an excuse to give the uniformed officers as to why he was there. "Do you think that'll work?"

"If it doesn't, tell them to radio Detective Superintendent Murphy so they can get an earful from him."

"I will do," Henry said; he had been on the receiving end of some of Murphy's 'earfuls' in the past. "Let's hope they'll believe me, for their sakes."

Chapter Three

Henry forced his eight-year-old Skoda Octavia to climb up the winding country lane towards the top of Addingham Moorside. The lane was narrow, only wide enough for one car, with hedgerows hanging over the crumbling drystone walls. He had to be careful at each blind corner not to drive headfirst into oncoming vehicles coming down the hill.

The glorious sunset hung over the plateau when he reached the top. With the valley on one side and the miles of wilderness on the other, he sped past gnarly trees in forgotten fields. When he joined a road wide enough for two vehicles, he realised he had no idea where Cragg Hall was. He headed straight towards the small hamlet along the road, assuming he would find it there.

He heard the ambulance's siren before it hurtled around a corner and drove past him at full speed. He watched it disappear in his rear-view mirror and heard more sirens approaching. Then a second one blew past.

What on earth had happened up here? A mass poisoning? A bad batch of burgers? He had never heard anything of the like.

He entered the small hamlet, made up of a few working farms, old cottages, and some barn conversions. He noticed a police patrol vehicle outside one of the properties and pulled up opposite.

He could only see one police car and assumed there would be two officers on the scene. Two ambulances were parked nearby, their back doors fully open. Ambulances were as rare as gold dust around here. He had no idea how so many had been scrambled.

Leaving his car, he crossed the lane and headed through the front gate of a large barn conversion. He walked down the footpath and peeped through the open front door. The rear of the house seemed to have glass bifold doors and he could see straight through and out into its large back garden.

Henry noticed two police officers standing in the middle of the scene, both gawping at the madness happening around them. One, however, appeared less flustered than the other and had gone to ask the four shell-shocked guests standing near a large outdoor table to get inside the house. Meanwhile, the other officer watched some paramedics dealing with two victims lying on the grass.

Henry counted two bodies on the ground. The one near the far wall was shrouded in a sheet, while the other was being worked on by a team of paramedics. One of them compressed the man's chest while another pumped air into his mouth though a bag valve mask.

"What the bloody hell has gone on here?" Henry asked himself, wishing he had an answer.

A shrill cry cut through the silence. The harrowing sound shot through Henry's spine like a burst of lightning. A woman broke through the team of paramedics and collapsed beside the man on the ground. The paramedic compressing the man's chest stopped and stood back to let the woman embrace her dead loved one.

The three remaining guests grew restless and started shouting. They demanded the police constables do something rather than stand around looking gormless. Henry sensed the situation was turning ugly. Of the three remaining guests, two of them were built like rugby players. Both were wearing polo shirts that strained to cover their pecs and biceps. They were clearly worked up and ready to blow. Henry doubted the two young constables could handle them. Well, neither could Henry, not physically.

The two rugby players went over to the outdoor table. It was built to seat twelve and was covered in glassware, bowls of salad, plates of meat and burgers, and bottles of alcohol.

"Please, don't touch anything," the alert constable said weakly.

One of the rugby players picked up a glass while the other touched plates. They were both searching for something within the food and drink. Henry's age-old instinct to preserve evidence took over him, and he rushed through the front door, bounded through Cragg Hall's interior, and stepped out onto the patio.

"Oi!" Henry shouted at the two men. "Don't touch a sodding thing and stand over there!"

The two rugby players were startled, and the police officers stared at him.

"Who are you?" the alert officer asked.

"I'm a consultant for the detectives," Henry said, vaguely remembering what he had to say.

The two rugby players looked at each other briefly, before continuing to tamper with the evidence on the table.

"Oi! I shan't tell you again!" Henry snapped. "Don't bloody touch a thing and get inside the house." When the two rugby players ignored him a second time, Henry added, "Do you want to get your fingerprints on everything, eh? Shall we start questioning you two as a matter of urgency?"

The taller of the two lowered a glass and replaced it on the table. "We just want to know what went on here."

Henry could see the blind panic in his eyes. One moment, he and his friends had been enjoying a nice May Bank Holiday barbecue, and the next, four of them had fallen deathly ill.

"We all want to know what's happened here," Henry said. "And we soon will, but if you keep touching the evidence, we won't, and you two will be our only suspects. So back off!"

Henry's point seemed to sink through their thick heads, and the two rugby players sloped off towards the bifold doors.

With one problem resolved, Henry turned around to face the next.

"Who are you?" the police constable asked, this time more assertively.

Henry crossed the patio to get closer to him. "DS Hargreaves sent me. She's on her way."

The officer looked confused and gripped his radio. "Who let you onto this crime scene?"

"You can double-check with Detective Superintendent Murphy if you really want to. Although, I doubt he'll speak to you very respectfully."

The officer didn't find the idea appealing and let go of his radio.

"I'm Henry Ward, a former DCI. Who are you?"

"PC Watkins. That's PC Smith." He nodded towards the other officer, who was still staring at the deceased.

Henry noticed the paramedics were packing up their gear.

"Ever seen anything like this before?" Henry asked.

Watkins shook his head. Of course he hadn't. He didn't look a day older than twenty-five, while PC Smith looked younger still.

Henry, however, pretended he was fully experienced in such situations. "Right, take the guests inside. Don't let them touch anything and keep them out of the kitchen. Then start taking their statements."

Watkins pulled a face, suggesting he was unsure if he should take orders from a retired detective who had just walked in off the street.

"Quick," Henry said, "or I'll tell DS Hargreaves you've left her crime scene in a state."

The officer blinked some recognition and shepherded the remaining guest inside the house.

Henry shouted PC Smith's name and ordered him to help Watkins. He did as instructed without asking Henry who he was.

Henry's eyes then took in the large back garden that sloped to a wall at the bottom. Beyond it were fields and woods that stretched into the valley below. Addingham and Ilkley seemed picturesque and calm, both settling in for a mild, quiet night.

The woman whose cry had sent a shudder down Henry's spine remained at the side of the recently deceased man, gripping his hand. Henry approached her slowly.

"What's your name?" Henry asked, standing over her.

The woman didn't look up. Her face was scrunched up; tears dripped down her red cheeks.

Henry tried again. "Excuse me, Ms…"

She noticed him. "I can't believe it!"

"I need you to get inside with the other guests."

She shook her head, unable to get the words out to say no.

"Please, Ms…" Henry caught the eye of a female paramedic, who had finished packing up her equipment.

She came over and placed her arm around the woman. "Let's get you inside, eh?" the paramedic said, pulling her up. "You can see him later on."

The woman didn't put up any resistance and wept on the paramedic's shoulder as she was taken into the house.

A cool breeze blew over Henry. Apart from the woman's weeping coming from the house and the occasional beep of a paramedic's radio, the garden was silent. He surveyed the scene. The recently deceased man was lying on the grass beside the outdoor table where wooden chairs had been knocked over. The second body, shrouded in a white sheet, was alone on a lower level of the garden, partially hidden by the railings around the patio.

Henry leant on the handrail to get a better look. It appeared as though the body had been sitting on the wall at the bottom of the garden, before falling backwards onto the lawn.

Henry blinked. This is as close to a massacre as he had ever been. The air was tinted with some visceral metallic compound that made his stomach churn.

There had been too much death here today.

"I suppose that's us then," said a male paramedic. He and his two colleagues had packed everything up and were looking at Henry, as if they needed his say-so before going.

"How many dead have we got?" Henry asked.

The paramedic took a breath. "Three. One was taken from here in a critical condition but died in the ambulance."

"So, four were taken ill, with only one surviving – for now."

"He might pull through, that one. Whatever it was that killed the others didn't seem to affect him that much."

Three dead? Henry asked himself. He went to speak but couldn't articulate any words. He watched the paramedics pull bags over their shoulders, and two of them traipsed into the house.

Henry stared at the dead man closest to him. He must be in his early forties, a similar age to Henry's own son. "Any idea how this happened?" he asked.

The male paramedic shrugged. "Extreme food poisoning or… intentional poisoning."

Henry glanced back at the table for twelve on the patio. It looked as though the guests had been enjoying a feast until the wind picked up and blew them away; as if they were made of nothing but spring blossom.

Henry gestured to the table. "We'll need to get all that tested, and then we'll need to find out what the hell happened here. Who did it, and why…?" His voice gave up on him. It all sounded beyond his capabilities.

The male paramedic looked at him with sympathetic expression, which Henry read as 'rather you than me'.

Chapter Four

Henry watched a paramedic cover the body of the recently deceased man with a sheet and then returned to examining the outdoor table. A few wasps buzzed around the bowls of salad. A large one sat on a plate of meat, sticking its mandibles into the congealed burger grease. Henry wondered if the meat had been poisoned and if the wasp would fly off. Just then, it fluttered its wings and flew into the sky without a care in the world.

There were eight dinner plates around the table, most were piled high with lettuce, potato salad, and meat. They had all been eating when the sickness or poisoning struck. Next to the seven plates were seven wine glasses – four glasses contained white wine and three held red.

Eight empty cocktail glasses – stained with a thick, yellow liquid – sat at the far end of the table. Henry strolled towards them.

He batted away some blackflies from inside the glasses, which were guzzling down the remnants of liquid. He couldn't persuade many to leave. The punch's sweetness caught on the breeze, attracting more insects. Henry peered under the table at the grass and couldn't see any dead flies, suggesting the punch was safe to consume.

A paramedic strolled along the patio towards Henry, carrying a large holdall.

Henry caught her attention with a wave. "Excuse me, what symptoms did the victims have?"

The paramedic batted away a fly that travelled off one of the glasses. "Apparently it started with abdominal pains, and then they dropped to the ground. Although, my colleague reckons it could be heart failure – it happened so fast. We won't know until they do the autopsies."

"And four fell ill out of the eight who were here?"

She gave Henry a knowing nod, as if she could read his mind. If it was poison, it must have been something only the four had consumed. Henry's eyes scanned the wine glasses on the table, picking out the four containing white. Three of them were half-empty, while one looked not to have been touched.

He grumbled to himself. "Thanks for your help," he said to the paramedic.

As she re-entered the house, Henry noticed the shrouded body at the bottom of the garden.

The odd one out.

He traipsed down the stone steps that led to the lawn lower down. The grass rustled around his boots until he came to stand next to the deceased. He lifted up the white sheet. It was a woman in her early forties. Luscious blonde hair cushioned her head. She was tanned and attractive. She appeared as if she was enjoying a nap. Her eyes were closed. Her lips – bright red with lipstick – were curled into a blissful smile.

Henry glanced up at the patio above him, and then back at the content corpse before him.

"Well, this makes no bloody sense," he said. "Why the hell are *you* so happy?"

After a few moments, he replaced the sheet over her face and returned up the stone steps.

Watkins was in the snug with the four remaining guests. Two lamps were on. The two rugby players occupied a three-seater sofa, while a man embraced a woman on a two-seater opposite. The house had stone flooring, and its walls had exposed brickwork with stylish embellishments here and there. The interior was both rustic and modern, and there was the pungent scent of lilies.

Henry approached Watkins, who held a notepad and pen in his hand. "How are you doing with the statements?" he asked, looking at the young constable's blank page.

Watkins pulled a pained expression. "They're refusing to comply."

"They're probably too traumatised," Henry admitted.

The four guests stared at the floor, each one in their own world.

"Where's your colleague?" Henry asked.

Watkins winced. "In the toilet. I think he's crying."

Henry shook his head. "Go talk some sense into him. If Hargreaves finds him in tears, she'll not take kindly to it."

Watkins left the snug and he heard him gently tapping the door further down the hallway. Henry observed the four remaining guests – the survivors.

"Well, I'd just like to say, I'm very sorry for your losses." None of them acknowledged him. "Listen. This might take a while to sort out."

The woman wept softly to herself.

"I need to know who was at this party and whose house we're in."

The taller of the two rugby players cleared his throat. He had piercing grey eyes and a chiselled jawline. The curls from his frizzy blond hair hung over his forehead. "This is Sarah and Mark Hardy's house." He spoke with a croaky voice.

Henry searched his pocket for his thin Moleskine notepad and pen. He flicked to a fresh page and noted down the names. "Right. And you are?"

"Tom. Tom Dixon."

"Okay, and you?" Henry pointed his pen at the rugby player sitting next to Tom, who was chunkier and had a round face. His head was shaven, and his left ear had become deformed from participating in too many scrums.

"Lee… Lee Combes," he said.

Henry scribbled down the name. "Okay, and who are those two over there?" Henry gestured to the man and woman sitting on the other settee – both oblivious to the conversation taking place before them.

"He's Pete Blackburn," Tom said. "She's Noura Emery."

Henry jotted down the names. "Did Sarah and Mark Hardy invite you here?" Henry asked.

Tom nodded.

"When was this?"

"What do you mean?"

"When did you receive the invitation?"

Tom frowned as he struggled to recall. "Earlier this week. Sarah invited both of us."

"How did you know Sarah?"

"Through friends in Leeds. I didn't know Mark that well. I was more pally with Sarah." He clenched his jaw shut. Lowering his head, he rubbed his eyes with his thumb and index finger.

All four of them were in a daze, so Henry decided to give them some space. He returned to the hallway, where he found PC Watkins and PC Smith. The younger constable wiped his eyes with the sleeve of his uniform.

"Are you alright, lad?" Henry asked him.

Smith sniffled and nodded. His eyes were red and blurry.

"Don't worry. You won't have many cases like this in your career."

Smith didn't seem buoyed by his statement.

There were some raised voices outside, and DS Hargreaves bounded through the door. She wore a dark-grey suit, and her jet-black hair was longer than when Henry last saw her. Her lips weren't their usual bright scarlet but a more muted red instead.

"Welcome to the house of death, Hargreaves," Henry said, catching her attention.

Hargreaves frowned at him and then looked at the two police constables. She stepped closer to PC Smith. "Have you been crying?"

"Hargreaves," Henry said. "You'd best come through to the back garden."

He led her away from PC Smith, through the living area, and into the back garden. He stood on the patio and gestured to the two bodies lying on the flagstones. Hargreaves stared at them. The garden had taken on the solemn respectful air of a graveyard. The wind had died down, and the birds sung gently at a respectful distance. Ahead, the sky was turning to night.

"Shit," Hargreaves said.

"Three dead. One in hospital in ICU. They're hoping he'll pull through. And four traumatised witnesses."

Hargreaves narrowed her eyes and then looked at the outdoor table loaded with food and drink. "We'll have to get all that tested, and everything in the kitchen."

"There's a whole long list of things to do."

She took her phone out.

"Who are you calling?"

"First order of business, I need to update Murphy. He'll have kittens over this. We're already at breaking point. There was a double murder in Halifax last night, and we're still dealing with a gang fight that took place in the centre of Leeds last week."

"I don't care if Murphy has puppies, as long as he promises us enough support to complete this investigation."

Hargreaves smirked. "Chance would be a fine thing. You're our only support, Henry. Why else do you think I let you on an active crime scene?" She stepped away from him with her phone pressed against her ear.

Henry surveyed the dining table and then the two shrouded corpses. He didn't have much hope of getting to the bottom of this. But didn't he always feel overwhelmed at the beginning of a big case?

This time, his motivational thoughts didn't spark much enthusiasm. Considering what had happened today at Cragg Hall, Henry had a nasty feeling that the whole truth would never come to light.

Chapter Five

Henry listened to Hargreaves' side of the phone conversation with Murphy. After explaining the key facts, she gave monosyllabic utterances that went from sounding very negative to quite negative. After she hung up, Hargreaves looked at the dining table on the patio. Henry followed her gaze and noticed more flies and wasps attacking the food and drink. The sun was slowly dying off in the sky, and the shadows on the patio were growing longer. They needed to preserve as much evidence as they could before nightfall.

"When will the scene of crime officers get here?" he asked.

"Not for another half an hour." She winced, as if she knew the task before them was too much to comprehend.

"Let's get PCs Watkins and Smith to do the lion's share of it?" Henry said.

Hargreaves nodded. "Aye, let's get Dumb and Dumber to do it all."

"What did Murphy say?"

"He's sending Barnes over. She's leading the major investigation team – under his oversight. I'll be her second-in-command."

"What about DCI Acton?" Henry asked, referring to the Mancunian detective chief inspector he had worked with recently.

"He's dealing with the double murder in Halifax."

Henry tutted. He was only just beginning to respect DCI Acton. "And what about Barnes? Is she okay with my involvement?"

"Isn't she usually?"

"Well… The last time I helped out on a case, she threatened to arrest me. She has a history of doing that, come to think of it."

"Well, she'll need your help with this, and Murphy expects you to get involved…" Hargreaves exhaled loudly and examined the table. "So, what killed them? Was it accidental… or are we thinking it was intentional?"

Henry shook his head. "We don't even know who was here. I've got the names of the survivors sitting in the snug but not the victims…" He regarded the two shrouded bodies on the patio. "We'll need to get a pathologist over here sharpish."

"Murphy's sending over Dr Anderson. All the autopsies and toxicology reports will be rushed through, Bank Holiday weekend or not."

Henry knew Dr Stuart Anderson very well. The prickly Home Office pathologist was of a similar age to him, and they had worked together on many cases over the years. "It takes something special to get that old sod off the golf course on a weekend… Though this might tickle his fancy."

Hargreaves read a text on her phone. "Barnes is on her way," she declared. She huffed again and then eyed the large dining table in despair.

"Come on," Henry said. "Let's get 'Dumb and Dumber' to protect the crime scene, and then we'll talk to the witnesses and start putting together a picture of what happened here."

They went into the house, and Hargreaves instructed PCs Watkins and Smith to carefully wrap up the food and drink with cling film. Henry then introduced Hargreaves to the survivors in the dimly lit snug. When she had worked out who was who, she explained that the police had launched a criminal investigation to learn what had happened at Cragg Hall that evening.

"But we'll need your help to do this," she said. She sat down in the centre of the snug so that she was at their eye level. "We need to build a picture of what happened before people started falling ill. Do you think that'll be possible?"

Tom and Lee nodded, but Pete and Noura looked too despondent to communicate.

Henry remained in the doorway, watching. Hargreaves was doing a good job. She usually got information out of witnesses by browbeating them and threatening arrest. This time, however, she was talking to them with a warmth Henry had never seen her utilise before. Had she undergone some training?

Hargreaves pulled her phone out of her bag and tapped on its screen. "Alright. Please can you give me the names of everyone present at the party?"

Tom and Lee did the talking and gave Hargreaves the eight names.

Sarah and Mark Hardy: Sarah had died at the barbecue, while Mark was in hospital clinging onto life.

Louanne and Pete Blackburn: Louanne had died on the way to hospital, and Pete was in the snug looking shell-shocked.

Noura and Allister Emery: Henry had witnessed Allister's death when he arrived at the scene, and Noura was in the snug with them, weeping softly.

Tom and Lee both appeared healthy and sound.

With all the names on her phone, Hargreaves sent Henry a text containing the list. He scrolled through them looking for patterns. If this had been an intentional poisoning, the killer would most likely be one of the survivors – unless they had intended to kill themself.

Henry focused on the four people in the snug more intently. "How were the other guests? Did they appear like their usual selves?"

His question provoked a despondent shrug from Tom but nothing else from the others.

"Did anyone, by any chance, attend the party but leave early?" Henry asked.

Tom attempted to think about it but shook his head.

"There was…" Noura's voice was barely audible. A bubble burst on her tear-streaked lips as she spoke again. "There was a baby."

Hargreaves' eyes bulged. "There was an infant here?"

Tom frowned. Then Lee elbowed him. "There was that bloke with his wife. The Huddersfield supporter."

"Oh, aye." Tom nodded. "He and his wife were here with their kid." He rubbed his forehead. "I forgot about them."

Hargreaves looked at Noura. "What are their names?"

"Ralph…" Noura said, tilting her head. "And Claire… and little baby William."

"Do you know if the infant ate or drank anything from here?"

Noura closed her eyes and shook her head.

"Where do they live?"

Noura, Tom, and Lee couldn't say.

"I know," said Pete. He stirred himself out of his stupor. "I'll write it down."

Hargreaves handed him a piece of paper from her notepad, onto which he scribbled an address in Leeds.

"Thank you." Hargreaves got up off the carpet and headed to the door. She called for PC Smith. When he appeared, she handed him the scrap of paper and ordered him to send a unit to the address immediately.

Hargreaves returned to the centre of the room. Her eyes were wide with concern.

The last thing they needed to add to this tragedy was a poisoned infant.

"Can we go soon?" Tom asked. "Or at least… I don't know. Get a drink–"

"I don't want to drink anything here." Noura spluttered, sounding terrified.

"The kitchen's out of bounds," Hargreaves said. "You'll need to stay a little while longer, and then we'll let you go."

"What about *them*?" Pete asked. "What about them? When do we move them?"

He pointed in the direction of the back garden.

"The Home Office pathologist is rushing over," Henry said. "Once he's examined them, he'll have them taken to hospital."

Pete nodded as if that made some kind of sense and went back to staring at the carpet. His fingernails picked the skin of his other hand, drawing blood.

Out in the hallway, two SOCO officers, dressed in white overalls, entered through the front door, much to Henry's relief. Hargreaves took them into the back garden while Henry stepped out the front door.

The street lights lining the lane were on, and moths and flies buzzed around them. A few cars drove by – more than Henry considered usual. Had word already spread that something terrible had happened here?

The awkward gait of a man in his mid-sixties walking past the wall caught Henry's eye. Dr Anderson ambled through the front gate, using his cane to walk. Despite the pleasant temperatures, he wore a grey tweed jacket and brown corduroys. His face was flush – a consequence of an overly rich diet – and his grey Victorian-style beard and moustache were in full form.

Dr Anderson raised a wizened eyebrow at Henry when he was halfway up the garden path. "Well, if I live and breathe, Henry Ward… back from the dead. Again."

"Dr Anderson. A pleasure as always. I'm not surprised you dragged yourself off the golf course for this."

"Golf course? I'm speaking at a conference detailing the rise of drug overdoses among the homeless tomorrow and needed to polish off my speech." As Dr Anderson walked, the point of his cane tapped the ground loudly.

"Sounds cheerful. Talking of drug overdosing…" Henry gestured towards the house.

Dr Anderson joined him on the front step and spoke in hushed tones. "Yes, it has been conveyed to me that we have two dead."

"Three now."

One of Anderson's owl-like eyebrows went up. "My current thinking is, apart from a mass poisoning event, we're looking at some bad meat or drink."

"Can food poisoning kill so quickly? It seems like they were dead within the hour."

"It's hard to say without looking at them."

Henry took him through the house and into the back garden. A SOCO officer finished setting up a light over the first body, while two others unwrapped the cling film PCs Watkins and Smith had hastily spread over the table.

Dr Anderson stood near the body of Allister Emery and knelt down. He pulled the sheet off the victim's head to show a man in his mid-forties staring blankly up at the sky. His mouth was curled into a painful snarl.

Dr Anderson touched his cheek with a latex-gloved hand and then felt underneath his chin. He lifted his head back and peered up his nostrils, and then moved closer to his mouth and sniffed.

"Hmmm," he said. "I've not smelt that in a while."

"What?" Henry asked.

Dr Anderson didn't reply and started unbuttoning the man's blue shirt. He pulled it open to show the top of his hairy chest. His skin was bright pink, as if he had nasty sunburn.

"Oh dear..." Dr Anderson said. He asked Henry to help him up off the grass and then glanced at the other body near the far wall. "I'll take a quick look at that one. But... I can't say for certain until I look inside. There needs to be signs of hypoxia, you see."

"Okay?"

"But if I'm right, and the toxicology reports confirm it, then we're probably looking at cyanide poisoning."

Henry paused for a moment. "Cyanide?"

"Is your hearing going?"

"They were all poisoned with cyanide?"

Dr Anderson nodded. "Well, this one, most probably. But I'll need to check the others, obviously. However, one may safely assume there was only one poison here."

Henry looked at the food on the table, from which the SOCO officers were taking swabs. "And how is cyanide usually administered?"

"It would've most likely been dissolved in a drink or some food. It's quite tasteless, you see. A simple white powder. It's very soluble."

"So, we're looking for a mass poisoner," Henry said, mostly to himself.

"Well, *you* are, Ward. Good luck with that. I'll have the bodies moved once Forensics have taken the necessary photos. Autopsies will be tomorrow, with toxicology reports coming back the day after. I understand Murphy has ordered one of the labs to stay open all weekend."

"And you're sure it's cyanide?"

"I could be wrong... but I'm fairly certain they were poisoned with it."

Henry regarded the two bodies in the back garden of Cragg Hall with trepidation, wondering who could have wished them dead.

Chapter Six

Henry drove down the hill towards Addingham. It was a relief to get away from Cragg Hall. The sickly-sweet scent of the punch haunted him, as did that atmosphere hanging around Addingham Moorside. It was after 9.30 p.m., and night had descended over the valley. All the Bank Holiday calmness Henry had experienced in his backyard that afternoon was long gone. He now felt very ill at ease.

The SOCO officers had free rein to carry out their work of snapping photos and taking swabs of all the food and drink on the property. Everything in the kitchen would have to be tested. The amount of work that needed to be done gave Henry a headache.

A meeting of the major investigation team was being held the following morning in Leeds Central police station, and Henry hoped he would learn more about how the poison had been administered. Cyanide? He shook his head. How the hell do people get hold of that these days?

The four heavily disturbed survivors had left the crime scene, and Hargreaves had given them strict orders not to leave the area, as the police would need detailed witness statements from each one.

Hargreaves had also heard back from the couple with the baby. All three were at Leeds General Infirmary being tested. Luckily, they all seemed to be in good health.

As Henry drove down the narrow country lanes, he wondered if it really had been one of the survivors who had poisoned the others. Logic told him to focus on the people who had prepared the food. However, both Mr and Mrs Hardy had fallen victim to the poison.

He wondered what it all meant as he headed down the road towards Addingham. He pulled up outside his cottage on Main Street and, as he got out of his car, heard people sitting outside the pub across the street enjoying the warm night. The urge to have a drink struck Henry. He could quite easily cross the street, order a pint, and sit outside with the other drinkers and forget all about the three people who'd lost their lives at Cragg Hall that evening.

But he couldn't cross the road and drown his sorrows. He knew one drink always led to ten. Besides, Hargreaves and Barnes were expecting him bright and early in Leeds the following morning.

After giving the pub a downcast look, he locked his car and headed into his cottage.

He stood in his kitchen waiting for his kettle to boil. His phone rang, and he was going to ignore the call, until he saw it was his next-door neighbour, Jean Whitehead.

She didn't wait for him to say hello and straightaway asked, "Have you heard about what's happened on Addingham Moorside?"

Henry pulled a chair out from under his kitchen table and took a seat, expecting this to be a long conversation. "I have. Why? What have you heard?"

"I've heard something about loads of people dying." She was outside somewhere. Birds were singing in the background, and it sounded as if she was standing next to a busy road.

"How's Cambridge?" he asked.

"Fine. Chris is taking us out for a curry. So… What have you heard?"

"There's been an incident."

"Like what?"

"We don't know yet."

"We? Who's we? Are you helping them out?"

"I am, as a matter of fact. Therefore, I can't go into details."

"Oh, go on! I won't tell anyone."

Henry imagined her ringing someone else to repeat what she had just learnt as soon as he hung up. "Well…

even if I could tell you, we still don't know what's gone on."

"I heard there were four ambulances. The police are still up there now."

"How do you know that? Who've you been talking to?"

Her voice quavered. "Nobody."

"Do you know someone who lives up there?"

"Erm… Well, I might have a friend of a friend who lives up there."

"Who's your friend?"

Jean exhaled. "Noel."

Noel Cleeves was a know-all arrogant toff whom Henry didn't care much about, but Jean had a teenage crush on, which wound Henry up no end. "And who does Noel know up on Addingham Moorside?"

"The Taylors."

They were members of the Addingham birdwatching committee. He'd seen them at a few meetings. However, he didn't know they lived up on the moorside. "Oh right."

"So," Jean said, sounding slightly desperate. "What can you tell me?"

The kettle clicked off, and Henry removed a clean mug from a cupboard. He put in a teabag and then poured the water.

"Henry? Are you there?" she asked. A large lorry drove past her in the distance.

He exhaled and traipsed to the fridge to take out the milk. "Alright, but this really must stay between us."

"Fine."

"There's been some kind of poisoning. We don't know what's gone on yet. It's pretty grim."

"Blimey! How many have been… poisoned?"

"Four. Three are dead… and one's still alive."

"Oh my…" She went silent a moment. "That's terrible. The Taylors… they said the couple who live in that house are really nice. Apparently, she's really friendly and has been organising loads of little events up there. She's Australian, did you know?"

"No, I didn't. What has she been organising?"

"Well, she makes jams and bakes all sorts of stuff. She's been running baking competitions in the hamlet up there and invites everyone into her back garden."

"She liked cooking and baking then?"

Jean fell silent. "Oh, so she died, did she?"

"Yes… unfortunately. Her husband's still in hospital."

"Oh, how terribly sad." The noise of the nearby road filled her line.

"Listen, Jean, I suppose you could tell the Taylors I might want a chat with them later? Or at least pass it along the grapevine?"

"Yes, I will, Henry."

"Alright, you go enjoy your curry."

She said she would and then hung up. Henry placed his phone on the table and imagined Sarah Hardy cooking and baking for her neighbours. Sarah Hardy again. The odd one out.

He fished out the teabag from the cup and went to take a sip but couldn't. He had heard too much about poison to want to drink anything. Instead, he poured the steaming tea down the sink and rinsed the cup.

Chapter Seven

Henry had ironed a white shirt and a pair of jeans for his trip to Leeds Central police station the next morning. The concrete and glass office building stood beside a busy road on the outskirts of the city centre; a stone's throw away from the Leeds United football stadium. The building's many sheets of glass reflected the bright morning sky.

The meeting was planned for 8 a.m. and Henry arrived ten minutes early. The roads had been free from traffic with it being a Bank Holiday Sunday; and the police station's car park was almost empty. Henry entered the building and introduced himself to the officer at the reception desk in the foyer. The officer was slouched in his chair and stared out the glass wall opposite. He begrudgingly picked up the phone and called Barnes. He then told Henry to wait in a seating area near a sweeping staircase with white metal banisters.

The comfy chairs were well-worn, and the television mounted on the wall showed the local TV news. Among that morning's headlines was news of another sighting of the kookaburra – this time in Ripon. Henry raised his eyebrows. It's getting closer.

Detective Inspector Kate Barnes eventually stepped out from a closed door. She wore a pale-grey suit over her lean athletic frame. Her blonde hair was cut very short, and dark bags hung under her eyes. She gripped onto a paper cup of hot coffee.

"Morning, Henry," she said, in her Kentish English accent. She gestured towards the stairs. "There's more coffee in the meeting room upstairs."

As she sipped her own drink, Henry said, "It looks like you're holding onto yours for dear life."

"I've not slept much."

"Any developments?" he asked, trying to match her pace up the stairs.

"A few. I'll give you them in the meeting."

They went into a white-walled meeting room with a view of the busy road outside. A large table took up most of the space. DS Hargraves had set up her laptop and was in full conversation with someone. Henry then heard Murphy's voice but couldn't see him in the room. He jumped when he saw the detective superintendent's bulldog-like face leer at him from a huge TV screen on the wall.

"Glad you've joined us, Ward," Murphy said, not sounding very 'glad' about it.

Henry greeted everyone and took a seat next to Hargreaves. Barnes remained standing and sipped her coffee.

"What do we have, then?" Murphy asked.

Hargreaves answered, sounding fully prepped. "We have three confirmed dead, and one in a stable condition at Leeds General Infirmary. The doctors reckon he'll recover."

"Right…" Murphy said, making notes. "Any idea how three died but this one didn't?"

"The doctors said he must've consumed less of the poison, so he wasn't as badly affected by it."

"And there's still no idea what contained the cyanide?" Murphy asked.

Hargreaves shook their head. "Forensics are still testing everything. They said this poison's usually dissolved, so we're not looking for an aerosol or anything like that."

"Just as bloody well." Murphy sniffed. "I've told them at the lab to rush through all the samples. They'll stay open all night, if need be, so we should have the test results asap."

"We also need to speak to the survivors to get a picture of what happened," Hargreaves said.

"Any news from them?"

"No, sir. They went straight back to their homes after they left the crime scene. Well, I think Noura went to the hospital to see her husband."

Murphy grunted his understanding.

"There's something about Sarah Hardy that's been bugging me," Henry said, attracting their attention.

"In what way?" Barnes asked.

"She was found near the wall at the bottom of the garden, a fair distance from the other victims."

"That doesn't mean much, does it?" Hargreaves said.

Henry grumbled. "Well, then there's that thing with the survivors."

"What about 'em?" Murphy asked.

"Surely a poisoner would know not to poison themselves, so, logically, we should be looking at them."

"The thought had crossed my mind," Murphy admitted. "What's your take on these survivors?"

Henry collected his thoughts. "Noura Emery is clearly too distraught to be considered a suspect, as is Pete Blackburn. Then we have the two rugby lads–"

"Who?" Murphy asked, frowning down his laptop camera.

"Tom Dixon and Lee Combes. They don't seem the type to go poisoning people."

"And what do poisoners look like?" Barnes asked. "We need to be looking at all of the people present at the party and then eliminate them from suspicion. Any one of them could've poisoned the others. We have ten people of interest, including the people who left early. That's assuming it wasn't someone else."

Henry accepted her point and remained silent.

"Aye, there were two who left the party early, weren't there? Ralph and Claire Gaskin and their baby," Hargreaves said, reading the names off her laptop. "I suppose we can rule the baby out."

Barnes picked up a blue marker pen from the table and went to the back of the room where she started writing on the wall. For an instant, Henry wondered what the hell she was doing, then realised it was a whiteboard-wall. They had all the mod cons these days. In his day, they had to make do with blackboards.

Barnes neatly wrote out the names of the ten people present at the barbecue.

"We need to interview the survivors and Ralph and Claire Gaskin," she said, putting the lid back on her marker.

Murphy and Hargreaves both agreed with grunts.

"How are we going to organise it?" Henry asked, looking at Barnes.

"I'll be with Dr Anderson most of the day while he does the autopsies," said Barnes, "and then I'll need to head back to the crime scene. You and Hargreaves can start talking to the survivors. When I'm no longer needed, I'll start interviewing some as well."

"What about the press?" Murphy asked. "They're already sniffing around this. Word spreads quickly in that little village of yours, Ward."

"Aye, it does," he said.

"I can do a press conference this afternoon when we have more information," Barnes said, her voice uncertain.

"No. I'll lead all the press conferences, but you can stand beside me to answer any details if needed," Murphy said. "Let's find out as much as we can by 1.30 so we can give the press something. Otherwise, they'll be on my arse. Have the next of kin been informed?"

"I've got two detective constables working on that," Hargreaves said. "They're also doing background checks on all the barbecue attendees."

Murphy shook his head. "No, no. At a horrendous moment like this, I think it would be better for these families to hear the news from a senior police officer. Barnes, why don't you personally inform them?"

Barnes's eyes bulged. "Erm. Surely, I should be with Dr Anderson all morning…" She blinked wildly and then said, "But, yes, sir… I'll handle it myself."

"Good." He inhaled. "God help the poor sods. They're about to go through something pretty rotten."

A moment of silence passed between them. Henry had the feeling someone had walked over his grave and shivered.

"It's bloody bad, this one," Murphy continued. "Let's do right by these victims and their families by finding out who did this as quickly as we can, and with as little fuss as possible."

Hargreaves nodded her head in agreement, while Henry crossed his arms over his chest.

"While I like your ambition, Murphy, Forensics need to test everything on that property for cyanide," he said. "I don't care if you force them to work day and night, it'll take them weeks to figure out where it came from–"

"Listen, Ward. Forensics have been read the Riot Act and know the score. They'll keep to their side of the bargain if you keep to yours."

"Aye, but this strikes me as more of a forensic investigation. I mean, aren't we dependent on them?"

"Are you saying you can't do your job without SOCO wiping your backside?"

"What? No, of course not–"

"Here, Ward. Why don't you do some of that detecting business and see if you can crack this case without those lab rats? Isn't that what we used to do in the old days?"

Henry shrugged. "Right. I'll do my best."

"Make sure you do. And, Ward, while you're out and about interviewing witnesses and reliving your heyday, don't forget DS Hargreaves is the serving officer. She pulls rank over you. You're only assisting with this investigation because we're short of detectives. Is that clear?"

Henry leant forwards in his chair. "Would you prefer if I went home? I was planning to go fishing today as it happens."

"Oh, don't get your knickers in a twist," Murphy growled. "Just show me you can respect her sergeant's stripes; not that you ever respected authority before."

Henry let out an exasperated sigh. "Aye, Murphy. You'll have no problems from me."

Murphy wished them luck and gruffly signed off.

Henry tapped the tabletop with his finger. "Always the massive pain in the arse, as usual?"

"Why don't you focus on these interviews, hey?" Barnes said, studying the names on the whiteboard. "And leave old rivalries aside. This is going to be a long and shit

Bank Holiday weekend." She rubbed her forehead. "I need to go find the addresses of the families."

Henry huffed. "Aye, you're right there. This could turn out to be one of the worst Bank Holiday weekends on record."

Chapter Eight

Hargreaves gave Henry a lift in her silver Audi to Tom Dixon's home. She had called Tom and Lee Combes beforehand, arranging for both of them to be there as it would be quicker to talk to them at the same time. Henry felt this could be a mistake, as speaking to witnesses individually garnered better results. However, as they were pressed for time, he hadn't made a fuss.

They arrived at Tom's address, which was a 1980s four-storey apartment building in a leafy suburb of Leeds. A busy high street filled with shops, cafés, and bars was a short walking distance away. The other houses in the street were Edwardian and well maintained with excellent paintwork, gleaming rooftops, and pristine front gardens.

Hargreaves pulled up outside the apartment building. A tree with lush green leaves stood in front of its entrance, and Henry observed something fluttering in its top branches. He got out the car and rushed to the foot of the tree. The bird was around the same size as a kookaburra.

Hargreaves stopped searching for Tom's apartment number on the intercom to look at him. "Is there a reason why you're staring at a tree, or should I start to worry?"

"It could be a kookaburra–"

The bird unfurled its wings to steady itself, showing off its black and white markings.

Henry harrumphed. "Never mind, it's just a magpie."

Hargreaves shook her head and buzzed the intercom. After a few moments, the front door opened and Henry followed her inside.

"Not a bad place," he said of the hallway.

The interior was sleek with shiny faux-marble flooring. They took the elevator to the fourth floor and found Tom Dixon standing outside his apartment door. He wore a white vest over his muscular upper body and had dark-blue rugby shorts on. His frizzy blond hair was messier than the last time Henry had seen him, and his complexion was pale.

Tom nodded dutifully at Henry and Hargreaves. "Come in, please."

He led them into an open-plan living area. A staircase went up to another floor at the end of the room. Floor-to-ceiling windows on both the east and south sides opened up onto wide balconies. Henry noticed the tip of the tree outside the front entrance. The magpie on its top branch had gone.

Two huge leather sofas took up the space and were positioned at a right angle in front of an enormous television on the wall. Lee Combes was sitting on one of them, wearing tracksuit bottoms and a hoodie. His hood was up, hiding his shaven, round head and cauliflower ears. He had paused the rugby match he had been watching.

"Erm… Can I get you a coffee?" Tom asked.

An espresso machine sat on the kitchen worktop in the distance, and Henry smelt freshly ground beans in the air.

"No, I'm fine," Hargreaves said, taking her phone out of her handbag.

Henry gave her a disappointed look and declined Tom's offer as well. They did have a lot of people to interview before the morning was out.

Tom slumped onto the sofa next to Lee and switched the television off. He sat forwards, with one leg crossed over the other. His thick, calloused fingers tapped his thigh.

He sniffed. His bulging shoulders were scrunched up as if he was preparing to enter a scrum. He was definitely anxious about something. The only question was what.

Lee cleared his throat and looked wearily at Henry and Hargreaves.

Henry gestured for Hargreaves to start the questioning, seeing as she was in charge.

"I'll record this, if that's okay," she said, tapping her phone and then placing it on the coffee table between them.

She took a seat on the arm of an unoccupied sofa, while Henry plonked himself down in the centre of it.

"So, we're here to ask you questions about what happened yesterday at Sarah and Mark Hardy's property on Addingham Moorside."

Both men nodded, wearing grim expressions.

"What can you tell us about what happened?"

They looked at each other.

"Tom," Hargreaves said, "why don't you start?"

"Well, we got there around 3 p.m."

"Okay. Sarah invited you, didn't she?"

"Yeah, and I invited Lee."

"And she was okay with him coming?"

"Yeah, she said 'the more the merrier'."

"Tell us what happened at the party."

"Well, it was fairly standard to begin with. It took a while for people to arrive, so we stood around in the back garden and chatted to the others a bit."

"Had you met the other guests before?" Henry asked.

"Aye, Sarah had invited me to dos like that before. I took Lee along with me, though, to have someone to talk to."

"You didn't get on with the other guests?"

"It's not that I didn't get on with them. I think it's mostly because they are all mates, and I don't have that much in common with them."

"They were Mark's friends?" Hargreaves asked.

Tom nodded.

"What happened when everyone had arrived?" she asked.

Tom glanced at Lee. "Well, that couple with the baby came shortly after us. We chatted to him. He was alright."

"Aye," Lee said. "Ralph was pretty sound."

"How long did they stay for?"

"About an hour or so," Tom said. "He had a couple of beers and then they headed off. She was getting ratty about feeding the baby and putting him to bed. It was only five o'clock, though, which is odd if you think about it."

"I think she was struggling with the baby," Lee said. "She looked shattered; so did he, to be fair."

Hargreaves scribbled into her notepad. "And when did you start eating and drinking?"

"Well, we'd been drinking beer since we arrived, and then Sarah brought out the punch and gave everyone a glass."

"I said I didn't want any," Lee said. "But she insisted. Said she'd made it herself."

"She *insisted* you drink the punch?" Hargreaves asked.

"Well, she was handing out glasses of it to everyone."

"We reckon…" Tom paused. "Well, it was just a thought…" He grimaced. "Do you know if it was the punch that made everyone ill?"

"We're still in the process of testing everything."

"Why would you think that?" Henry asked.

Tom and Lee shared a look.

"Not everyone drank much of it. We didn't," Tom said.

"I took a sip to be polite," Lee said. "But I hate sweet stuff like that. So, I poured mine down a drain."

"Me too. I drank a few sips but just left it on the table." Tom frowned. "Looking back, Sarah was a bit insistent about everyone drinking some. She asked, 'Why are you not drinking this?' when she found my glass. I told her I wasn't a fan, and she gave me a dirty look."

"You think she wanted to poison you?" Hargreaves asked.

Tom let his shoulders drop. "Of course not. She'd probably just spent all afternoon making it. Plus, she drank loads of it herself. She was rat-arsed by six o'clock."

"Aye," Lee said. "She'd been crying as well."

Hargreaves and Henry glanced at one another. "When was this?" she asked.

"Around 6.30," Tom answered. "She came out of the house; she'd been inside for a while, long enough for me to start thinking about going to look for her, and then she came out crying."

"Do you know why?" Hargreaves asked.

Tom shook his head forcefully.

"What did you eat at the barbecue?"

Tom shrugged. "Same as everyone else."

Lee nodded. "I had two burgers."

"I'm cutting carbs," Tom said, "so I just had some meat and a bit of lettuce."

"When did you start eating?"

"Just after Sarah came out of the house. She told us all to help ourselves to food. So, we took some seats at the table. We were sitting at the far end near Allister and Noura."

Lee cleared his throat and bit his knuckle. He looked out the south window at the tree outside.

"Then…" Tom heaved a sigh. "We realised Sarah wasn't there with us, and Lee…"

Lee continued staring out the window.

"He was facing the railings. He saw her lying on her back near the wall," Tom said.

Hargreaves focused on Lee. "You saw her unconscious on the ground?"

He sniffed. "I don't know if she was or not. I just happened to glance through the railings and saw her lying on the grass. I thought it was odd so… I walked down the steps to see if she was alright. I thought she was just drunk and had passed out, but–"

"He called me down," Tom continued, "as I was watching from the table. I just thought she was being 'Sarah'. She was always a bit kooky, but he was–"

"I thought something bad had happened to her," Lee said.

"Eventually, I got out of my seat and went down to help Lee wake her up… but she wouldn't open her eyes."

"Where was everyone else?" Hargreaves asked.

"Still at the table. Eating and chatting. When we realised she was ill… I rushed up the steps and shouted for Mark, her husband."

"What did he do?"

"Erm…" Tom said. "He tried to ignore me until I had to raise my voice and interrupt the dinner. Then he came, and everyone went silent. Some stood by the railings, looking down. They panicked when they realised she wasn't well."

"So, you and Mark went down to check on Sarah?" Henry asked.

Tom wore a pained expression and shook his head. "We didn't, because that's when people started falling ill."

Chapter Nine

Hargreaves jotted down what Lee and Tom had just said in her notebook. Henry remained seated next to her on the large sofa, watching Lee and Tom give their witness statements. The sun had burst through the haze outside and splashed bright light over the living area.

Squinting in the daylight, Hargreaves asked, "Can you talk me through what happened when people started falling ill?"

Lee picked up the television remote and gripped it tightly, tapping it against his thick thigh.

Tom pursed his lips and glanced back at this kitchen. "Are you sure I can't get you a coffee?"

"Aye, why not," Henry said, believing Tom needed a moment to regain his composure.

Tom jumped off his sofa and rushed to the espresso machine across the room, while Lee turned the remote control around in his hands – his eyes transfixed on the blank TV.

Hargreaves gave Henry an annoyed look and tapped her phone to stop the recording.

When Tom had returned with strong black coffee for everyone, he sat down crossed-legged and sipped his drink.

Hargreaves restarted the recording. "So, let's get back to you, Lee, and Mark walking towards Sarah," she said.

Tom slurped his coffee and scrunched up his nose. "He… Mark… suddenly lost his balance halfway down the garden."

Lee stopped spinning the remote control.

"I thought he might be pissed as well, but it was only, what… 6.30?" Tom said.

Lee grunted affirmatively.

"And he could barely stand up straight. Then, he gripped his stomach and said he was going to be sick."

"And more people started doing the same around the table." Lee shook his head. "They were wailing and saying their insides were on fire," he said.

Tom nodded. "Mark said the same. He retched like he was about to throw up. He leant forward, trying to be sick, but then toppled over."

"The others around the table got out of their seats and fell over, as well. Some staggered a few steps before they fainted." Lee was gripping the TV controller so tightly, his knuckles went white.

"Did they all collapse at the same time?" Hargreaves asked.

They both nodded.

"And what time was this?"

"Like I said, just after 6.30," Tom said, with Lee nodding in agreement.

Hargreaves flicked through the pages of her notebook. "You both made calls to 999 around that time?"

"Aye," Lee said. "Tom rang first, and I called as well when they put him on hold."

"They were struggling to get enough ambulances. I don't think they believed me at first. I had to get Lee and then Pete to ring them as well."

Henry placed his empty cup on the coffee table. "What did you think had happened to the other guests?" he asked.

Tom shrugged. "I'd not a clue. Food poisoning?"

Lee shook his head. "No. I felt something bad had happened."

"Like what?" Henry asked.

"Like it'd been intentional."

"And what made you think that?"

"Well…" Lee looked at Tom, who shifted in his seat.

Henry narrowed his eyes. "What is it, fellas? What are you not telling us?"

"There was a bit of friction…" Lee said, rubbing one hand over the other. "Between Tom and Mark."

Tom clenched his jaw.

"Why's that?" Hargreaves asked.

Tom didn't answer. His cheeks reddened.

"Might you, by any chance, have had a relationship with Sarah?" Henry asked, sensing that was the root of his distress.

Tom raised his eyebrows. "Is it that obvious?"

"Come on, it wasn't that hard to notice. What I couldn't tell was whether you were in a relationship or if it was just an attraction."

Tom went to speak but his voice was too weak. He cleared his throat. "I… We…"

"How long for?" Henry asked.

"On and off for about three months." He scrunched up his nose. "It was stupid of us. I'm single, so I can do what I please. But she wasn't."

"And Mark found out about this?" Hargreaves asked.

Tom nodded. "He found our text messages two months ago on her phone."

"He checked her phone?" she said.

"Yeah, I know. To be fair, I don't think he looked at it intentionally. He didn't spy on her or anything…" Tom bit his lower lip, and his eyes teared up. Pulling a pained expression, he willed his emotions away. "She was a nice lass, Sarah. We even talked about getting together and her leaving him… but in the end she never did."

"Why?" Hargreaves asked.

"I don't know. I think she loved him as much as she hated him. It was an odd marriage. I didn't really get it myself."

"Didn't I say you'd be best off out of it?" Lee said, his eyes on Tom.

Tom gave a slight nod.

A moment's silence passed between them.

Henry tilted his head to the side. "Are you trying to suggest that Mark Hardy was involved in this poisoning business?"

Tom and Lee shared a concerned look.

"Mark is still in intensive care," Hargreaves reminded them.

Tom accepted her point. "I know he is. It's just… when I saw Sarah lying down in the garden, my first thought was…"

"Mark had harmed her?" Henry asked.

Tom looked him in the eyes and nodded.

"Alright," Hargreaves said. She stopped the recording. "That's all we need for now, but we will be in touch later with more questions, so please don't leave the area."

"We're hardly going to go off on our hols, are we?" Tom asked, frustrated. He then closed his eyes. "Sorry, I know. You need us to be around."

Henry and Hargreaves saw themselves out. When they were outside the front entrance, walking past the tree, Henry craned his neck to look at the penthouse apartment.

"Nice place he has. What was it he does?"

"Professional rugby player, I think, and a personal trainer on the side. So's the other one."

"Who do they play for?"

"Leeds."

Henry was impressed.

"Though, I'd like them more if they played for Bradford," she said. "I bloody hate Leeds."

In Hargreaves' silver Audi, they drove down the busy street away from Tom's apartment building. The cafés were doing good business, with people sitting on the outdoor tables, some chatting with friends while others stared at their laptops.

"So, what do you think of all that?" Henry asked.

Hargreaves shook her head. "I don't really know." She chewed her lower lip, which, like the previous day, was a muted red colour and not the normal bright scarlet. "Like them, I reckon it was the punch that had the poison in it."

"We'll see later, but I think I agree. Who poisoned them, though? Sarah? And why would she? A mass murder-suicide?"

Hargreaves groaned. "I bloody hope not. But it's starting to become an option, isn't it? She made all the food. She insisted they drink her punch."

Henry wrinkled his nose. "I don't buy it. Why would a happy-go-lucky woman suddenly murder her husband and friends before killing herself?"

Hargreaves frowned. "I'm sure we could find a reason."

"Aye. You just might." Henry sighed and stared out the window for a moment. "Here," he said, broaching a subject that had been bothering him. "You're looking a bit more… presentable these days."

She frowned. "Are you saying I didn't before?"

"No. Well…" He regarded her longer hair, more natural make-up, and more professional clothes. When he had first met her, she had looked like someone who had got lost on the way to Whitby's goth festival.

Hargreaves gave him a look. "I've had to change my appearance a bit."

"Aye, I'd noticed. Why?" Henry then added, "You're also more compassionate with witnesses, which is new for you. I didn't know you could do compassion."

She exhaled. "Yeah, it's bloody knackering trying to be nice all the time. I can see why Barnes doesn't bother."

Henry looked at her, his head tilted. "What's it in aid of? You've only just become a detective sergeant; you surely can't be expecting to move up the ladder already?"

She arched an eyebrow. "Can't I?"

"The standard is three or four years minimum between ranks–"

"Are you calling me standard, Henry?" She smirked. "I've been taking some extra training and have already started revising for the inspectors' exam. I want to be a DI before I'm thirty-three."

Henry guffawed. "I was well over forty when I hit inspector rank!"

"Aye, but you're not me."

Henry shook his head and looked out his window at the pavement. They had hit a red light and were waiting behind traffic. "So, when do you turn thirty-three?"

"Are you asking a lady her age?"

"No. I'm asking *you*."

"Very funny," she said, accelerating when the light turned green. "I'm thirty-three next June."

Henry tapped his chin. "In one year? You're confident."

"Fortune favours the bold, Henry."

Henry grumbled at that. "Well, I've noticed the difference. You're a lot more professional." He nodded his head approvingly. "I hardly recognise you. You used to get information out of people by barking at them."

She smiled. "Aye. And it worked sometimes, but now I know it's probably not the best technique."

"And you didn't before?"

She shrugged and pulled a face as if she wasn't bothered either way. "Well, I have found being nicer gets more information out of people, though I do keep my hard-nosed-bitch personality as backup, just in case. But like I said…" She shook her head. "It's bloody hard work being nice all the time."

"Aye, I can see it doesn't come naturally to you."

"You can say that again."

Chapter Ten

Their next stop was Ralph and Claire Gaskin's small suburban house on the other side of Leeds. The Gaskins' street was residential but less leafy than the one Tom Dixon lived in. With it being a Bank Holiday Sunday, the residents' cars lined both pavements, reducing the space for passing vehicles. Hargreaves managed to squeeze her silver Audi into a gap further down the street. As they got out, Henry could smell petrol fumes and cut grass as someone mowed their lawn nearby.

The Gaskins' modest semi-detached house had been spruced up in the past few years, with some of its pebble-dash exterior being replaced with wood cladding. The patio at the front of the house was free from dirt, as if it had been recently power-washed, and the grass on their little lawn was cut short.

The door opened almost as soon as Hargreaves knocked. Ralph Gaskin's eyes were red and bleary. He was in his early forties but appeared older on account of being bald on top and short round the sides. He wore a black T-shirt and classic blue jeans, and slouched as he peered at them.

He waved them in after Hargreaves introduced her and Henry, and led them into a living room on the right.

Claire Gaskin rose from the sofa on seeing them enter. She was of a similar age to Ralph but looked younger. Despite her energetic 'nursery teacher' vibe, she had lines under her eyes from exhaustion. She wore a denim dress marked with stains and had a pink blouse on underneath. Her blonde bob was unbrushed. She blew her nose into a tissue and nodded a hello.

Ralph sat beside her on the settee, while Henry and Hargreaves seated themselves in armchairs across the room. Primary-coloured toy blocks littered the beige rug in front of the television, but apart from that, there was no sign of baby William.

Claire grabbed Ralph's hand and sniffed. Her eyes were redder than her husband's, and she wiped tears from them with the tissue.

"I hope you didn't stay too long at the hospital?" Hargreaves asked. She was sitting up straight with her handbag on her lap.

Ralph hugged his wife. "They finally let us out at four in the morning…" he said. "They said we're fine, which I'd told them when we arrived."

"Better safe than sorry," his wife said.

Husband and wife pressed their foreheads together.

"Is little William, okay?"

Claire sniffed. "He's fine. Just tired."

Hargreaves looked at Henry. Had they come too early, she appeared to be asking.

Henry observed the married couple. "Would you mind answering a few of our questions?"

Ralph lifted his head away from Claire to reply. "We can try."

Claire blew her nose again.

Henry looked at Barnes and gave a slight nod.

She opened her bag and removed her notepad and phone. "I'm going to ask you a few questions about yesterday," she said. "I know it's still very raw, but any information you can give us will be very valuable." She tapped her phone to start the recording and listed who was in the room. "Now, can you tell us who invited you to the barbecue?"

Claire sniffed and spoke with a weak voice. "Sarah did."

"When was that?"

"Last Monday. We have a messaging group, and she invited us."

"Is that how she invited you in the past?"

Claire nodded.

"When had you last seen Sarah and Mark Hardy before yesterday?"

Claire shook her head as if she didn't know, and turned to her husband.

"About three weeks ago," he said. "It was a party at Allister's."

Hargreaves made a note of that. "How did you know Sarah and Mark?"

"I went to school with Mark," Ralph said. He stroked his wife's hand, who'd fallen into tears again.

"So, you've known him for a long time?"

Ralph nodded.

"Were you friendly with Sarah?"

They both said they were.

"She was lovely," Claire managed to say. "Full of life. Always having fun. A burst of sunshine… It's just so sad."

Hargreaves let Ralph console his wife and glanced at Henry. She arched an eyebrow.

Henry leant forwards. "Your son?"

They nodded.

"Where is he?"

"My mum's taken him," said Ralph. "We thought it might be best if he wasn't in the house. We won't be any use today."

"He'd realise we are sad," Claire said. She wiped her eye with a fresh tissue Ralph had given her. "I don't want him to know we're sad." She cleared her throat and spoke with more strength. "He's good at picking up on things. Even if he's barely one."

Henry smiled. "Kids can be like that, can't they? My eldest could always sense the mood of a room." He chuckled. "What do you think little William picked up at the barbecue yesterday?"

Claire's eyes widened at the question, and she blinked. "Well, I don't know. He seemed happy enough."

"He was…" Ralph said. "Until around 4 p.m., and then he got ratty."

"There were too many people there," Claire said.

"Had you taken him to parties before?" Henry asked.

They both fervently shook their heads.

"I'd never wanted to," Claire said. "But as it was during the day, we thought it'd be worth trying. Plus, we wanted to get out. Well, you did, didn't you?" She stared at her husband.

He nodded. "Aye. I was feeling a bit down."

"How come?" Hargreaves asked, sitting forwards.

Ralph flared his nostrils as he looked at her, then turned to his wife. "Well… William's nearly eleven months old, and I don't think we've been to a party or anything since…"

Claire shook her head. "We hadn't."

"Hadn't you seen Sarah and Mark at Allister's party three weeks ago?" Hargreaves asked, reading her notes.

"Oh, that…" Ralph smiled away his mistake. "That didn't feel like the same."

"I didn't go then, did I?" Claire said. "I looked after William. He slept all night, which was a first." She attempted a laugh. "Maybe you should go out more often, he might sleep more."

Ralph laughed weakly and then gave Hargreaves an apprehensive look.

Hargreaves leant forwards. "How do you get on with your friends, Ralph?"

He frowned. "How do you mean?"

"Are you on good terms with them?"

"Of course."

Hargreaves studied her notes. "I understand you're in marketing?"

"A marketing manager, yes. Claire's a nursery-school teacher."

"I'm still on maternity leave," she said. "I go back in a few weeks."

"What does Mark do?" Hargreaves asked.

Ralph stared into the distance. "He's a director of a company or something."

"He runs his own IT company, doesn't he?" Hargreaves corrected.

Claire answered for Ralph, who'd fallen silent. "Mark's family is very well-off," she said. "I think his dad helped fund his company to begin with, didn't he?" She looked at Ralph to back her up.

Ralph frowned at his wife. "He's done well, has Mark. He works really hard. He's a workaholic." He grimaced. "I just hope he'll pull through this."

"He should do," Hargreaves said. "The hospital's fairly positive about that."

Ralph's shoulders relaxed. "What a relief."

He squeezed Claire's hand. She wiped her eyes again as fresh tears came.

"Did you eat anything at the barbecue?" Henry asked.

Ralph exhaled frustration. "We've been asked that countless times over the last twelve hours."

Claire answered for him. "We nibbled on a few snacks, but we left early."

"What time did you leave?"

"I don't know," Ralph answered. "Around 5 p.m."

"Why did you leave so early?"

"Well, William was causing a scene, and we couldn't quiet him–"

"I thought it best we went. Get him back home and calm him down," Claire said.

Henry nodded his head thoughtfully. That was probably all they were going to get. He glanced at Hargreaves and then the door. She understood.

"Well, thank you for your time," she said. "We will be in touch later today or tomorrow."

Henry and Hargreaves rose out of their armchairs, and Ralph and Claire did the same. As Hargreaves put her phone and notepad in her handbag, Henry asked, "Oh, just one question. Did you drink any of the punch?"

"The punch?" Claire looked at Ralph. "I had a bit, but I don't like passion fruit."

"I was driving," he said. "So, I had non-alcoholic beer that I brought with me. Why? Is that what you think it was?" His eyes searched theirs for an answer.

"We're still waiting for confirmation," Henry said.

"Oh, God," Claire said, gripping her stomach. "I drank some of that."

Ralph turned to her. "You've been checked over."

"What if they missed something?"

"Have you felt sick or had any symptoms?" Hargreaves asked.

"No... Well, come to think of it, I felt a bit dizzy last night, but other than that–"

"You're fine." Ralph sighed. "The hospital did all the tests they had."

Claire swallowed hard and nodded.

"Do you have any idea who did it?" Ralph asked. "Assuming someone poisoned the punch?"

"We don't know who yet," Henry said. "It's only a matter of time until we find out, though; isn't it, DS Hargreaves?"

Hargreaves' eyes locked onto Ralph's. "Aye, Henry. Only a matter of time."

Chapter Eleven

Henry got in Hargreaves' Audi and fastened his seatbelt. She pulled out of the parking space and into the narrow street. As Henry watched the small semi-detached houses pass by, the sun pierced the haze again, casting a god-like beam from the heavens over the residential street.

Henry squinted out his passenger window before looking at Hargreaves. "So," he said. "What did you think of the Gaskins?"

She scrunched up her lips and then checked her rear-view mirror before turning onto the high street. "I don't know yet."

"Aye, that's the conclusion I've come to." He rested his elbow on the door's armrest and cupped his chin in his hand.

He watched the high street zip past. The bakers' window was boarded up with battered bits of wood, and the beer adverts outside the newsagents were peeling off from the wall.

Hargreaves took a pair of large designer sunglasses from the centre console and put them on. They made her look bug-eyed.

"Ralph isn't as wealthy or successful as Mark, is he? And he seemed a bit touchy about it, despite pretending not to be." She paused. "Then if you're thinking about logistics, he brought his own drinks to the barbecue, didn't he? And they would have taken the pushchair and a nappy bag filled with everything a one-year-old could need."

Henry regarded her. "Are you suggesting he kept a vial of cyanide next to the sippy cup?"

Hargreaves ran her tongue along the inside of her cheek as she considered it. "I don't know. Maybe not. What do you think?"

Henry huffed. "He seemed cut up about it all, and so did she… But there definitely was some tension over Mark's wealth. And you're right. He didn't sound that believable when he said Mark had earned his success." He frowned. "But I can't see him obtaining a controlled substance and poisoning his friends."

"We don't have to see it, do we? We just have to prove it."

"So, you think he was bitter about not being as successful as his friends and decided to kill them all?"

Hargreaves scrunched up her nose. "Nah, I suppose not. But maybe he didn't intend to poison them *all*."

Henry lifted his head slowly. "Ah, well. That's different, isn't it? Did he intend to kill Mark, but then somehow ended up poisoning the rest of them?"

"He might even have poisoned his wife, if it really was the punch that killed them."

"Aye… that's a possibility."

Hargreaves concentrated on driving her vehicle as it sped onto the Leeds Inner Ring Road. "Actually, let's see if we've had any news from those lab rats yet." She clicked the screen on the console and selected 'messages'. "Ah, it won't let me read them while driving. Can you check them?"

Henry took up her handbag resting between them and pulled out her large, pink phone. There were several notifications, but none seemed to be from Barnes. "You've had messages, but I can't tell who they've come from."

She tutted before snatching her phone from his hands, opening its lock screen, and reading her messages while glancing up at the road.

"You know it's illegal to text and drive?" Henry asked. "Especially when you're on a dual carriageway."

She sniggered under her breath. "I'd like to see a woodentop with the balls to fine me for it." She placed her phone on the console between them. "No news from the lab rats yet."

"So, we have two possible theories so far. Either Sarah Hardy poisoned everyone in an act of murder-suicide, which would be pretty grim. Or Ralph Gaskin attempted to kill Mark Hardy, for reasons unknown – but possibly out of jealousy – and accidentally spiked the others."

Hargreaves mulled over his summary. "I suppose that's all we've got at the moment, which isn't bad as it's not even 11 a.m. We've got two more survivors to talk to. They might be able to add more insight."

"Aye. Let's see what they have to say for themselves," Henry said. "And afterwards, maybe we could get some lunch. I had my rolled oats at six and now my stomach's starting to rumble."

* * *

Pete Blackburn lived in a cottage up on the moors to the west of Leeds, just off the main road towards Ilkley. Henry could see the tall towers in Leeds city centre on the horizon, as if the large buildings had mushroomed across the countryside – growing bigger and bigger.

Hargreaves turned off the main road and into a country lane, and, after a few moments, her sat nav declared they had arrived. She turned into an open gateway between crumbling walls and drove up a short gravel drive. Henry studied the stone cottage squatting underneath the boughs of an old oak tree. Ivy spread across the house's exterior like a bad rash, and its leaves flittered in the gentle wind.

The property seemed to have once been an inn, converted into a home many decades ago. The driveway went up to the house and was barely big enough for two modern-day vehicles. A family-sized Burgundy-red Renault was parked outside and Hargreaves parked just behind it. Henry got out of the car and heard passing traffic on the road in the distance, and the faraway bleats of sheep.

Pete Blackburn answered Henry's knock on the door. He wore a brown shirt, unbuttoned at the collar, and black khakis. He looked a state. His brown hair was clumped up, and his dark-green eyes were bleary. He studied them for a moment before muttering that they should come in.

A collection of men's and women's shoes lined the hallway – running trainers, hiking boots, pumps, and wellies. The clay floor tiles were chipped in places, and the house looked to have been decorated by the previous occupants; unless Pete and Louanne had the same decorating tastes as a middle-aged couple from the late 1980s. Henry recalled having stencilled flowers on his walls in the home he'd shared with his wife many moons ago.

Pete asked them to take a seat on an old beaten settee in the living room. He pulled out a wooden chair from the dining table and placed it opposite. The room was cluttered, with too many magazines, ornaments, and trinkets everywhere. The air was thick with dust.

"How are you doing, Mr Blackburn?" Hargreaves asked, peering at him.

He scratched the sleeve of his brown shirt. "I've been at the hospital most of the night. They told me to leave, eventually. She's now in the morgue."

"I'm very sorry for your loss," Henry said. He noticed the scabs on the back of Pete's hands from where he must have picked at them. Henry then signalled to Hargreaves to start the interview.

"We need to ask you a few questions," she said, removing her phone and notepad from her handbag.

Pete squinted and squeezed the bridge of his nose. "Yes… sure." He crossed one leg over the other and folded his arms, looking awkward sitting on the chair opposite them.

Hargreaves started the recording. "Can you tell us what happened yesterday?"

"Well… from when?"

"From when you arrived at the barbecue."

"Erm… What can I say? We arrived around 2.30, as Louanne wanted to help Sarah get things ready."

"She helped prepare the food?"

"Well… Not really. Sarah said it had mostly been done beforehand." Pete chewed a well-bitten fingernail.

"Sarah had already prepared everything?"

He nodded.

"How do you know Sarah and Mark Hardy?"

"I went to school with Mark."

Henry leant forward. "Which school was this?"

"St George's Grammar. It's a private school."

"Oh, that place over on Rawdon?" Henry asked.

Pete's tired eyes lit up. "Yes, do you know it?"

"I've come across it a few times before now. I certainly didn't go to school there, though."

The light in Pete's eyes faded, and he attempted a smile. "Yes, well… It's an okay school."

Hargreaves got her pen and notepad ready. "Mr Blackburn, did all the guests at the barbecue know each other from the same school?"

He gave a slight nod. "Well, me and my friends did. The wives didn't go, obviously. It's a boys' school."

"And what about Tom and Lee?"

Pete found that mildly funny. "No, they didn't go there."

"Do you all get along? Your circle of friends?"

"Yes. We're still very close."

"How do you stay in contact with each other?"

"We have a chat group on our phones. We meet up every other month or so."

"You had a party three weeks ago, didn't you?" Hargreaves asked, checking her notes.

"Yes, I think they did, but we were on a hiking holiday. Every spring we try to get over to Wales to go for walks around Snowdon."

"Did you and Louanne enjoy hiking?" Henry asked.

Pete slouched and stared into the distance.

Henry noted there weren't many pictures of Louanne or Pete around the living room. Instead, the mantelpiece above the stove and the windowsill were covered with figurines, snow globes, and ornaments. Henry spotted one of the snow globes was a souvenir from Snowdonia; the rest were from French and German locations.

"Can you tell us what you think happened yesterday?" Hargreaves asked delicately.

Pete stirred himself out of his thoughts. "I don't know. We were having fun, chatting about this and that, then someone said Sarah had collapsed, and then everyone fell ill."

"Do you know why you didn't fall ill? Can you think of something you didn't drink or eat that the others did?"

He shook his head while gazing at the ground. "I've absolutely no idea. I've spent the last fourteen hours thinking about it. What could it have been? I ate the same as Louanne, the salad and a burger, we both shared a bottle of wine we brought."

"What about the punch?" Henry asked.

Pete folded his arms across his chest. "Yes, the punch. I keep coming to that."

"You didn't drink any?"

He shook his head. "I might have had a sip to be polite in front of Sarah, but no… I didn't touch it. I hate sugary stuff."

"Did Louanne?"

"Well, that's what I keep wondering… as she barely touched it, too."

"Really?" Henry asked. "Are you saying she didn't drink any?"

"She had some. Maybe half a glass…" Pete gripped his forehead. "I can't for the life of me believe that sipping that punch killed her."

"What did you think when you heard Sarah had collapsed?" Hargreaves asked.

He frowned. "What do you mean?"

"What was your opinion of her?"

"Of Sarah?" He lifted up his nose. "Not much."

"Were you on good terms with her?"

Pete started scratching his hand, picking at the scabs. "Not really. I tried to avoid her, to be honest. She was just so bloody…" He exhaled. "She was always full-on and making a noise. Just the opposite to me and…" He looked down at his hands.

Henry leant forwards. "So, what did you think when you saw Sarah had collapsed at the bottom of the garden?"

"Truthfully? I thought, oh here we go, another round of the 'Sarah Hardy' show." Pete clenched his jaw and pulled a large scab off his hand.

"What do you mean by that?"

"She was always playing jokes, trying to 'liven up' the parties." He affected an Australian accent. "'We need to liven up this party, guys!' She'd always say that. She'd hold up a bottle of vodka and make us do shots."

"And you didn't like that?" Henry asked.

Pete scrunched up his face. "No. None of us bloody did. Not one bit."

A stream of blood ran down from the open wound on his hand, and Pete watched it drip onto the carpet.

Chapter Twelve

Henry and Hargreaves turned to each other as blood streamed out of the top of Pete's hand and dribbled onto the beige carpet. It wasn't clear if Pete was aware it was happening.

"Maybe you should see to that?" Henry said eventually, but Pete didn't respond. His eyes were transfixed on the blood leaking out of him.

Hargreaves took a tissue from her handbag and went over to Pete. As she covered the wound, she bent down in front of him. He stirred himself out of his daze and blinked.

"Are you alright, Mr Blackburn?" she asked.

He nodded lightly and swallowed. "Yes…"

"You're bleeding."

He noticed the tissue under Hargreaves' hand and touched it. "Right."

"Do you want to take over?" Hargreaves asked, removing her hand. "Press down on it hard."

Pete did as instructed.

Hargreaves returned to the settee and gave Henry a sideward glance. He read it to mean she thought Pete was in need of a psychologist.

"Have you got any family around here, Mr Blackburn?" Henry asked. "Or someone who can come and keep an eye on you?"

Pete lifted up the bloodstained tissue and peered underneath.

"Mr Blackburn?" Henry asked. "Do you have someone who can come and look after you?"

Pete replaced the tissue over the wound. "Louanne could… if she were here."

Henry and Hargreaves exchanged looks. "Best get on the phone," Henry said to her quietly.

Hargreaves excused herself and stepped into the hallway.

"We're going to see if we can get someone to check you're alright," Henry said, putting on a smile.

"I'm fine," Pete said. His eyes were still transfixed on his hand.

"I'm sure you are, but as you've suffered a big shock, it might be best if someone takes a look at you. These very stressful situations can get the better of anyone."

Pete observed him with calculating eyes. "You think I've lost my mind?"

"Of course not, Mr Blackburn. We just want to make sure you're getting all the support you need."

Pete's eyes rested on the window. "It's a nice day out again," he said. "It was nice yesterday, before all that happened." He lowered his head. "I'll have to start arranging her funeral, won't I? I wouldn't even know where to begin…"

"I'm sure others can help you with that," Henry said, optimistically. "Did Louanne have family around here?"

He sucked in a breath. "Christ, I have to tell her family. I don't think they even know…"

"It's alright, Mr Blackburn." Henry raised a hand to calm him. "We have a senior detective informing the next of kin of all the victims. If you can let Hargreaves have Louanne's family's address, she'll make sure they're told."

Pete's eyes watered, and he nodded. He wrapped his arms around his thin chest. "I don't think I could manage telling them."

Henry nodded his understanding and heard Hargreaves in the hallway talk to someone on the phone.

"You mentioned something about Sarah Hardy earlier," Henry said.

Pete frowned. "Did I?"

"You suggested that people didn't like her."

"We didn't. She was… you know, so in your face."

Henry cleared his throat and glanced at the door. "What did Louanne think of her?"

"In what way?"

"Did she get on with her? Usually at such events, the wives get together and chat."

"I suppose they do," Pete said. "Though, Louanne and Sarah didn't really get on. Louanne was quiet, like me. We kept ourselves to ourselves. While Sarah was the type to force you into having 'fun'."

"And it was never your sort of fun?"

"God no." Pete shook his head. "Do you think downing colourful shots and surfing on Bondi Beach are my ideas of fun?"

Henry glanced around the fairly austere living room, at the trinkets from hiking trails across Europe. "I suppose not."

Pete clenched his jaw.

"Would you know anyone who'd want Sarah dead?" Henry asked.

Hargreaves walked into the room just then, catching the end of his question. She raised an eyebrow at Henry but then looked at Pete, who shoved his hands between his thin thighs and shifted in his chair.

"It's hard to say…" Pete trailed off.

"What do you mean?" Henry asked.

Hargreaves returned to her place on the settee and restarted the recording.

"It's hard to be certain… I mean," Pete said. He wasn't looking at them. Instead, he studied his bloodstains on the carpet. "She… had a past. A bad one, apparently."

"Do you mean Sarah? Can you give us more details?" Hargreaves asked.

Pete observed her. "She had an odd past in Australia, I believe. Before she met Mark."

"And how did she meet Mark?"

Pete smirked. "That's something of great speculation."

"Meaning?"

"You'll have to ask him."

"Mark's still unconscious in hospital," Hargreaves said.

"Well…" Pete lifted up the tissue on his hand and peered at the staunched wound. "I heard that she had an unpleasant experience with an ex-husband over there."

"In Australia?"

"Sydney, to be exact." Pete nodded, as if something had clicked in his mind. "Mark had been very worried recently."

Hargreaves and Henry frowned at each other.

"What about?" Henry asked.

"He said to Allister, a few weeks ago, that her ex-husband was in the country."

"Whose? Sarah's from Sydney?" Hargreaves asked.

Pete narrowed his eyes and gave the slightest nod.

"Do you know his name?"

"I never heard it. He was just referred to as 'the Aussie'."

"And what had Allister heard about him?" Henry asked.

"Apparently, Mark told him about it three weeks ago at the party I couldn't go to. I saw Allister last week…" He swallowed hard. "Allister's gone now, as well. Hasn't he?" Pete fell silent, and his head hung low.

Hargreaves gestured to the door, and Henry nodded.

"Someone will be over in the next half an hour, Mr Blackburn," she said loudly to Pete. "It's my colleague, DS Claudia Forrester. She's very nice and will keep an eye on you. A doctor is also on his way. He'll ask you some questions and see if you need any medication. Is that alright?"

Pete didn't answer. He breathed shallowly.

Henry and Hargreaves got up off the settee. "I'm very sorry about your loss, Mr Blackburn," Henry said.

Pete stirred out of his stupor. He fixed his bleary eyes on Henry. "I don't need sympathy, Detective. I need you to find out who did this to me and my friends."

Henry winced.

Pete stretched out his bloody hand as if he wanted Henry to hold it.

Henry looked at Hargreaves, who was frowning at the situation. He stepped closer to Pete and reluctantly touched his hand.

Pete gripped his in return. He peered up at him, pleadingly. "Please. Will you find the person who did this to us… to my Louanne?" He gulped. "I don't know how I'm going to… move on."

Henry gave a curt nod. "I promise, I'll put my all into finding out what happened and make sure the person who did it pays."

Pete scrunched his eyes closed. "I hope you do, Detective. I hope you do."

Chapter Thirteen

Hargreaves drove along the country lane, going way faster than Henry felt was safe. She accelerated round a blind corner and then gunned the motor as if they were in a rally race. Her black sunglasses were fixed on the road in front of her, and she chewed gum loudly.

"Well, that was bloody depressing," she said, checking her rear-view mirror. "I hope you washed his blood off your hand."

Henry grunted in response. He had applied some hand gel before getting back in the car. He watched the green fields beyond the drystone walls flash by. Yellow buttercups speckled the long shards of grass. The hazy cloud had cleared up, and the early-May sun shone down on the moorlands around them. A line of traffic was on the main road in the distance. People were clearly making the most of the weather by visiting the local beauty spots.

"What do you think of this business about Sarah's ex-husband?" Henry asked.

Hargreaves shrugged. "Who knows. The guy needs a mental health assessment first. He's clearly having some kind of breakdown, so I'd take what he says with a handful of salt."

"I accept all that; however, we haven't considered a third party yet, have we? We've been focusing on the survivors."

"Suppose so. And it could also have been one of the victims. Talking of the survivors, I doubt it could have been the two rugby lads or Pete Blackburn – unless they're bloody good actors."

"Aye. The two rugby lads seem sound enough. And Pete… Well, he's in a state, as you said. I also very much doubt Noura was involved, considering the state she was in yesterday. But we have Ralph Gaskin to look at, don't we?"

Hargreaves pouted. "We do. I don't know why, but there's just something about him I don't like."

"So, we have Ralph as a person of interest, possibly Sarah, and then Sarah's ex-husband–"

"Who may or may not exist. We'll have to confirm that, first. I wouldn't be surprised if Pete was making him up."

Henry shook his head. "I think he was fairly lucid then."

"What? When he did the weepy hand-holding thing and asked you to promise him we'd charge someone for this?"

"Well, yes… he seemed more lucid then than he did before."

Hargreaves grunted. "We need to see if this ex-husband is a living and breathing human being."

"Well, let's see if Noura can confirm if he's real."

Hargreaves looked down at the Audi's console and tapped on its screen. "I'll check in with Barnes, see if she has any updates."

A ringing tone vibrated out of the car's speakers until Barnes answered.

"Yes?" she asked.

"Hiya, it's us. We've done the Gaskins, the rugby lads, and we're on our way back from Pete Blackburn's," Hargreaves announced.

"Right," Barnes said. She spoke quietly as if she were somewhere she couldn't speak.

Henry leant forwards to talk into the car's front console as he was unsure where the microphone was. "Pete Blackburn asked if you could call his in-laws, but we didn't have the chance to get their details."

"It's alright," Barnes said quietly. "I've broken the news to Louanne's family."

"Where are you now?" Henry asked.

"In the mortuary. They're just wrapping up Sarah Hardy's autopsy."

"How did it go?"

"Inconclusive."

"What do you mean?"

"The cause of death."

Hargreaves scrunched up her face. "It wasn't poison?"

"It could be. Toxicology will have to tell us tomorrow. Possibly poisoning or natural causes."

"What kind of natural cause?" Henry asked.

"Heart failure."

"But that's the cause of death from cyanide poisoning, isn't it?"

"Yes, but there were no other signs of it. Normally, the internal organs are damaged. But Sarah's were fine, apart from her heart. Dr Anderson's stumped."

Henry bit his lower lip. From past experience, it wasn't good when Dr Anderson couldn't work out a victim's cause of death. He was one of the best pathologists in the

North of England, and if he didn't know how someone had met their end, it was unlikely anyone else ever would.

"Wish Anderson my luck, then," Henry said. "I hope he finds out what happened to her."

Barnes mumbled a reply.

"We're heading over to Noura's home to question her," Hargreaves said, her bug-eyed sunglasses fixed on the road ahead. "Then we'll stop somewhere for lunch and head back to HQ."

"Don't bother heading to Noura's," Barnes said, "she's here at the hospital."

"Oh, right. Have you questioned her yet?" she asked.

"No, I'll do it in a moment."

"Make sure you ask her about Sarah's ex-husband," Henry said.

"What's this? She had an ex?"

"Aye, Pete Blackburn stated there could be an ex-husband with a potential history of violence."

"That's interesting," Barnes said. "I'll make sure I'll ask her about that."

Hargreaves pouted. "You'd best make sure he exists first. Pete was away with the fairies when he spoke to us. Where do you want us next, then?"

"You can head over to Leeds General Infirmary, where Mark Hardy was taken," Barnes said.

"Right? How come?"

"The doctor rang earlier; he's awake."

Henry bowed his head. "That's interesting news. Let's go see what he has to say."

"Go easy on him," Barnes said, "the doctor doesn't want him to deteriorate."

"Don't worry," Hargreaves said, gripping her steering wheel. "We'll handle him with kid gloves."

"What else have you found out, apart from the ex-husband?" Barnes asked.

Henry briefly explained his hunch on Ralph Gaskin.

"Do you have anything else on him, apart from the fact you don't like him?" she asked.

Hargreaves came to Henry's defence. "Well, he brought his own drinks to the barbecue, and they had the baby with them, so he could've slipped the poison into the nappy bag or something. He also didn't drink any of the punch."

"The punch?" Barnes asked.

"Aye. We're trying to work out what had the poison in it," Henry said.

"Oh, we might have an answer to that after lunch," Barnes said. "Murphy's been ringing the crime lab every hour, demanding updates and threatening them with reprisals if they don't deliver."

"Well, I'm glad I'm not them," Henry said.

"Alright," Hargreaves said, as they came to the end of the country lane to join a main road. "We'll grab some quick lunch and then head over to the Leeds General to speak to Mark Hardy. Maybe we can find out if this ex-husband exists."

"Okay," Barnes said, "go check if it's a solid lead and then meet me back at HQ. I'll speak to Noura before I go."

"We will do." Hargreaves hung up on Barnes and glanced at Henry. "That adds something else to the list."

"Which one?"

"Reasons to suspect murder-suicide."

Henry pulled a face. "Sarah's inconclusive cause of death doesn't mean a thing."

"Think about it. She prepared the food, had a difficult relationship with her husband, was disliked by his friends, and her ex-husband might be back in the picture – if we're to believe Pete."

"That doesn't mean she's behind all of this."

"Not necessarily… But we might need to start heading in that direction. Don't you think?"

Henry grumbled and peered out at the passing fields. His eyes were on the lookout for any birds.

"I agree it's another reason to suggest she's the odd one out," he said, eventually. "But I'm not ready to call this murder-suicide. Not yet anyway."

Chapter Fourteen

They stopped at a petrol station on the way to the hospital to refuel and pick up sandwiches. Henry had checked the fridges inside the shop for something that tickled his fancy, but there wasn't much. In the end, he'd settled for a ham and pickle sandwich on brown bread that came in a plastic packet. Hargreaves positioned her Audi to the side of the shop near the air pump, and they ate their lunches in their seats. Henry's sandwich wasn't great. The bread was hard at the corners and soggy in the middle.

"What's our game plan with Mark?" Hargreaves asked, biting into her sandwich. She had bought a large coffee from the machine, while Henry had a cup of steaming tea in the holder next to him.

"Let's see what he knows about Sarah's ex, and then get his account of the barbecue."

"What are your thoughts on him?"

"In what sense?"

"He could be a suspect," Hargreaves said, taking a bite and chewing. "If he knew about Sarah and Tom's fling, maybe he had decided to act?"

Henry pursed his lips while chewing. "It's a bit risky to pull something like that with all their friends present. Why not wait for a less public occasion? He could have taken Sarah walking along the moors and pushed her down a ravine? Make it look like an accident."

Hargreaves finished her sandwich and rubbed her hands on a napkin. "I suppose that would make more sense. Let's go see him and find out."

Henry nodded and dropped his half-eaten lunch back into its packet. "That was the worst sandwich I've ever eaten."

"Ah, don't be so snobby. There's nothing wrong with a petrol-pump lunch."

"There's nothing bloody right with it."

Hargreaves tsk-tsked, then started the engine and rolled her Audi out of its parking place.

They arrived at Leeds General Infirmary forty minutes later. At reception, they received directions to the intensive care unit, which was on the third floor. They found Mark Hardy half-asleep in a hospital bed in the corner of the ward. Monitors and machines crowded around him; wires and tubes were attached to his hands, arms, and bare chest. As Henry stepped towards the bed, Hargreaves drew the cubicle curtain closed.

Mark was deathly pale, his skin the milky colour of bone. His black, shaggy hair was tousled. He opened his bloodshot eyes and peered at them. "Who are you?" he asked through chapped lips.

Hargreaves introduced herself and explained Henry was assisting the investigation. "We're here about what happened yesterday," she said.

Mark rotated his head on the pillow to look at the drawn curtain. He closed his eyes.

"Mr Hardy?" Hargreaves asked.

He didn't stir.

Henry raised his eyebrow. "Are you alright, Mr Hardy?"

"I'm not well enough to talk to anyone," he said weakly.

"Well, your doctor says you are, and we really need to talk to you." Hargreaves stepped closer to his hospital bed. "What can you tell us about yesterday?"

"Are you aware of what happened?" Henry added.

Mark raised and lowered his head slowly.

"So, what can you tell us?" Hargreaves asked.

Mark turned to look at her. His lips left traces of blood on the pillowcase. "I fell ill."

"That's correct," Hargreaves said. She gripped her hands together, and Henry guessed she was doing her upmost to remain polite and calm. "What else can you tell us?"

"We were sick. A lot of us," Mark said. "And Sarah collapsed."

"Can you tell us what happened? Who collapsed first?"

Mark focused on the ceiling panels. "I can't quite… I think… Sarah was ill first. Then I went to help her and didn't feel well." He swallowed hard. "I then…" He took a breath. "I woke up here."

"Do you have any other recollections, Mr Hardy?" Henry asked.

Mark shook his head and then turned to face Hargreaves.

"Are you sure that's everything?" she asked.

Mark nodded, appearing not to notice her hardened tone.

"Can you remember Tom Dixon telling you that Sarah had collapsed?"

"I can't."

"Are you sure? He said he and Lee Combes informed you that Sarah had fallen down in the garden."

Mark shook his head; his eyes narrowed with suspicion. "I can't remember him talking to me. I saw her collapse, and I jumped up from my seat at the table and ran towards her, but…" His hand rose to his forehead, pulling the tubes and wires with it. "I couldn't walk. My legs wouldn't work…" He kicked his feet under the duvet to check they still worked.

Hargreaves frowned and stepped away from the bed.

Henry stepped closer. "Mr Hardy, are you saying you saw your wife collapse?"

He nodded.

"Where were you when you saw this?"

"At the head of the table."

"And who was around you?"

"My friends."

"And when you stood up and walked across the garden to Sarah, you collapsed?"

He nodded. "I never made it."

"And you didn't see Tom or Lee? Are you certain they didn't come to you?"

He nodded shallowly. "They were at the other end of the table…"

Henry chewed his lip and then asked, "Where was Sarah from?"

Mark frowned. "Australia?"

"Did her family or friends from Australia ever come to visit?"

Mark shook his head automatically, and then his eyes flickered. "Why?"

"Had you heard rumours about an ex-husband being in town?"

"Never. No."

Hargreaves approached him. "We've heard rumours that Sarah's ex was on the scene."

"From whom? That's not true."

"Are you sure?" Hargreaves asked, her voice almost a warning.

"Yes. I've never heard anything like that."

The two detectives frowned at each other. "We heard you and your friends have a chat group," Henry said. "Would you mind us looking at it?"

"Of course you can."

"Good," Hargreaves said. "We'll take your phone and look through it–"

"My phone?" Mark scratched his cheek. "Why do you want to look at my phone?"

"It might help us find out who poisoned you, your wife, and your friends," Hargreaves said. Her glare suggested she was coming very close to letting her hard-nosed-bitch persona out.

Mark considered her remark before facing away from her glare. After a pause, he said, "That's fine. Look at whatever you want."

Henry spotted Mark's phone in a plastic bag. It was on top of a neat pile of clothes resting on a chair next to the bed. Hargreaves picked it up and placed it in her handbag.

"Is that all?" Mark asked, his eyes flickering. "I'm very tired now."

Henry nodded at Hargreaves. "Aye, we'll let you get some sleep."

"We'll need to talk to you again later, Mr Hardy," Hargreaves said.

Mark closed his eyes. "I want to go back home," he whispered.

Henry grimaced. "You won't be going back there for a few days. Forensics will need it. Besides, I doubt the doctors here will let you out of their sights for a while."

Mark's eyes shot open. "I suppose you're right. I detest hospitals."

Hargreaves opened the cubicle curtain. "We'll see you soon, Mr Hardy."

With that, they walked out, leaving Mark to drift off into a less-than-blissful sleep.

Chapter Fifteen

They left Leeds General Infirmary and crossed the city centre to return to the police station. Despite it being a lazy Sunday afternoon, traffic was dense. Perhaps it was people wishing to visit the city's shops and museums –

why they weren't out in the Yorkshire Dales enjoying the sunshine, Henry didn't know.

He shifted in his seat and glanced at Hargreaves, who furrowed her eyebrows as if struggling to solve a mathematical formula.

"I don't know what to make of that," she said. "Mark Hardy's just contradicted two separate witness statements."

"Three, if you count Lee's," Henry said. "Well, maybe that is two, as Tom and Lee basically said the same thing."

Hargreaves slowed her car as they came to some traffic lights. "So, according to Mark, Tom and Lee didn't approach Mark to tell him that Sarah had collapsed. And he says he knows nothing about the ex-husband Pete mentioned."

"Hmmm," Henry said. "One contradiction could be accepted, but two…"

"Who's lying then?"

"Well, who has more reason to lie?" Henry asked.

Hargreaves clenched her jaw. "Why would Tom and Lee make up that story about telling Mark that Sarah had collapsed? What's in it for them?"

"Maybe they didn't lie. Mark will still be up to his eyeballs on medication."

"I think it's more likely that the ex-husband story isn't true, as we only have Pete's word on that. And, as I've said, that man's not far off from being sectioned under the Mental Health Act."

"Well, let's get back to HQ and look at everything we've gathered so far," Henry said. "Something might stand out."

"Besides Sarah Hardy."

"Aye, besides her."

Hargreaves patted her handbag, which rested between them. "We'll learn more when we get into Mark's phone."

"What do you think we'll find?"

She huffed. "No idea. I'd like a look at the group chat to see what they've been talking about. We could also get a look at his social media and browsing history."

"Do you see Mark as a poisoner?"

She tilted her head; her bug-eyed sunglasses reflected the afternoon sun. "It could be that Mark is telling the whole truth, and it's Tom and Lee who are lying."

"Aye, but why? What difference does it make whether they told Mark that Sarah had collapsed or not?"

"Well, they're among the survivors."

"Aye, that's a point." Henry rested his chin on his hand and stared out at the shop windows that passed by – a procession of chain coffee shops, fast-food restaurants, and betting shops promising big wins. "But for me, the rugby lads were the most believable ones."

"Me too, to be fair."

Henry mused on what this could mean, and then a new thought came to him. "What about their phones?"

"The victims'? We've collected Allister's and Louanne's from the scene."

"What about Sarah's?"

"She didn't have it on her. Forensics are still searching the house for it."

Henry tapped his chin. "That's interesting."

"I know," Hargreaves said. "Who knows where she put it."

They made it back to Leeds Central police station within twenty minutes. The building had more life in it than earlier. Several officers rushed around the corridors, and the sound of ringing desk phones echoed off the walls.

Henry and Hargreaves stepped into the meeting room they had occupied that morning. The sun must have shone through the window since then, making the air in the room uncomfortably warm. Barnes's handwritten list of the barbecue invitees was still on the whiteboard. Hargreaves picked up a marker pen and started scribbling down what they had learnt in their interviews that morning.

Sitting in a chair at the table, Henry saw that it was already 1 p.m. Murphy's press conference would begin in thirty minutes, and the detective superintendent would want a list of details to announce so he could pretend they were on top of things. As Henry watched Hargreaves jot down her notes on the whiteboard, he doubted they had much of anything to say. The witness statements were contradictory, and Henry and Hargreaves had come away more confused than before. They had three or four persons of interest, and each had a perfectly good reason why they might be innocent.

Henry sighed and spun his swivel chair round to face the window. The busy street outside bustled with traffic. This might be a case where there were more motives than people, Henry felt, which was common when a group of old friends were involved. Henry hated such cases, as they became bogged down in hearsay and lacked hard evidence. Any of these old friends could have harboured secrets, frustrations, and grudges that had lasted for decades – until yesterday, when all those years of built-up negativity culminated in an atrocious act.

Henry could relate to holding grudges. He contemplated his own history with Murphy. They had once been close, working well together as young detectives back in the late eighties, but now Henry suspected his old partner was involved in an investigation that got him pushed out of the police force twelve years ago. However, up until now, thankfully, there hadn't been any outbursts of violent rage. Well, not yet anyway.

Henry absent-mindedly tapped his chin with a finger while staring at the deep blue sky above the traffic outside. Going back to the case at hand, two things needed to be taken care of quickly. First, how had the poison been obtained? Who had got hold of it, stored it, and brought it to the party?

The second thing that needed urgent exploration was the relationship between the group of friends. They had been in contact with each other since school. Henry believed most grudges that fester into motives to kill often start at school, when egos are less developed, and people can be mentally harmed by the simplest of slights.

Had, as Henry suspected, one of these friends harboured resentment against the others for twenty years? Resentment that, to the killer, justified murder?

Hargreaves popped the lid on her marker pen and stepped back to reread her notes on the whiteboard. "I think that's everything," she said. "Anything to add?"

Henry stirred himself out of his thoughts. "No, that looks fine." He stood up, took another pen from the table, and walked to the whiteboard. "I want to add two things."

He wrote down 'school' and 'poison' and drew large circles around them.

Hargreaves frowned. "What's this?"

"If we look at the group of friends and their pasts, we can find a motive."

Hargreaves lifted her head up. "I don't think we're short of possible motives, Henry. We've got three already."

"I know. That's why we also need to be looking at the poison. Where was it located, stored, and how was it brought to the party?"

"And how was it administered?" Hargreaves added, her arms crossed over her chest, head tilted to the side. "Alright. But if it was just a vial of powder, any of them could have hidden it in their pockets and brought it to the party."

"That's true. That's why we need to be looking at people who have access to cyanide or who can easily obtain it. To my mind, it's hardly something you can pick up at your local chemist."

"Isn't cyanide in rat poison?"

Henry shook his head sternly. "No, not for ages. We'll need to see who had access to laboratories or industrial sites, and then work it from that angle."

Hargreaves narrowed her eyes and studied the names on the whiteboard. "Right. I suppose we start a file on each possible suspect and then accumulate as much info as we can on them." She sighed. "That could take bloody days. I'll see if I can lump one of the detective constables with that task. I'm sure they'll be happy to crack on with it."

Henry chuckled. "You sound like an inspector already."

She glowered at him.

The door opened, and Barnes stepped into the meeting room. Her tanned face was flushed red, and she loosened her shirt collar.

"Alright?" Henry asked her.

She nodded, breathing hard, and checked her phone. "I've just spoken to–" she took a breath "–the lab."

"Right? Do they know about the poison?" he asked.

Barnes nodded and sucked in a breath. "Salad dressing."

Henry pulled a face. "Salad dressing?"

Barnes nodded curtly. "They found–" she took another breath "–a very high dose of cyanide in it… Over five grams."

"Is that a lot?" Hargreaves asked.

"Enough to kill a herd of elephants," she said. She took a deep breath and waved air into her face. Her beathing eventually calmed down. "Sorry, I ran up the stairs while talking on the phone. And the high pollen count isn't helping."

"So, it wasn't the punch?" Henry asked.

"No, that was clean. It had a very high volume of alcohol, but no cyanide."

"So, it was the salad dressing…" Henry frowned and bit his thumb knuckle. "And no news on what killed Sarah Hardy?"

Barnes shook her head.

"Well, this case just gets odder and odder," Henry said, feeling Hargreaves' and Barnes's eyes on him.

Chapter Sixteen

Henry and Hargreaves watched the press conference on the big television in the meeting room. It was being broadcast through the nation's live news channels. Henry leant forwards in his chair while Hargreaves reclined in hers and plonked her feet on the table. The points of her high heels scraped the surface.

On the live TV feed, Murphy was stood at a lectern, which had a bouquet of colourful microphones on it. He wore a fitted dark-navy uniform with a silver crown on each epaulette. After a brief discussion with Barnes, which wasn't picked up by the mics, Murphy gripped both sides of the lectern and puffed out his chest. Barnes remained visible in the background, her head bowed slightly, doing her best not to look at the cameras.

"She's not a natural TV personality, is she?" Hargreaves asked, almost sneering at the screen.

"It's something you grow into, I suppose," Henry said. "I wasn't very good at it to begin with." He stopped himself from asking Hargreaves if she thought she could do a better job; he already knew the answer.

Murphy did his best to sell the meagre details they had obtained since the investigation at Cragg Hall had started. A small crowd of journalists typed the information down on their laptops. After his brief speech, Murphy foolishly opened up a Q & A instead of rushing off stage. With a few pointed questions, Murphy's spin quickly unravelled under the journalists' scrutiny.

"So, you don't know what happened at all?" one journalist for a national paper asked after a brutal line of questioning, her tone of voice mocking him.

Murphy cleared his throat. "My detectives are working hard on this investigation, and as quickly as they can, and we're doing our best to find out what happened here and to ensure the guilty party faces justice."

Sighs of exasperation came from the press and were picked up by the microphones.

Murphy pointed at another journalist, who stood up and introduced himself as, "Roy Parker, *Yorkshire Gazette*."

Henry recognised the voice and the name. He had dealt with Roy on a recent case – saved his life, in fact – and hoped he would repay the favour by going kindly on Murphy.

Roy read from his notepad. "So, you've got three dead, one in a critical condition, and you believe foul play was involved but you don't have any suspects or any ideas what happened?"

Murphy cleared his throat. His bulldog-like face grew redder than it already was, and his shirt collar looked ready to snap open around his thick neck. "We are investigating what happened and should know more presently."

"How many detectives do you have on the investigation?" Roy asked, smirking.

Murphy's upper lip twitched. "We have a full major investigation team and a full lab working on this."

"A full MIT?" Roy said. He then paused, before asking, "Is it true that you have a retired former senior detective on the MIT working in an unofficial capacity?"

Murphy's eyebrows shot up. "I don't know who you're referring to."

"A Mr Henry Ward. Do you know him?"

"Oh, bother," Henry said, huffing. Why the bloody hell was Roy outing his involvement in this investigation on live TV, he wondered.

"I shan't be answering questions about personnel," Murphy said. He made a show of collecting the few papers on his lectern and thanked the press for their time.

But before Murphy had stepped away from the microphone, Roy asked, "Just one further question, Superintendent! Is there any truth to the rumours that the man who owned the property is also being investigated for fraud and embezzlement?"

Murphy scrunched up his face at the question and then glared at Barnes behind him. She went pale and didn't speak. Murphy looked back at the press. "As I've said, we are still carrying out our investigation and will update you all shortly."

With that, Murphy spun on his dress shoes and stormed away from the lectern, with Barnes following behind. Henry feared the berating Barnes would get from Murphy as soon as they had stepped off stage.

Hargreaves took her heels off the table and picked up the remote control. She turned off the TV and huffed. "That Roy Parker is bad bloody news."

Henry was staring into the distance and agreed with a grunt.

"I mean, was he really trying to drop you in the shit?"

Henry stirred himself out of his trance. "I don't know. I can't think why he would. I did save his life not that long ago."

"Aye, the ungrateful git."

Henry glanced at her. "What about that other thing? The detail about Mark Hardy being investigated for embezzlement and fraud?"

"Lord bloody knows."

"Nothing like that has come up yet?"

She shook her head as she leafed through her notebook. "We've not heard much about his company at all."

"What's the name of it again?"

"Erm… Sales Expedited."

Henry tapped his chin. "It doesn't have a link to chemicals or science, does it?"

Hargreaves shrugged. "The Gaskins said he did IT stuff, didn't they? But who knows what that really means." She pulled a face. "I guess we'll have to find that out, won't we?"

Henry rose from his chair and picked up a marker pen. He went to the back of the room and wrote 'Sales Expedited' on the whiteboard. Then, he drew a big circle around it.

"We've got three things to look at now: poison, motives, and Hardy's company, which could also help us with the first two."

"Aye, alright," she said, nodding slowly.

Murphy stormed through the door, loosening the top button of his shirt collar. He cut a very distinguished figure in his tailored suit, despite his bulky figure. He breathed noisily through his nostrils and paced the room like a bull about to cause havoc. "What the shitting hell are you lot up to?"

Hargreaves and Henry shared a confused look.

"I wanted facts for this press conference, and what do I get? A load of possibilities and Lord knows what. The bloody journalists know more than we do."

"Roy's an investigative journalist," Henry said. "He enjoys digging up dirt."

"Aye," Murphy said, focusing all his rage on Henry. "He has been digging something up: your zombie career. How the bloody hell does he know you're involved?"

Henry raised his hands in the air. "I've no idea."

"Who have you been talking to about this case?"

"Nobody. Apart from the witnesses we spoke to today, and Hargreaves was with me then."

As Murphy glared at him, his lower lip quivered slightly, and then he looked at Hargreaves. "And what have you learnt this morning then, seeing as you've spent it chatting with folk and having cups of tea?"

Barnes drifted into the room looking drained after presumably suffering the first round of Murphy's bollocking.

Hargreaves sat erect in her chair, clearly not one to be intimidated by Murphy's bark. "We've spoken to all the witnesses, and we have a group of persons of interest–"

"A group?" Murphy asked dubiously.

"And three clear lines of inquiry." She pointed at the whiteboard.

Henry gestured at the three circles he had drawn. "We need to find out which person of interest could have obtained and transported the poison to the barbecue. Then, we need to find out which one had a clear motive. And thirdly, we want to look into Mark Hardy's business and see if these accounting issues are true or not."

Murphy took in the writing on the whiteboard, his arms crossed over his large chest.

"We also know the poison was put into the salad dressing," Hargreaves added.

"So I've heard. Who the bloody hell puts cyanide in sodding salad dressing?" Murphy tutted. "Anyway… what's wrong with a bit of salad cream? Bloody poncy salad dressing." He huffed through his nostrils again as he inspected the whiteboard.

Henry didn't know if they had given him enough to quell his anger.

Murphy walked to the window and looked out at the street outside. "I don't like this case," he said. "I don't like poisoners; they're pathetic. I wouldn't say it's a woman's method of murder, as I respect women too much. But let's just say, it's for the weak and snide. Aye… the snide. The passive-aggressive sort who pretend they're your friend and then slip bloody cyanide in your sodding… what was it? Salad dressing?"

He exhaled before continuing. "Let's focus our efforts on these three areas you've outlined, and I'll give another press conference tomorrow, where I want to say something more than just 'we're looking into it'."

"But it's only the first day," Henry said. "Nobody expects us to know much in the first twelve hours."

Murphy glared at him. "Oh, people do, Henry. People expect results in a day. Not even that. As soon as they hear a murder's taken place, they want to know we've caught some bugger for it. Otherwise, they think we've failed, that we'll never find the killer, that we're a bunch of incompetents who don't know our elbows from our sodding backsides. And then they start questioning why we cost so much. Why do we need all this money to fund our pensions, the PFI building payments, salaries, and equipment. And that, Henry, gives those twats in Westminster the cover to reduce our budgets another ten sodding per cent."

Henry shrugged. "It wasn't like that in my time."

"Well, excuse me, Henry. Why don't you wake yourself up from your afternoon nap and look out the sodding window. Because out there, it's 2024 – not 1997. There's a whole bloody world of difference. We've got these sodding things for a start." Murphy pulled his mobile from his pocket and held it in the air. "We've got social media, the dark web, sodding AI. We've got hundreds of new ways for people to commit crime, only now, we've got fewer sodding detectives worth any salt."

Murphy then turned to Hargreaves and Barnes. "Well, you two are alright." He then looked at Henry. "And you, I suppose, even if you have one foot in the grave."

"Cheeky sod!" said Henry, appalled. "We're the same bloody age."

Murphy ignored him and went back to staring out the window. "You've got twenty-four hours to get me a suspect I can parade on live TV," he said.

Henry waited for a 'or else', but it didn't come. He then realised it was implied.

Murphy turned to the whiteboard with his arms folded over his chest. "Can I ask why murder-suicide isn't on here?"

Henry glanced at Hargreaves before answering, "We're not quite sure–"

"I don't care if you're sure or not, it should be on here. By all accounts, it's a strong likelihood." His face soured. "I admit, however, that parading the suspect on live TV would be a challenge in that case. But it'd be a quick, clean resolution to this shitshow."

Henry went to argue but held his tongue.

"Twenty-four hours!" Murphy thumped the whiteboard as punctuation.

Hargreaves and Barnes wore downcast expressions.

Henry didn't know why, but he had some hope that this mess could be cleared up quickly – and without resorting to framing Sarah for the murders. All they had to do was get to the bottom of a few things, and the rest would fall into place.

Chapter Seventeen

It was 2 p.m., and they had the rest of the afternoon to find out as much as they could about their three new priorities: 'school', 'poison', and 'Mark's company'. Barnes told them to look into the company angle first, seeing as they had been blindsided by Roy Parker's question on the topic. So, Hargreaves and Henry set off to the headquarters of Sales Expedited.

As they were in Hargreaves' silver Audi speeding along the dual carriageway out of Leeds, Henry searched the internet for details of the company on his phone. He felt slightly carsick as he read the search results while Hargreaves overtook cars and swerved between lanes. However, he managed to focus long enough to get the relevant details.

Sales Expedited was a distribution company that sold international products from origins unspecified, which were shipped across the UK. All of its transactions were done online, which seemed to be its only link to IT. The company also used to distribute products across Europe before Brexit but had since stopped that activity.

What the company distributed was a mystery to Henry, as the website didn't have much information. The stock images included photos of packages and cardboard boxes, but something did pique Henry's interest: there were images of test tubes and vials.

"Do you think this company deals with chemicals?" Henry asked Hargreaves.

She had her sunglasses on, as the sun was shining brightly. "I guess we'll know when we get there," she said.

"Will anyone be there? It is Sunday on a Bank Holiday weekend."

"Barnes has called someone in – Curtis Quaker. He's agreed to meet us."

"Quaker?"

She nodded. "He's a friend of Mark's and apparently helps him run the company."

"Alright, let's see what he knows then."

They arrived at the company headquarters, located in a business park to the east of Leeds city centre. The company's name was on a sign near the entrance of an empty car park, and Hargreaves pulled up in front of a two-storey office building. The premises were surrounded by security fencing and at the back of the building was a warehouse. Its large roller shutter doors were firmly locked.

They went to the front entrance of the office building, which had the company's name and logo on, and rang the bell. No one came. The windows showed a dark interior, and Henry wondered if this Curtis Quaker was even here. He double-checked the empty car park.

"You do realise your Audi is the only car here?"

Hargreaves grunted. "Aye. I've just seen."

"Did Barnes ring that Quaker or not?"

"I thought she had."

The sun shone down on them, and Henry squinted at the busy road in the distance. As he let the sun settle on his skin, he realised he could be sitting in his comfy camping chair in his backyard, instead of standing outside a nondescript office building waiting to talk to some bloke.

"Do we know any more about this fraud accusation?" Henry asked her.

Hargreaves shook her head. "I was hoping Curtis would enlighten us."

"Why would he do that if he fears it could implicate his friend and business partner?" Henry bit his lower lip. "You know what? I think I'll try something."

"I'd prefer if you didn't."

Henry ignored her and walked a few paces away from her into the car park. He took out his mobile and searched for Roy Parker's number. When he found it, he dialled, and his call was answered instantly.

"Mr Henry Ward?" Roy said. Henry could almost hear his smirk.

"Roy? How are you? Recovered well after what happened last time we spoke?"

"Nothing two weeks in the south of Spain and some therapy can't fix."

"The south of Spain? I'll remember that for the next kidnapping victim I come across."

Roy snickered. "What is it you want?"

"I'd like to know about this fraud business. Are you winding us up?"

"No, I'm just doing a better job at uncovering what happened."

"Is that right?" Henry paused. "How did you know I was involved?"

"I didn't for sure, until you just rang me now."

Henry grinned. "Nice try, but you wouldn't have asked Murphy if you weren't one hundred per cent sure I was working on this case, would you? If Murphy had denied it, you'd look silly."

"Murphy didn't deny it, and he still looked silly."

"He can't help that. That's just the way he looks." Henry heard Roy typing on a keyboard. "Are you writing down what I'm saying?"

"I didn't start the voice recorder, so yes."

"But this is all off the record."

"You need to say that at the beginning, Henry. You know the rules."

Henry pursed his lips and glanced back at Hargreaves in the distance. She watched him carefully. "I've not said anything worth printing," he said to Roy.

"Well, you've confirmed you're working on this case and that you've no idea about the fraud investigation into Mark Hardy's company. I'm looking forward to seeing what else you'll let slip."

Henry clenched his fist and tapped his knuckles on his forehead, in the hope he could knock some sense into himself. What was wrong with him? He used to be a master at dealing with the press.

"Well…" Henry said, unsure where to go from here. "Is it such a problem if I'm working on this case?"

"You mean, you don't think it's a problem that a retired detective, who's got no business being involved in a real police investigation, is handling evidence and interviewing suspects?"

"Well… no. Not if he's a consultant."

"A consultant? Is that what they're calling you? That's an interesting way of spinning it." Roy sighed. "Apologies for getting serious on you, Henry; but weren't you at the centre of a corruption investigation before you retired twelve years ago?"

The question landed like a punch in Henry's gut, but he did his best to pretend it hadn't affected him. "I was cleared of all charges–"

"You were forced to resign, weren't you?"

"The accusations were without merit."

"If you're saying West Yorkshire Police pushed you out, why are you helping them now?"

Henry's mouth gaped. He couldn't think of an answer. He saw Hargreaves scowling at him as if she was aware he was badly messing something up. Thank the Lord she was too far away to hear the conversation.

"Why did you ring me, Henry?"

"To see what you knew–"

"Listen, let's come to an arrangement."

"What do you mean?"

Roy took a breath. "I can keep your involvement in this out of the press."

"And what will that cost me?"

"I want an inside line into this investigation."

"I can't do that!"

"I don't need you to spy or anything, I just want titbits every now and again."

"I can't…" Henry shook his head. "I have never – and never will – leak details about an investigation to the press."

"Oh, really? Because I've found out a lot of details already, thanks to you."

"I beg your pardon?"

"I've been talking to the Taylors, who've been talking to your friend, Jean Whitehead."

Henry snarled for an instant. "You spoke to the Hardys' neighbours?"

"They were very helpful and very willing to talk. They mentioned your name and said they'd heard 'confidential' details about the investigation, thanks to you."

"That's not true."

"So, you haven't spoken to Jean Whitehead today about this case?"

Henry didn't answer.

"You don't deny leaking details to her?"

"Listen, fella! I bloody saved you from being killed, remember. What's all this in aid of?"

Roy paused. "This is my job, Henry. This is who I am."

"So, you've found a way to get more information from a live investigation by pressuring me?"

"Pretty much."

"And you're not going to tell me who was investigating Hardy's business or why?"

"No. But I'm sure you can find that out. Aren't you back with the police now?"

"Maybe I shall look into that myself."

"Good luck with that. HMRC is closed today."

"How did *you* get the information, then?"

"All my sources remain strictly confidential. As you would be if you became one."

"Don't make me laugh," Henry said. "The only way you could know about this is if you were illegally accessing confidential tax information."

"As I said, all my sources are private. Are you sure I couldn't twist your tail? No one would ever know anything came from you."

"You know what? Forget I ever bloody rang."

"I wish I could. However, you've given me so much to look into, I think–"

Henry hung up on him.

Hargreaves' suspicious glare intensified as Henry made his way back to the building's entrance. "What was all that about?" she asked.

"Nothing," Henry said, shoving his mobile into his pocket.

He really wished he was sitting in his backyard in his foldable chair, minding his own business and keeping his nose clean. And, more importantly, avoiding all conversations with journalists.

Hargreaves didn't take her eyes off him. "No, really. What just happened? Who did you ring?"

"Nobody of any import."

"What does that mean?"

A navy-blue Rolls-Royce appeared at the entrance to the car park and Henry jumped at the chance to change the subject.

"Oh, here we go. This must be the Quaker."

Hargreaves watched the grand four-door saloon roll to a stop and then glanced at Henry. "Let's make it clear that you'll tell me who you've just spoken to after we've dealt with this idiot."

Henry gave a non-committal grunt and avoided her hard gaze.

He really hoped he could salvage the situation with Roy Parker before the sodding journalist did him any damage.

Chapter Eighteen

Henry assumed the person driving the Rolls-Royce would be a chauffeur and that some elderly businessman was seated in the back. However, a man younger than Mark Hardy bounded out of the front seat. He wore a light-grey sweatshirt and had bright-blue tracksuit bottoms and flashy pink-and-white trainers. His blond hair had a centre parting, and his curtain-style fringe framed his face.

For reasons Henry couldn't specify, the man's good looks and infectious smile were oddly unsettling.

The man introduced himself as Curtis Quaker and shook Hargreaves and Henry's hands. He took out some keys from his pockets and opened the office's front door.

Henry noticed he didn't bother to lock up his Rolls-Royce.

Curtis apologised for the delay as he let them into the building, explaining he had been at his house in the country. The front hallway was stuffy, the industrial carpets were grimy, and the walls were chipped from where furniture had banged into them.

Henry noted the solitary reception desk lacked a phone and computer.

Curtis took them into a meeting room, which had broken blinds over the single-pane windows, and smelt of heated plastic. He offered them coffee, but Hargreaves and Henry both declined and sat opposite him at a table. Curtis leant his elbows on the tabletop and rested his head on them, looking at the detectives expectantly.

"So, what is this all about?" he asked.

Henry felt Curtis' tone and demeanour were oddly chipper for someone whose business partner had been involved in a mass poisoning. He frowned and then caught Hargreaves looking at him. She nodded at him to start.

"We're here about what happened yesterday at Mark Hardy's home," Henry said, gravely.

Curtis raised his head slowly, but his buzzing enthusiasm didn't die down. "Right, oh yes. That was wack. No cap." He then stared at them. "And is that all?"

Henry double-blinked. He only understood half of the words Curtis had used.

"We're looking into Mark's life to see what could have motivated the poisoning," Hargreaves said.

"Right. Yes. I couldn't really help you there."

"Oh?" Henry said.

Curtis nodded. "I don't know much about his personal life."

"You've never met his wife?" Henry asked. "Or visited his home?"

Curtis shook his head through Henry's questions.

"What about these accusations of fraud?" Hargreaves asked, glaring at Curtis.

His enthusiasm deflated somewhat. "Excuse me, these what?"

"We've heard rumours about fraud taking place in this company."

Curtis was shaking his head again. He tried a smile, but it wasn't as convincing as before. "That's caps. I've never heard anything like that. Besides, I wouldn't know anything."

"Aren't you involved in this company?" Henry asked, scrutinising him.

"This one? Hardly at all."

"So, what is your involvement in it?"

"Well… I seeded the capital to help Mark get started in the beginning."

"I thought it was Mark's family who helped him start the company," Henry said, checking with Hargreaves who nodded in agreement.

Curtis shook his head again. "No, no. My BS meter's going off the charts. That's complete caps–"

Henry slammed his hand onto the table. "Please, could you stop speaking in riddles and start telling us the bloody truth?"

Curtis' eyes widened.

Hargreaves turned to Henry, giving him a look of warning.

Henry gathered his nerves. The conversation with Roy Parker and dealing with this idiot had gotten the better of him. He closed his eyes for an instant, took a breath, and then asked, "Please, would you answer our questions in standard English? Now, what is your involvement in this company?"

Curtis glanced at the two detectives in turn and then shook his head slowly. "You know what, this is all sus. I'd feel better if I had a lawyer present."

"Why?" Hargreaves asked, offended.

"I'd just… yeah. I'd much prefer it if my lawyer were here."

"Can't risk telling us the truth, eh?" Henry asked.

Hargreaves tutted at Curtis. "We're only having an informal discussion here, Mr Quaker, to help us with our inquiries. This is a time-sensitive investigation and making it more formal will only waste your time and ours."

Curtis nodded as if he understood. "Yeah, but I'd still prefer it if my lawyer was here. I mean, I am allowed to do that, aren't I?"

Henry nodded. "Aye, you can have a lawyer. It just makes you look guilty."

"So, having legal representation makes people look guilty, does it?" Curtis asked, crossing his arms over his chest.

"Mr Quaker," Hargreaves said, "we can make this more formal, and you can bring your lawyer into it, but that'd mean you spending the rest of the day at Leeds Central police station. I'm sure you're a busy person and have better things to do. The alternative is that you tell us what we need to know now, and we can let you enjoy the rest of your afternoon."

Curtis tilted his chair back, balancing it on its rear legs. "I don't know…"

"Listen, Mr Quaker," Henry said, pressing his hands together. "We're dealing with a very serious crime here. Ten friends met yesterday afternoon to enjoy a barbecue on Addingham Moorside. Only seven of them survived. Your business partner is in a critical condition in ICU. Three people are dead. Murdered." He leant forward. "We need to find out what happened and locate the guilty party as quickly as possible. And we believe this company may or may not be involved. If it isn't, then we'll leave you be. If it is, then you can help us discover why someone wanted those three people dead. Does that make sense to you?"

Curtis scrunched up his nose. "I don't want to get involved in anything." He narrowed his eyes as he considered something and then nodded to himself. "Yeah, I definitely want a lawyer present."

"Can you get one here now?" Hargreaves asked.

Curtis shook his head. "Well, no. It's Sunday. And tomorrow's a Bank Holiday, so it'll be Tuesday or Wednesday at the earliest." He clicked his fingers and pointed at Hargreaves. "You know what? I'm off on a business trip to Dubai for the next three weeks. I set off Tuesday morning. So…" He sucked air through his teeth. "I wouldn't be able to talk to you for a couple of weeks at the earliest."

Henry huffed and crossed his arms. He glanced over at Hargreaves, who leant forwards. "Can you at least tell us what this company does?"

"I don't know, but I'm pretty sure that if my lawyer were here, he'd tell me to end this conversation right now." Curtis nodded to himself again. "You know what, that's just what I'll do." He flopped his chair forwards, planting the front legs on the carpet, and jumped out of his seat. "I'll have to ask you to contact my people and arrange a meeting when I'm back from Dubai."

Hargreaves and Henry remained seated at the table. "I'm sorry, Mr Quaker, there seems to be a misunderstanding," Hargreaves said, tilting her head. "You seem to have mistaken us for people who are not detectives investigating a mass homicide."

Henry could feel the rage buzzing off Hargreaves and winced slightly. How bad was this going to get?

Curtis must have also sensed it, as his false smile disintegrated, and he inched towards the exit.

"Sit down, Mr Quaker, or I'll arrest you for withholding evidence and for pissing off a detective sergeant."

Curtis guffawed. "You can't do that!"

"I can do what I want. We'll drag your lawyer from wherever the heck he is and have our interview at six o'clock tomorrow morning, after you've spent a night in a holding cell."

Hargreaves rose out of her seat.

"Have you ever been in a police cell, Mr Quaker?" she asked.

He didn't respond. He just gawped at her.

"They're tiny," she said. "They stink of piss and shit. You can't get comfy in them. Your shoelaces and belt will be taken from you, so you can't hang yourself like others have done, and you'll sit there all night, trying your hardest to get to sleep, but the screaming drunk in the cell next to yours will do their best to keep you awake, all… night… long."

"Aye, especially if I pay him a tenner to do it," Henry said, chuckling.

"And then at six in the morning, after a crap breakfast and a weak cup of tea, we'll interrogate you all day long until we find out what we want to know. Your lawyer will be sitting next to you, pissed off and unhelpful, as you'll have ruined his lovely weekend. So don't expect him to be much use. Now, does any of that sound like a good plan, Mr Quaker?"

The two detectives glared at him. Henry noticed his left leg was wobbling.

"Right, I'll take that as a no," Hargreaves said. "Now, could you sit back down so we can finish our conversation?"

Curtis nodded weakly and lowered himself into his chair.

Chapter Nineteen

As Curtis Quaker leant forwards in the seat, strands of his blond fringe fell around his forehead. He looked pale. His eyes glanced around the dusty tabletop, and he ran a finger down the collar of his light-grey sweatshirt.

Henry observed Curtis and wondered how old he was. He guessed him to be in his early thirties, as he lacked the puffy face and wrinkles of a man of Mark Hardy's age. There was still a strong sense of vibrancy about him.

Henry glanced at Hargreaves, who'd calmed down a little from her rage. She pulled out her notebook and mobile from her handbag. She started recording their conversation and then placed her phone behind her bag; probably in an attempt not to perturb Curtis.

"So, are you happy to speak to us?" she asked him, for the benefit of the tape.

He glanced up at her and nodded.

"Can you say 'yes' or 'no'?"

"Yes," he said, in a croaky voice.

"We're speaking to you today to clarify some facts about the multiple murders that occurred yesterday at Cragg Hall."

Curtis didn't speak.

Hargreaves looked at Henry, who asked the first question. "How old are you?"

Curtis frowned and sat back in his chair. "Why?"

"I'm just curious."

"I'm thirty."

"How did you meet Mark Hardy?"

Curtis exhaled. "What do you mean?"

"Well… when did you meet him?"

Curtis shrugged like he didn't understand the question.

Henry turned to Hargreaves. "I don't know how I can ask that more clearly."

She nodded in agreement.

"I met him through school," Curtis eventually admitted, after rolling his eyes.

"Ah, would this be St George's?"

Curtis nodded slowly.

"Aren't you a bit too young to be in Mark Hardy's year?"

"I met him through Allister."

Hargreaves looked at her notepad. "Would this be Allister Emery?"

Curtis nodded slowly.

"Are you aware that Allister died yesterday at Cragg Hall?" Henry asked.

Curtis lowered his eyes.

"Mr Quaker, are you aware he died yesterday?"

"Yes…" he said, through tightened lips.

"And how do you feel about that?"

"About what?"

"Allister being killed yesterday, along with three other people." Henry pulled Hargreaves' notepad across the table so he could read from it. "Louanne Blackburn, Allister Emery, Sarah Hardy. All killed yesterday in what's turning out to be a mass poisoning on a scale never seen before in our county."

Hargreaves confirmed Henry's assertion with a nod.

"How am I supposed to feel?" Curtis asked. He scratched his shoulder. "I don't know… Sad, I guess. Upset. I mean… how am I supposed to feel?"

"I don't know," Henry said. "You tell me."

Curtis shrugged. "I dunno… I didn't really know them."

Henry tilted his head forwards. "Are you saying you started a company with Mark Hardy, whom you met through Allister, and didn't really know either of them?"

Curtis exhaled. "Listen. I own thirteen companies. I don't know everything about the people running them. Just as I don't know the personal life of the woman who cleans my toilet."

"So, would you place Mark Hardy as low as a cleaner?" Hargreaves asked.

"Not as low, but…" Curtis clenched his jaw. "I have lots of people working for me. I don't know them that well. I keep myself away from–"

"The help?" Henry asked, raising an eyebrow.

Curtis didn't say anything.

"What about this company? Why did you meet us here on a Sunday afternoon if it's not that important to you?"

"I felt like I needed to be here."

"Is that because of the fraud investigation?" Hargreaves asked.

"I don't know anything about that."

"Right, pull the other one," Henry said. "That's what you thought we were going to ask you about, wasn't it? Hence you rushing over in your Rolls-Royce and bringing us here."

Curtis narrowed his eyes. "No, I heard about the murders this morning, like everyone else, and knew you'd only ask me about that."

Hargreaves raised her palm in a sign of peace. "Here, let's just make a deal. Tell us the general gist of this fraud investigation, and we'll stay well clear of any specifics. As you can see, we're investigating a murder and not your tax affairs."

Curtis folded his arms across his chest and set his jaw.

"We're detectives investigating the murder of your business partner and friend. We're only here collecting background information on the off chance it's relevant–"

"But it's not," Curtis said.

"Let us be the judge of that. If what you say isn't relevant to our investigation, it'll all be forgotten. However, if it *is* relevant–"

"But it really isn't."

Hargreaves glared daggers at him. "Tell us what you know, so we can work that out ourselves."

Curtis chewed the inside of his lip as he considered his options.

Henry expected him to play more games and wanted the jumped-up toerag to spend a night in a cell, but they needed to find out as much as they could as quickly as possible.

"Choose wisely," Henry said. "Either let us help you or take the harder path."

Curtis' expression eased. "Alright. How about this… can I speak hypothetically?"

"Whatever you want, just give us the broad strokes," Henry said, casually.

Curtis appeared to collect his thoughts. "Okay. Let's say, for example, a company was accused of falsifying documents."

"Right," Henry said, frowning.

"Well… this company has apparently – and this is all hypothetical – been sending imaginary shipments of goods to a network of other fake companies."

Henry looked at Hargreaves and then back to Curtis. "So, Sales Expedited is a shell company?"

Curtis shook his head feverishly. "No. No. Not at all! And if you accuse us of doing that, I'll sue you." He pushed his chair back from the table. "In fact, I've said enough already." His fingers cut through the strands of his blond fringe, and he scratched his scalp. "I need to get going."

"Hold on," Hargreaves said. "Did you forget what I said earlier about the police cell?"

"No, I didn't; but this stuff is serious. I really–" His eyes bulged as he noticed the mobile on the table behind Hargreaves' bag, recording their conversation. He jumped at it and pulled it away from her. "Turn it off!"

His trembling hands dropped her phone onto the floor, and Hargreaves shot up in a flash, pulled his arm behind his back, and pushed his face into the plasterboard wall. She was the same height as him but bulkier, and as young Curtis had been caught off guard, he submitted quickly.

"Right, I've had enough of this," she said. "Curtis Quaker, I'm arresting you on suspicion of tampering with evidence."

Curtis gave a faint attempt to struggle free while Hargreaves explained he was under caution. She instructed Henry to get the handcuffs from her bag. He did as she asked with a grin on his face.

She took them from him and slapped them around Curtis' wriggling wrists. He squealed as Hargreaves clicked them tightly closed. She forced Curtis back into his chair and bent down to pick up her phone from the floor.

"Keep an eye on him," she said, out of breath. "I'll go call for backup."

She stepped out of the small room and into the hallway, while Henry remained standing opposite the table, leaning against the wall.

Apart from snarling and staring daggers at Henry, Curtis didn't put up any more resistance.

"You chose poorly there, didn't you?" Henry asked, crossing his arms. "Care to tell us what the hell you hoped to gain from that?"

"I'll make sure my lawyer rips you both to pieces. I haven't done anything wrong."

"We'll see about that. It sounds as though your company's up to no good, for starters."

Curtis snarled at him.

"And… it sounds like you're afraid of someone. You don't want them to know you've been talking to us."

"Bollocks!" Curtis shouted. However, he didn't raise his head to project his outburst.

Henry grunted. "So, who's scaring you? Someone in the UK or someone abroad?"

When Curtis didn't answer, Henry recalled seeing the empty reception desk at the entrance, with no phone and no computer. The stale, dusty air hung heavy in the room. "This whole thing really is a shell operation, isn't it?"

Curtis didn't stir; his head was still lowered.

"So, you bring in products from other countries and then move them around, but the whole thing isn't real. Do you even import products or is this just a massive money laundering operation?"

Curtis lifted his head. "I don't know what it is." He sounded beyond exhausted. "But none of it is linked to me."

Henry scanned the office and then peered down at Curtis. "Why the hell did you let us in here if it's a front for something?"

Curtis couldn't meet Henry's eyes. He exhaled. "I have the right to remain silent, right?"

"Aye, you do."

Curtis pressed his lips together.

"Alright, but you'll have to talk sometime, Mr Quaker. Either you or your business partner, Mr Hardy."

Concern flickered in Curtis' eyes, then he sat back in his chair, clearly not willing to give anything else away.

Chapter Twenty

PCs Watkins and Smith arrived in a patrol car a short while later and put the subdued Curtis Quaker into the back seat. PC Smith looked less bewildered than he had done inside Cragg Hall the previous day. He had more colour in his cheeks and gave Henry a smile, before getting into the passenger seat to keep an eye on Curtis, who was sulking in the back.

The mid-afternoon sun shone down from a cloudless sky. Watkins approached Henry and Hargreaves, who were standing near Curtis' Rolls-Royce.

"Whose is this?" Watkins asked with his hands on his utility belt. He ogled the navy-blue luxury cruiser. Its bonnet glinted in the sunlight. "Nice bloody ride," he said. "Does it belong to that young fella we've just nicked?"

"Maybe ask him if you can drive it to the station," Henry said, pointing at Curtis.

"Who says I need to ask? I've just bagged his keys." Watkins smirked as he shook a plastic sachet in the air.

"Ah, well, I'd be careful. He looks the type to sue quite easily, and I don't think West Yorkshire Police will pay the legal fees if you damage his car," Hargreaves said, raising an eyebrow.

"I guess you're right," Watkins said, becoming more serious. "So, what have you arrested him for?"

"Tell your desk sergeant to book him for withholding evidence. If Curtis wants to call in a high-powered pain-in-the-arse lawyer, tell him I won't be free until tomorrow morning."

"Alright. What if he wants to talk this afternoon?" PC Watkins looked at both of them.

"Well, if he sounds sincere, give me a ring. But my guess is a night in the cells will make him more talkative," Hargreaves said.

"And if he does stay overnight, please put a noisy drunk in the cell next door. Tell him you'll give him this if he makes a racket all night long." Henry slipped Watkins a ten-pound note.

PC Watkins scoffed at it. "They'll want more than that. I'll see if I can swipe some more from the office kitty." He snatched Henry's money and pocketed it. "Anyway, you can trust me. I'll make sure it happens." He winked at Henry before returning to his car, and they drove off with the siren on.

"You probably shouldn't have done that," Hargreaves said.

Henry waved off her comment. "It'll be fine," he said. "Well, that went down differently than I expected."

"You can say that again."

"Are you really sure Curtis will be more talkative after a night in a cell? I've got a feeling he's not that clued up on what's going on here."

"Why have you just spent a tenner to cause him a restless night, then?"

Henry chuckled. "I suppose he got under my skin."

"I think he knows more than he's letting on. At least, I hope for his sake he does."

Henry pointed at the Rolls-Royce. "What shall we do with that? Do you think we can just leave it here?"

Hargreaves sniffed as she sized up the gleaming vehicle. "Nah, he'll be pissed off if it gets nicked. Let's have it towed. If we're really lucky, they might scratch it on the way."

Back in Hargreaves' car, she made the relevant call to the Roads Policing Unit, asking them to tow Curtis' Rolls-Royce as soon as possible. Henry gazed out the passenger window at the office buildings and warehouses in the rest of the industrial area. Something from his interaction with Curtis was niggling at him.

"He can't be very sharp, that Curtis Quaker, for someone who owns thirteen companies," Henry said. "I mean, for starters, why the hell let us into that office building?"

She grunted in agreement.

A heavy silence fell between them. Henry looked at her as he sensed she was annoyed at something. "Are you alright?"

"What happened before Curtis showed up in his Rolls-Royce?"

"When?"

"Who were you on the phone to?"

"Oh, that..." Henry smiled. "That was nothing important."

"It looked important."

Henry nodded; his eyes fixed on the junction ahead. "I... erm. I called Roy Parker–"

"What!?" She gave him a death glare. "Why did you ring a journalist? Especially *that* one?"

"I wanted to know what he knew about–"

"And what did you find out?"

Henry swallowed. "Not that much, really."

"I bet he found out more from you, didn't he?" She shook her head and swore under her breath. "I can't bloody believe it. What did he find out?"

"He knew I was involved, obviously, as I'd phoned him."

Hargreaves rolled her eyes.

"Also, he knew that we didn't have much of an understanding of this fraud business."

Hargreaves exhaled sharply. "Well, that's not true anymore," she said. "We know something went on there. You don't have to be high-up in the Serious Fraud Office to figure that one out." She shook her head in disbelief. "Did Roy Parker get anything else out of you?"

Henry shook his head. "He tried pressing me into leaking information from the investigation, but I told him to get lost."

She scrutinised Henry for an instant, before refocusing on the road. "Let's see how he retaliates to that."

"You think he'll get back at me?"

"Why wouldn't he? You're his only bet for getting an exclusive story."

Henry shook his head. "I thought he was an alright bloke."

"He's a bottom-feeder journalist! He's as desperate as they get." She drew in a breath and exhaled. "Well, that'll teach you. You might think twice before saving his life again."

Henry rolled his eyes at her comment and stared out of the window. He wasn't sure what Roy could do except write an article about him helping out the investigation. And surely that wouldn't cause much of a fuss, would it?

"Shall we go and see how Mark Hardy's recovering, and start asking him about his company?" Hargreaves asked.

Henry grunted. "And what are we going to ask him about?"

"I don't know… We could ask him if he runs a shell company with possible links to money laundering?"

"Oh, you mean, 'Hello, Mr Hardy, what can you tell us about the industrial fraud you're committing?' I doubt he'll be very forthcoming."

"Alright, then. What do you suggest?"

Henry pinched his lower lip. "Someone else in the police, or maybe even the tax office, must have been investigating this company. We need to find out who that was so we can get the low-down from them."

"How do we do that? A group email to the Serious Fraud Office?"

"I don't know. We've just arrested someone, so hopefully that'll raise a flag. Assuming any of them work weekends."

"That's very doubtful."

Henry grunted his reluctant agreement.

"Right, so back to HQ then?" she said.

Henry shook his head. "No. We've got three priorities, don't we? The poison, the business, and the school."

Hargreaves raised her eyebrow. "Do you know where it is?"

"Aye. And it's not too far from here."

Hargreaves sat tall in her seat. "Good. Then, you can direct me."

Chapter Twenty-One

St George's Grammar School had originally been an orphanage built in the late 1800s. Its austere stone structure rose out of marshy moorland between two rounded hills. Nothing but heather waiting to bloom and stretches of tall grasses between rock formations surrounded it. Despite it being a sunny Early May Bank Holiday in the valley below, the wind up here was fierce. Henry wondered what school days in winter were like when the mist layered these moors, and the air was bitterly cold. Even on a late-spring day like today, the area looked bleak.

They parked in front of the school's cast-iron gates. Metal fencing surrounded the compound, which included newer buildings made of steel and glass alongside the original Victorian one. Henry spotted netted tennis courts, rugby and football pitches in the distance, and suspected the school had all the amenities required for a good education. The school's motto – *In Adversitate, Virtus Invenitur* – was written on the coat of arms, which was welded to the arch of the school gates. Henry had learnt enough Latin at his state grammar school to guess it meant, 'In adversity, one finds virtue'. The coat of arms included a shield and a serpent-like dragon that had been pierced with a spear.

Hargreaves sniffed as she looked at the school between two metal bars in its fence. The gates were chained shut and the buildings were lifeless.

"So, people really spend money to send their kids here?" she asked, wrinkling her nose at the bleak Victorian building.

"Aye, they pay good money at that," Henry said.

"It looks depressing. Is it a boarding school?"

Henry checked the sign to the left of the gate. He shook his head. "Day school only. It used to do boarding, however."

"So they bus the kids up onto this moor?"

Henry scanned the bleak surroundings. "They must do."

"I don't see the attraction," she said. "When I have kids, I'd prefer just to send them to the local academy."

"Some parents think sending their kids to schools like this gives them more opportunity."

"I know… but look at Ralph and Pete. He's only in marketing and the other lives in the run-down old cottage. Was all that money really worth it? And then look at Tom Dixon and Lee Combes. They're professional rugby players; Tom has a huge flat near Leeds city centre, good prospects, and both of them went to state schools."

"I think you're looking at the exceptions there, and not the rule."

Henry narrowed his eyes at the stern building and spotted gargoyles crouching along the parapet. The dark stone gremlins glared down from their haughty positions. Their lifeless eyes were filled with hate. Above them, hidden among the slate roof tiles, was a tiny, barred window, most likely for some dingy attic room.

He shivered. "I wouldn't have sent my kids to this school, though. Not after what I heard about its history."

Hargreaves frowned. "What did you hear about it?"

Henry felt a chill from the wind and wished he had brought his fleece with him, as he was only wearing his white shirt. "Let's get back into the car."

With the doors closed, Henry started to feel warm again. "About thirty years ago, there was an investigation into kids being abused."

Hargreaves grimaced. "Sexual abuse?"

Henry shook his head. "We didn't hear anything like that. It was kids being severely beaten. Students receiving lashings."

"Lashings? As in, whipped? When was this?"

"Early nineties. I got involved in the investigation after a father came to see us about his fourteen-year-old son coming home with gouges in his back. The son didn't want to complain about the school and never identified who'd done it – he was too scared – but the father, a lawyer, insisted we investigate it anyway."

"How had the father found out it'd happened?"

"Apparently, he heard his son crying in the bathroom. Those whelps on his son's back had got infected, and the son eventually came clean about what had happened to him. Well, he told his dad he'd been whipped, at least."

"But not by whom?"

"No. Me and DI Ashford, an old colleague of mine – a great copper he was – we went to interview the school's headmaster, Mr Jessop. He denied everything and said the lad must have made it all up. When we showed him pictures of the cuts on the lad's back, he admitted it might have been another student who'd done it. That he'd heard about some secret club in the school."

"A club?"

Henry nodded. "Of students. There was this cult-like clique within the school, apparently run by the most popular pupils in the final year. There were initiations for younger students and punishments for those who didn't obey. I suppose you could call it fagging taken to extremes, and none of it was apparently known by the teachers."

Hargreaves pursed her lips and looked back at the school. "Did you ever charge anyone?"

Henry shook his head. "The students wouldn't say a thing. The school was borderline obstructive. The young lad who'd been whipped kept shtum on what'd actually happened to him." He shrugged. "There wasn't much we could do. Eventually we closed the file, despite receiving other reports about lads who'd been whipped. But if no one talks and we can't get a suspect or any evidence… well, you know yourself, there's not much we can do."

"Do you think this might be related to what happened yesterday?"

Henry shrugged and looked back at the school. "I don't know. It might just be coincidence."

"And why haven't you said anything about this before?"

"Well, the only link we have is that they went to the same school. We don't know for sure the people at the barbecue yesterday were involved in this 'hazing' club… if it ever existed."

Henry observed the austere structure. Apart from the foreboding Victorian main building itself, the rest of the compound looked like any other school in the area. "All we knew was that a few lads had been whipped… and that was all."

Hargreaves narrowed her eyes. "Mark Hardy and his friends are in their forties, aren't they?" She counted on her fingers. "They would have been teenagers back then. When did your lad with the welts make his complaint?"

"I can't quite remember exactly. I'd have to read the case notes, but I don't think they'll be easy to find."

Hargreaves tutted.

"Of course, there's a strong chance it has nothing to do with Cragg Hall," he said.

"Why bring it up, then?"

"I don't know." He looked down at his hands on his lap. "I just felt it could be relevant somehow."

"What about this DI Ashford you worked with? Can't you ask him what he remembers?"

"No, he died a few years ago. Pancreatic cancer."

"Is there anyone else who might know something about it?"

Henry scrunched up his lips. "Aye, there was another detective on the case with us, as a matter of fact. And you know him pretty well."

Hargreaves frowned. "Murphy?"

Henry nodded. "He was just a dogsbody back then. A DC looking to get promoted who was pretty useless." He shook his head decisively. "I doubt he'd remember a thing, but you can ask him…"

Hargreaves dialled a number on her phone. "Hi, it's me," she said, when her call was answered. "I'm with Henry outside St George's school. Can you remember a case about it from the early 1990s?" She paused.

Henry heard Murphy's voice faintly coming out of the phone.

"It's something about abuse. Pupil on pupil." She glanced at Henry. "Some kind of cult?" she said.

"Tell him we started an investigation when a lad said he'd been whipped," Henry said. "Ashford led the investigation."

Hargreaves relayed the message. Murphy said something to her, and she nodded. "Alright, tell us if it rings any bells." She hung up. "He says he can't remember but will have a think."

"Let's see how that goes," Henry said doubtfully. "You know what? Let's go pay Ralph Gaskin another visit."

"Why?"

Henry tapped his chin. "I don't know… something about him suggests that if there was a secret club run by the popular kids…"

"He might have been bullied by them?"

Henry shrugged. "Very possibly. What do you think?"

"It's worth a shot. Besides, I want to get away from this creepy moor."

She started her engine and drove away from the school, heading back down into the sunny valley below.

Chapter Twenty-Two

It was just after 4 p.m. and the Gaskins' narrow street was lined with more parked cars than earlier. Hargreaves huffed as she drove past their address, until she eventually found a spot several houses away. They walked back along the pavement, passing the modest semi-detached houses with their small front gardens, some of which were filled with kids' outdoor toys and empty paddling pools.

Ralph Gaskin stood on his drive, watering his lawn with a hosepipe. He squinted in the sun at Henry and Hargreaves and attempted to hide a concerned expression. He stopped the flow of water and held the hose limply in his hand. "Hello?"

Hargreaves and Henry positioned themselves around him, causing him to step back against the vehicle parked on his drive.

"We have a few more questions for you, Mr Gaskin," Henry said, smiling.

Ralph nodded, shading his eyes from the sunlight. "Sure, whatever I can do to help."

"What can you tell us about St George's?" Hargreaves asked, frowning at him.

"What about it?" He glanced between Henry and Hargreaves.

"Did you have a good time there?" she asked.

"Ah… I suppose I did. Why?"

"Mr Gaskin," Henry said, "you were at St George's in the early 1990s?"

Ralph nodded.

"And did you have lots of friends there?"

"Yes… well, I had an okay time. I wasn't the most popular person, but I did alright."

"Did you ever hear about students' clubs?"

"Like the rugby one?"

Henry narrowed his eyes. "Were you in any clubs?"

"Well, I wasn't very sporty. But I was in the chess and debating clubs."

"Debating?" Hargreaves asked, raising both eyebrows. She looked Ralph up and down doubtfully. "Were you good at it?"

"I was alright…"

"Did you ever hear of a more clandestine club, run by students in the top year?" Henry asked.

"A 'clandestine' club?" Ralph shook his head.

"A club you had to join through initiation."

Ralph blinked twice. "I never heard anything like that…" He cleared his throat. "Do you think what happened yesterday was linked to our school somehow?"

Henry shrugged. "It's a possibility."

"But… how?"

"We're looking into it. It's one of many lines of inquiry." Henry looked at Hargreaves, who was observing Ralph.

"You're in marketing?" Hargreaves asked.

Ralph nodded.

"In an agency or in-house?"

"In-house."

"For whom?"

"Oh, just some international company." He shrugged dismissively. "No one's really heard of it."

"Isn't that your problem if you do its marketing?" she said.

Ralph laughed and nodded. "Good point, but not really. It's B2B."

"What's the name of this company?" she asked.

"International Synthetics." Ralph watched her unchanged expression and forced some laughter. "See, you've never heard of it, have you?"

"I can't say I have," she said. "Does it deal in chemicals?"

Ralph nodded. "Synthetic products, mostly – plastics, fibres, polyesters and nylons. There's also some pharmaceuticals and cosmetics we do."

Henry nodded. "Very interesting."

Ralph gave Henry's interest a concerned look. "Is that all?" he asked, lifting up his limp hose.

Hargreaves stepped away from him. "We might drop by again to ask more questions." She looked at his small, semi-detached house. "How's your wife doing?"

"She's sleeping. She was worn out."

"Of course, you were at the hospital until late."

Ralph nodded. "I suppose it was for the best. We had to make sure William was alright. Luckily, he was fine in the end."

Hargreaves glanced at Henry and said, "Yeah, thank God he was."

They left Ralph on his drive, looking downcast, and headed back to Hargreaves' car.

With the doors closed, Henry asked, "So, what did you make of that?"

Hargreaves pulled the car out of its tight parking spot. "I think he's even more suspicious."

"Aye. I believe he knew something about that secret club–"

"How so?"

"Just an impression. And then he also works at a company that handles chemicals."

Hargreaves grunted. "We do need to check that out. Though there's a chance he works in some boring office miles away from the production sites. He only works in marketing."

"But he could have visited a site recently, and taken the cyanide."

Hargreaves shrugged and focused on the road.

Henry checked the time on the car's console, which said 4.30 p.m. "Shall we head back to HQ?"

"Might as well."

She indicated at a junction, and they joined Leeds Inner Ring Road.

Henry lost himself in his thoughts until Hargreaves interrupted. "So, we've got until tomorrow to find a suspect. How likely do you think that is? And be honest."

"Well, I agree there's a lot of lab work to do, and lots of leads to follow up on. But" – he shrugged – "if we give it our best shot, you never know."

Hargreaves moaned. "I bet you a tenner we miss this deadline."

"That's very fatalistic of you."

"I'd say more realistic."

Henry pursed his lips. "Ten quid? That's a bit much. How about one?"

"A quid?! One pound? There's no point betting on one quid. Who cares if you lose a quid?"

"Hey, I do. I'm retired. And there's a cost-of-living crisis."

"Sod off. You own a poncy cottage in Addingham worth three hundred grand. You're hardly poor."

"Hey, some might say I'm cash poor."

"You can afford to pay PC Watkins a tenner to keep Quaker up all night."

Henry shifted in his seat. "Aye, well. That's a different matter."

"In what way?"

"I wouldn't bet a tenner on missing the deadline or not."

"Aye, 'cause you know you'd lose it."

Henry held his tongue.

Hargreaves' phone rang through her car's speakers. She huffed at Henry and then answered.

"Hi, where are you?" Barnes asked, her voice coming through the speakers. She sounded flustered.

"Just heading back to HQ. Why?"

"Get back here quickly. IT have sent in the initial report on Mark Hardy's phone."

Henry's eyes lit up. "And?"

"It's mostly clean, but there are a few things that make for interesting reading."

"Right, we'll be there asap." Hargreaves ended the call and then pressed a button on the panel next to her indicators. A police siren blared and blue lights came on.

"I don't think this calls for blue lights, do you?" Henry asked.

"There's loads of traffic ahead. Do you really want to lose half an hour sitting in it?"

Henry guessed not. He looked out the window. "Is it too late to shake on that bet?"

She hissed. "What? Now you know we've got a break in the case? Am I bugger shaking on that…"

Henry sighed. "Oh well… I might have just lost out on a tenner."

Chapter Twenty-Three

Henry strode into the meeting room at Leeds Central police station to find Barnes slouched over a laptop at the table. Her light-grey suit jacket was hung on the back of her chair, and she had loosened the collar of her white shirt. A cable from the TV on the wall was connected to her laptop, and it mirrored her screen. She scrolled through messages, which appeared to be in a group chat between Mark Hardy and his friends. Henry approached the table, reading the messages.

Barnes glanced up at him. "It's all quite interesting, this," she said. "Where's Hargreaves?"

"She had a call. She's just outside."

Henry suspected Hargreaves was speaking to Murphy, as she had interrupted their discussion to answer the call, ignoring Henry's existence in the process.

Henry read the text on the screen. He quickly got the gist of the fact that most of the messages mocked someone who they referred to as 'Rat face'. 'Reeky twat head' was also mentioned a lot.

"Are they talking about Ralph?" he asked.

Barnes nodded. "I think so. IT found numerous group chats on Mark's phone. This one is called 'Crew without the rat'."

"And is there any chat group with Ralph in it?"

"Yes, and in that one they don't use the word 'rat'. Though it's still quite racist and homophobic."

"Oh, great," Henry said sarcastically.

He pulled out a chair from under the table and sat down. Each new message seemed to insult Ralph as badly as the previous one. The friends were clearly competing to make up the most offensive insults about him, poking fun at his house, his clothes, his car, his job. Some even mentioned his wife and child, calling baby William 'rat spawn'.

"Bloody hell," Henry said. "Why the hell do they put up with Ralph if they hate him so much?"

Barnes shrugged.

"Are there any group chats that exclude other friends?"

"There are lots of chats. Oddly, some of them are completely empty."

"Empty how?"

"There are no messages in them. The techies think they've been using disappearing messages."

"Which we can't access?"

"Clue's in the name. They disappear as soon as they've been read."

"And that's it, they're gone forever?"

She nodded.

"That's suspicious."

"It could be. They're growing more and more common these days." Baines refocused on her laptop screen. "What we can say for certain is Mark seems to be the ringleader. He organises the events they have: the parties and meet-ups. He controls the discussions. He's also the admin of all the chats."

Henry recoiled at a disgusting comment about Ralph's personal hygiene that was up on the screen. "Any idea why they invite Ralph to these events if they hate him so much?"

She nodded and gestured at the TV. "It seems to be him."

A message from Allister said:

> *Come on. We'll have to invite the rat. He'll only weep and moan if we don't.*

There were two emoticons, one a weeping face, the other a rat.

"Allister convinces them to invite Ralph to every event they have. The others seem to disagree, but Mark gives in and says they'll invite him."

"Allister Emery," Henry said to himself, his eyes narrowed. "He seems to have been someone who liked bringing people together."

"What do you mean?"

"Allister introduced Curtis Quaker to Mark Hardy."

"The rich guy Hargreaves arrested?" Barnes asked. Her eyebrows went up. "I need to talk to her about that. He's threatening to sue her personally for false imprisonment."

"I'm glad to learn he's perked up a bit. Have you told him he can't make civil suits against individual officers? He'd be up against West Yorkshire Police's lawyers, which will be an entirely different matter."

"Hmm. But aren't you a private citizen?"

Henry scrunched up his face. "*Me*?"

"Yep. He mentions you, as well. And seeing as you're working on this case in an unofficial capacity, you're not entitled to legal protection from the police."

She had a point. Henry bit his lower lip.

"This is why I hate you being involved in cases, Henry," she continued, sitting back in her chair. "Not because I don't value your input, but because it's not above board. Legal cover like this, insurance policies, the question of whether evidence becomes inadmissible if you touch it – everything gets overly complicated when you're around."

"Right… I didn't know you 'hated' my involvement."

She tilted her head. "'Hate' is too strong a word. Let's say, I'm uncomfortable with it."

Henry grunted. "I didn't arrest this Curtis, though, did I? I only asked him questions in the presence of a detective sergeant, who was the one who nicked him." He scratched his chin. "Besides, he's only lashing out because he's scared; we'll find something on him."

"Like what?"

Henry pointed at the TV screen. "Let's see if there are any messages between Mark Hardy and him on there."

She typed on her laptop. "What am I looking for?"

"There's something wrong with Mark's company, Sales Expedited. It's a front for something, and Curtis doesn't want us to find out what it's hiding."

"Alright," she said, focusing on her laptop screen. She leant her head forwards to get closer to it.

Hargreaves barged in the room as she ended her call. She dumped her phone in her handbag and looked at Henry. "That was Murphy. He couldn't remember St George's but sent someone to locate the case file in the archive."

"Oh, right?" Henry lifted his eyebrows. "It's unusual for Murphy to be so keen."

"He wants this case sorted quickly, doesn't he?" Hargreaves sat down at the table and placed her handbag in front of her. "Someone's scanning it now, and they'll email it over. Apparently, four lads, aged between thirteen and fifteen, received wounds from being whipped on their backs. The cases started in 1993 and finished in 1995. There hasn't been another one mentioned since, so possibly the school closed this club down–"

Henry frowned. "Or the student holding the whip left the school in 1995." He gripped his chin. Could that old case really be linked to this?

He looked at the messages on the TV screen from Mark Hardy to his friends.

> *That creepy rat twat is the prime example of someone who needs a good flogging.*

Henry's stomach turned. "Do we have the names of the lads who were abused?"

Hargreaves shook her head. "I'll pass you the file when I receive it."

Henry gestured to the TV screen. "You should see how Mark Hardy and the others speak about Ralph behind his back."

Hargreaves scrutinised the TV screen, which was now showing other messages from Mark Hardy's phone. "Why? What do they call him?"

Henry relayed the rodent theme to her.

"Sounds interesting," she said.

"Here," Henry said, "I bet you a tenner Ralph was one of those lads who was whipped."

Hargreaves studied his face and pouted. "Nah, you worked on the original investigation. I bet you've remembered he's one of the lads and want to rip me off."

Henry chuckled and rolled his eyes, then caught Barnes staring at them.

"Are you two gambling on the outcome of an investigation?" she asked.

Henry shook his head. "Not at all. We've not shaken hands on anything."

"Aye, 'cause Henry's too chicken," Hargreaves said.

"What's this business with a school?" Barnes asked, her face wearing a look of distaste.

Henry explained their suspicions surrounding St George's school and Ralph Gaskin being a potential abuse victim.

Barnes tilted her head. "Why would that be a motive for murder?"

"It could show he has a deep-seated loathing for them," Henry said. "That he was a victim of their abuse and has held a grudge ever since."

Barnes tapped the desk with her knuckle. "Possibly. But why now? Why not get his revenge twenty or thirty years ago?"

"Maybe this all got stirred up when he had the kid?" Hargreaves suggested. "He's sleep-deprived and isn't thinking straight. Or having the kid has forced him to come to terms with what happened to him in his past, and he's decided to take action now. Right old wrongs." She shrugged, not sounding too convinced by her own words.

Barnes pulled a face. "Why would he remain friends with his bullies, though?"

"It's male social hierarchies, isn't it," Henry said. "The weaker subservient types are drawn towards the powerful ones. If the alpha males bully them, it's the victim's fault for not being good enough. Sometimes they're even just happy for the attention."

"Bloody hell, that can't be true?" Barnes asked.

"I don't know. Sending kids off to abusive boarding schools can cause all kinds of problems. Just look at our recent crop of politicians." Henry snickered.

"Well," Barnes said, "see where it goes, but please avoid focusing on the wrong angle and wasting time." She went back to studying her laptop's screen.

Henry and Hargreaves shared a look, then Hargreaves rolled her eyes.

"Here, look at these text messages," Barnes said.

Messages between Mark Hardy and Curtis Quaker filled the TV screen, and Henry whistled when he saw the hate-filled language in them. "Clearly Mark and Curtis weren't good friends."

"Did Curtis Quaker write these messages?" Hargreaves asked, staring at the text. "Well, that makes me even more glad I've just nicked him!"

Chapter Twenty-Four

Henry wasn't allowed to participate in the interview. Barnes said that his presence would cross the line into professional misconduct. So, he had to make do with sitting in a side room, watching proceedings on a small television.

On the screen, Henry had a wide shot of the interview room, which had four chairs positioned around a black table. He guessed the room stunk of stale sweat and apprehension, like they had done in his day. Although, back then, they had also stunk of cigarette smoke and hangover-breath, usually his own.

In contrast, the side room Henry was now in had clean, conditioned air and a bank of TVs mounted on the wall. As he nursed a paper cup of tea, he could sit there and watch the interviews happening in the station's other four rooms all at once. However, only one room was booked that evening, the one Barnes had just entered.

She held open the reinforced door for Curtis Quaker, who stepped inside cautiously. He looked far too fresh-faced for the interview. He hadn't endured a full night in a holding cell, so his resolve would still be strong. However, needs must. They couldn't wait until tomorrow morning.

A middle-aged man in a grey tailored suit followed after him. Going by the man's miffed expression and terse body language, Henry guessed he was the expensive lawyer Curtis planned to sue him with.

The lawyer placed his briefcase on the black table and straightened his wonky tie. Henry hoped he had received the call to represent his client while playing a round of golf or having a picnic with his family. The more pleasant the activity ruined; the happier Henry felt.

The lawyer introduced himself as Sebastian Thornton and shook hands with the two detectives. All four took their seats, with Curtis and Sebastian one side, and Hargreaves and Barnes on the other. Hargreaves started the recording and introduced everyone around the table for the benefit of the tape, then they got down to business.

"Can I just ask," said Sebastian, his voice nasal and his accent rich with privilege, "why have you arrested my client?"

Barnes answered. "Your client can help us with our inquiries into a mass murder but has chosen not to. We also want to learn more about this company he's involved in."

Hargreaves stared at Curtis, who was slumped back in his chair. "Aye," she said, "Sales Expedited seems to be a front for something. And your client pretty much confirmed our suspicions when questioned earlier today."

Sebastian turned to scowl at his client.

"It's not true," Curtis said to him. "I was talking hypothetically."

The lawyer looked back at the detectives. "My client said that you denied him legal advice earlier."

Barnes turned to Hargreaves, but Hargreaves ignored her questioning look.

"Your client agreed on tape to talk to us without you being there," Hargreaves said. "He didn't speak to us under duress, and I explained his rights to him."

Sebastian turned his nose up at Hargreaves. "I don't like police heavy-handedness–"

Hargreaves scoffed, but Barnes jumped in before she could respond. "We don't like people who threaten the victims of serious crimes," she said, withdrawing pieces of paper from a file.

Henry was relieved to see they were finally getting to the phone messages. He wouldn't have let the lawyer bang on for so long.

"Can you read these messages and confirm if you sent them to Mark Hardy?" Barnes asked, passing a sheet of paper to Curtis.

Sebastian scanned it first and then pushed it towards Curtis, nodding his head in approval.

Curtis picked up the sheet of paper and ran his eyes over the text. He then flicked the sheet away. "So, what?"

"Do you have a habit of speaking to people like that?" Barnes asked.

Sebastian picked up the discarded sheet from the table and glanced over it. "There's no proof that my client sent these messages."

"Is that your telephone number, Mr Quaker?" Barnes asked.

Curtis nodded.

"And does anyone else use your phone?"

Curtis frowned. "Which phone–"

"What my client meant to say, was that he can't be sure if someone else used his phone or not. He might have left it somewhere, for example."

Barnes placed a plastic bag on the table, which contained Curtis' mobile. "His phone was locked when he handed it in to us. If you're suggesting someone else used it, they must have known his passcode."

The lawyer didn't quibble over her point.

"Don't you own thirteen companies?" Barnes asked Curtis. "I would expect someone in your position to be careful not to share their personal login credentials."

Curtis pouted like a sullen child.

"Did you send these messages to Mark Hardy last week?" Barnes asked.

Both lawyer and client looked at each other.

"I can't remember," Curtis said, eventually.

Hargreaves leant forward to read the messages on the sheet of paper. "You can't remember sending Mark Hardy a message that said 'you're a thieving twat! I'm going to hunt you down and kill your whole family'?"

Curtis bowed his head.

"You are aware that someone poisoned Mark Hardy and three other people yesterday, including his wife? And that those three people are now dead?"

"I didn't poison them," Curtis mumbled.

"What my client meant to say was, while he is aware that such a tragedy occurred yesterday, he wasn't involved in it and has no knowledge of what happened, other than what has been reported in the press," the lawyer said.

"Can you tell us where you were yesterday between five and seven o'clock?" Hargreaves asked.

"What?! I didn't poison anyone!" Curtis said.

"Can you tell us where you were–"

"My client will issue you with an explanation of his whereabouts after this interview has been concluded," the lawyer said.

"Can't your client confirm where he was to us now?" Barnes asked him.

The lawyer pinched his brow. "Detectives… Would you please give us the courtesy of having a few moments alone–"

"We need to talk to your client now, not later," Hargreaves said.

"Please. Just ten minutes."

Barnes stood up. "You have five. We also want to access all the phones he has."

"All of them?" Curtis asked, startled.

"That's what I said. You've just suggested you have more than one phone, so we wish to see them all."

The lawyer lifted his palm in the air. "Five minutes, please, Detective Inspector."

Barnes gathered her files and Curtis' bagged phone from the table. Hargreaves paused the tape after explaining that the detectives were stepping outside. They left the interview room, and it took them a few moments to join Henry in the side room.

"Doesn't seem to be going well," he commented.

Barnes huffed. She bent over to get a better view of interview room three on the small TV screen, while Hargreaves hung around the door, checking her phone.

"Do you think you'll get anywhere with them?" Henry asked.

"I don't know. Maybe," Barnes said, watching the screen. "I'm not sure this lawyer knows much about young Curtis' business activities."

"I don't think even Curtis does," Henry said, sipping his tea.

He glanced at the TV screen and saw the lawyer and Curtis leaning close to each other, talking quietly so their voices weren't picked up by the microphone. Curtis nodded after the lawyer finished a long utterance and smiled.

"Okay," he said. He then leant closer to Sebastian's ear and whispered something.

The lawyer considered Curtis' words and then shook his head.

Curtis seemed taken aback. He folded his arms over his chest and huffed.

"I wonder what that's about. You'd better get in there and find out for yourselves," Henry said.

"I suppose so," Barnes admitted. She turned to Hargreaves, who was staring at her phone as if it was on fire. "What's up?" Barnes asked her.

"Erm… so, that scanned case file from Murphy has come through."

"Oh right?" Henry peered up at her from his chair.

Hargreaves scrolled through the document on her phone. "Well… three of the pupils aren't linked to this case, but one is."

"Who?" Henry asked. "Ralph?"

Hargreaves shook her head. "Pete Blackburn."

"Pete?" Henry's eyes widened in surprise.

He tapped his chin with his finger. What did this mean? Pete had tried to enter this secret club and failed, or had he passed the brutal initiation and ended up a member?

Barnes checked her watch. "Their five minutes are up." She went to the door. "Are you coming?" she asked Hargreaves.

"Aye, just two seconds," Hargreaves said, still studying the document on her phone.

"So, we need to speak to Pete after here?" Henry asked.

Hargreaves nodded and then scowled at the TV. "After I've dealt with that little pipsqueak."

Chapter Twenty-Five

Hargreaves and Barnes returned to their seats in interview room three, which Henry now suspected really did smell of Curtis Quaker's anxiety and apprehension. Curtis and his lawyer separated from their huddle and faced the detectives. Curtis ran a hand through his long blond fringe. Hargreaves restarted the tape and announced they were continuing the interview. In the side room a few metres away, Henry chewed on the lip of his empty paper cup, watching the proceedings take place on the TV screen.

"So, we'd like to clarify what we think has happened here," said Sebastian. "You detectives are lost at sea – you have no idea what happened yesterday – and you are clearly clutching at straws."

Barnes glared back at him, visibly unimpressed with his mixed metaphors.

"You have latched onto my client," the lawyer continued, "who's innocent and wasn't even in Yorkshire yesterday, and you insist on wasting our time and yours with this fruitless arrest."

Barnes lowered her stare. "Have you finished?"

Sebastian shook his head. "Oh no. I shall be lodging a complaint with the Independent Office for Police Conduct on Tuesday morning, when they're open again."

"Right?" Barnes opened the file in front of her. "Your client has a history of sending offensive and threatening messages to someone who became a victim of attempted murder. That victim remains in intensive care, recovering from cyanide poisoning. Three people were also murdered in the same criminal act." She lifted up the sheet of paper on the table. "Here are messages sent from your client's phone – who we believe is its sole user – threatening to kill this victim and his friends and family." She paused. "So, please, go ahead and make your complaint to the IOPC. To me, this seems like a fair arrest, wouldn't you agree?"

Sebastian leant his elbow on the table. "You only found those messages after the arrest had taken place–"

Hargreaves chimed in. "Has your client agreed to have all his phones searched, or do you want us to get a search warrant?"

"Get one," Sebastian said, sitting back in his chair. "You won't have it until Wednesday morning, at the earliest."

"I'll be out of the country by then," Curtis said, struggling not to grin.

Hargreaves held up her phone. "All I need to do is call my detective superintendent and tell him we need this warrant. He'll see to it that it arrives in a few hours." She leant forward. "I'll also request we search your house and any other properties you own." She slid a piece of paper and pen across the table to him. "Could you be a star and start writing all the addresses down for us?"

"We won't be doing that," Sebastian said, disdainfully.

"Oh, shame. Well, I'll just have someone look them up on the Land Registry."

All traces of Curtis' grin disappeared.

"Do you have a lot of houses, Curtis?" Hargreaves asked. "Imagine all the little goodies we could find in them. If there's so much as a spliff, or anything that's been imported illegally – like ivory or furs, or whatever it is you rich people buy – we'll charge you for it."

"This is threatening behaviour," Sebastian said.

"Requesting a search warrant is standard police procedure," Barnes said. "There's nothing threatening about it… unless your client has something to hide."

Sebastian turned to Curtis, who had lowered his head. His blond fringe covered his eyes. The lawyer then turned to Barnes with calculating eyes. "Is there some kind of deal we could strike?"

"A deal?" Barnes tilted her head. "Are you ready to bargain, already?"

Sebastian cleared his throat loudly. "Is there something my client could give you that could aid your investigation?"

Barnes took a breath. "Well, we want to see all his phones. But we'll drop the other search warrants if he complies and tells us what we want to know."

"And what's that?" Sebastian asked.

Barnes focused on Curtis. "Can you tell us why you sent threatening text messages to Mark Hardy last week?" She pushed the sheet of paper with the messages on towards him – as if he might need reminding.

But Curtis didn't look at it. "We fell out…"

"Clearly," Hargreaves said.

"What over?" Barnes asked.

"The company…" Curtis glanced at his lawyer, who was concentrating on the messages Barnes had pushed towards him, as though he hadn't seen them before. Then, he continued, "The company isn't doing well. I wanted to know what the issue was. It was thriving as far as I could tell. And then I saw Mark last week and he said it wasn't. No cap! He was deadly serious. So, I asked him why, and he tells me that… the fraud cops are looking into us and the money's gone, and he wants to close the company down."

Henry, in the TV room, bit the rim of his paper cup. Finally, they were getting somewhere. He pulled out his phone and texted Hargreaves a question to ask Curtis.

Hargreaves' phone buzzed on the table in the interview room, and she looked at it.

Barnes continued her questioning. "Why had the company lost its money?"

Curtis shrugged. "I don't know… Bad management."

"How much have you lost?"

Curtis exhaled through his teeth. "I don't know. I put in seven hundred and fifty at the beginning. All that's gone. Mark asked me for another five hundred last year as he wanted to invest in the future, and I suppose all that's been wiped out, too."

"So, you've lost nearly 1.3 million?" Barnes sounded scared for him.

Curtis looked sulkily down at the table as if he were a child who had lost a board game.

"Can you survive such a loss?" Barnes asked, with a furrowed brow.

"It's seriously bad. But it's not a fatal–"

Sebastian raised his hand. "We're not here to discuss my client's net worth nor his financial arrangements."

Barnes raised an eyebrow at him and then refocused on Curtis. "When was the last time you spoke to Mark Hardy?"

"Last Tuesday."

"Where was this?"

"At his house."

"Was that the first time you'd visited his home?"

Curtis nodded.

"How long were you there for?"

He raised his palms to the ceiling. "Half an hour?"

"Did you know he was going to deliver bad news to you before you arrived?"

"Obviously not. I thought we were smashing it."

"You didn't know the company was haemorrhaging money?"

Curtis shook his head and sat forward, leaning his elbows on the table. "That was the clever thing he did. Mark sent me reports that must have been fake, as they showed me we were making a killing. Growth was over fifteen per cent year-on-year, two to three per cent growth every month. I mean, wouldn't you invest in that?"

No one answered his question.

"Why did you meet Mark Hardy at his home?" Barnes asked.

"I don't know."

"Was it odd that you met him at his home and not the office?"

Curtis clasped his hands in front of him. "I don't know. I suppose, thinking back. But I just wanted an update."

"So, what happened when Mark told you the business had gone under and was being investigated by the fraud squad?"

Curtis cracked his knuckles. "What do you think? I… I got angry."

"What happened then?"

"I lost my cool… I shouted at him. I had a fit. He asked me to leave, but I said I wanted to stay and talk it out. He threatened to call the police if I didn't go." He shrugged. "I had no choice… and I left."

Barnes narrowed her eyes. She turned to Hargreaves, who looked up from her phone.

"Curtis, I have one question for you," Hargreaves said. "When we arrested you earlier today, you appeared to be afraid of something."

"Well, I've lost over a million pounds because some dick's been lying to me, of course I was worried."

"Worried? I'd say you looked more like you were bricking it. And I'd say you were more afraid of *someone* than of losing your money."

Curtis bit his lip and turned to his lawyer.

"My client doesn't need to answer that," Sebastian said. "You're speculating about his emotional state."

"I'm asking him to explain the reasons behind his emotions," Hargreaves retorted. She fixed her eyes on Curtis. "Who are you afraid of?"

"Nobody."

"Where do you get your money from?"

Curtis' eyes flashed with annoyance. "No comment."

"Can you explain whose money it is you've lost–"

"It's my money!" he snapped.

"Then why are you so scared?"

Curtis bit his lip. "Who says I'm scared?"

"Your face."

"I think we should end this interview here," Sebastian said.

Barnes held up her hand. "I say when we finish. Not you."

Hargreaves' eyes were still on Curtis. "Tell me, who's got you so scared? If the money's all yours, like you've said, then is it a business partner or someone Mark knows that's unsettling you?"

"I think we'll finish here, thank you–" Sebastian rose out of his chair.

But Curtis had fallen for Hargreaves' hypnotizing gaze, which up until then he had done a good job of avoiding.

"Curtis," Hargreaves said. Her eyes locked on his. "We will find out everything that happened. We will request all your digital devices. We will get expert forensic teams to scrutinise every single message, email, tweet, Snapchat, photo, TikTok DM–" she took a breath "–you name it. We'll go through everything with a fine-toothed comb. Every business and personal interaction you've had for the last few years will be queried. If you want to avoid all that, I suggest you start helping us."

His blue eyes widened.

"Come on, Curtis. I thought you were a successful businessman. Do you really want us to make your life hell, or would you prefer to make a deal?"

He pulled his eyes away and rubbed them. "A deal." His shoulders sagged. "It's not someone I know. It's someone Mark knows."

"Who?"

Sebastian slapped the back of Curtis' chair. "Come on! We're going."

"He's under arrest!" Barnes said. "He's staying in that chair."

Hargreaves intensified her gaze. "Tell me who they are, Curtis."

"I don't know his name. All I know is that he's Australian."

"What's his role in all of this?"

Curtis swallowed hard; his arms were hugging his chest. "I'm getting warm in here. I need some fresh air."

"Who is he? This Australian?"

Curtis shook his eyes free from Hargreaves' trance. "I want some fresh air."

"You're under arrest," Barnes said.

Hargreaves sat back in her chair and winked at the camera on the wall.

Henry chuckled as he watched her on the small TV screen.

Chapter Twenty-Six

Hargreaves entered the side room with a smirk on her face. "I think we're getting somewhere," she said. "Maybe arresting Curtis in a fit of rage wasn't such a bad idea?"

"You might be onto something there," Henry said.

He then concentrated on the door. He could hear Barnes arguing with Sebastian over whether Curtis should be released or not. It sounded like Barnes was winning – but only just.

Henry refocused on Hargreaves. "Could this Australian be Sarah's ex-husband? But why would Mark Hardy be in business with his wife's ex? Especially if he's dangerous?"

"I guess we'll need to take a trip to ICU to ask Mark Hardy himself."

"Aye. We also need to find this Aussie and bring him in for questioning. Wherever he is." He paused. "Pete Blackburn was the first one to mention him to us, wasn't he?" He raised his head knowingly. "We also need to talk to him about what happened at St George's back in the nineties, if he'll say anything to us about it."

"Alright. I suggest we head over to see Mark Hardy first and disrupt his beauty sleep, and then head over to Pete Blackburn's." She checked the messages on her phone. "DS Forrester is still with Pete. A doctor's arrived and given him some sedatives."

"Will he be compos mentis when we get there?"

"More than he was earlier, I hope. Apparently, he's stopped picking the flesh off the back of his hand, so that's a start." She tapped on her phone. "I'll tell Forrester we'll be over in the next hour so she can lay the groundwork. I'd prefer him not to freak out when he learns why we really want to talk to him."

"Sounds like a plan."

Barnes stormed into the room, looking haggard and distressed. "I bloody hate lawyers. Especially that one. He's nothing but a parasite who's latched onto a dim-witted millionaire."

Henry chortled. "And, luckily for him, Curtis is a prime host. He has loads of money but lacks the brains to know how to spend it wisely. Anyway, speaking of Curtis' millions, do either of you know how he made his fortune? He doesn't strike me as a business mogul, no matter how much he tries to pose as one."

Barnes nodded wearily. "I looked into it earlier. His parents won the lottery twenty years ago and invested most of it. Curtis got a lump sum when he turned twenty-one, and it sounds like he's burnt through most of that. He now makes a living off his YouTube channel."

Hargreaves pulled a face. "A channel? What on?"

"Business and investing."

Hargreaves burst out laughing. "Him? He's just gone and lost a million quid!" She struggled to gather her composure. "I wish you'd told me that before the interview started. I'd have loved to have quizzed him on his business acumen."

"Yeah, well I'm glad I didn't." Barnes ran a hand through her short blond hair. "Let's not forget why we're here. There's a mass murder to solve by tomorrow lunchtime. So, what did we learn from Curtis?"

Hargreaves rolled her eyes.

Henry cleared his throat. "Well, we learned Curtis seems more concerned about this Australian fella than losing a million quid. And this Australian could be Sarah's ex-husband."

Hargreaves outlined their plans to Barnes, who gently massaged her temples.

"Fine," Barnes said. "I'll hang around here and start making a dent in the paperwork. Remember, it's nearly 6 p.m. and we need to present Murphy with a suspect tomorrow."

"Understood," Henry said, rising out of his chair. "I do feel like we're making progress."

Barnes exhaled. "Really? 'cause I feel like we've just lost an hour arguing with a thirty-year-old adolescent and his overpaid lawyer. We need to step it up a gear. I've already received a bollocking from Murphy today, I don't want to get another one tomorrow."

Hargreaves huffed. "Alright, bloody hell. We'll see what we can do."

Henry followed Hargreaves out the door. He highly suspected that Barnes would receive another telling-off the following day, and probably the day after that, but he wasn't worried for her. Murphy's bark was always worse than his bite, as Henry knew all too well.

* * *

Henry left Hargreaves near the lifts at the intensive care unit. She was talking to someone on the phone, presumably Murphy, and complaining about Barnes. Not wanting any involvement in it, Henry walked towards Mark Hardy's bed. The cubicle curtains were drawn, and Henry paused a moment to see if Hargreaves would catch up with him.

As Henry waited for her outside Mark's cubicle, he glanced around. Some of the other beds on the ward had their curtains pulled, while others didn't, and the patients within were on full display. The beeps of monitors filled the air, and Henry found the chatter from the hospital staff and the footfall of people traversing the centre of the ward very disruptive. Wasn't this supposed to be a place that encouraged rest and healing?

He saw Hargreaves at the lifts still chatting on her phone, and decided he would get started with Mark. He pulled back the curtain and blinked. It took him a moment to realise what was the matter.

Mark's bed was empty.

He accosted a nurse in green overalls who happened to be walking past. "Excuse me. Where's this patient gone?"

The nurse frowned. "What do you mean?" She looked past Henry and gawped at Mark's empty cubicle. "Erm… Well, he's supposed to be there."

The monitor at the side of the bed was still on, its screen showing flat lines and its wires trailing over the floor. The sheets had been thrown back.

"There's no drip stand," the nurse said, pointing at the right side of the bed.

The neat pile of Mark's clothes on the chair had also been taken.

"He couldn't have got far," Henry said. "Get security on the case."

The nurse nodded. "He shouldn't be out of bed. He could do himself harm."

She ran towards the nearest nurse station and picked up the phone while Henry swept his eyes over the ward.

There was no sign of him.

Hargreaves finally strolled over. She gave the stressed-looking nurse a puzzled look before noticing Mark's empty bed. "Shit! Where's he gone?"

"AWOL," Henry grunted. "He couldn't have gone far. He's still connected to the IV drip. The nurse is calling security now."

Hargreaves held her phone to her ear and stepped away to call for backup.

Henry focused on the hospital bed. Mark must have leapt out of it, grabbed his drip stand, collected his possessions, and headed off somewhere without being seen. He couldn't have taken the lifts as he would have been spotted. Henry's eyes then alighted on a fire exit between Mark's bed and the nurses' station.

Henry burst through the fire door and stepped onto a landing, with staircases above him and below. The ICU ward was on the third of five floors. Mark could have gone down to find an exit, or he could have gone up, changed into his clothes, and possibly descended to the ground floor in a lift. Considering Mark's deteriorated state, however, Henry suspected he had gone down. Going up a flight of stairs might have been too much.

As Henry descended to the second-floor landing, he noticed some translucent fluid spilt on the floor. He knelt on the concrete and touched the cold liquid. More puddles had formed on the stairs leading down to the next landing.

He reached the first floor, where the puddles had a hint of red to them. Blood speckled the wall, and Mark's drip stand lay askew on the concrete. He descended the rest of the way, discovering a man's hospital gown by the bottom fire escape.

Henry's mobile buzzed in his pocket, and he answered with a grunt.

"Where the hell are you?!" Hargreaves asked.

"On the ground floor, down the fire escape." His voice echoed off the walls. "Mark came down here and left his hospital gown and IV drip."

"Right, I'm coming down."

Henry clasped his mobile in his hand and checked the landing around him.

Why the hell had Mark felt the urge to cut his recuperation short and flee his hospital bed?

If they ever caught him, they might just find out.

Chapter Twenty-Seven

Henry and Hargreaves waited at the ground-floor reception for Bryan, the head of security for Leeds General Infirmary. The main entrance had been rebuilt a few years earlier and had a glass roof that curved down from the second floor to the automatic front doors. Daylight pored through the thick glass, creating a greenhouse effect that Henry suspected, on hotter days, could be quite unbearable.

A bulky man in his late fifties, with a shaved head and the look of a nightclub bouncer, approached them. Henry vaguely recognised him but couldn't think from where. He wore a blue shirt, and a rainbow-coloured lanyard identifying him as Bryan hung around his neck.

"We've double-checked the CCTV everywhere," Bryan said, using the antenna of his walkie-talkie to point out one of the bauble-like cameras on the ceiling. "And he's not turned up anywhere."

"We'll need that footage from you as soon as we can," Hargreaves said.

Bryan nodded. "And you'll soon get it."

"Are you suggesting he's not left the building?" Henry asked.

Bryan narrowed his eyes at Henry as if he recognised him too. "It's a possibility, but we have ten exits on the ground floor. It's not improbable that he's left through one of them."

"Do they all have cameras on them?" Henry asked.

"Most of them do, yes. However, there are a few fire exits that don't. I'm having them checked to see if they've been opened."

"Aren't they alarmed?"

Bryan shook his head. "They should be, but some haven't been fitted with alarms yet, and some others are faulty… we don't have the means to have them all correctly installed."

Hargreaves stepped away from them, staring at the buzzing mobile in her hand. "I need to take this."

Henry guessed she was off to talk to Murphy again. He then caught Bryan staring at him.

"Are you *the* Henry Ward? The DCI in Bradford?" Bryan asked.

"I was. I'm a consultant on this investigation."

Bryan held out his chubby hand. "I thought it was you. I'm former Inspector Samson. I used to be stationed at Littlemoor, near Bradford."

Henry shook his hand. "Oh, yes. I thought you looked familiar."

"I worked on some of your big cases with you."

"I expect you would have done if you were at Littlemoor." Henry gestured to the hospital's front entrance. "So, this is your retirement, then?"

"I did my twenty years on the force and decided to get out with my pension." He looked round the brightly lit space. "This isn't that bad. Pays alright, and I still get to see some action every now and then."

"Like today, I expect."

Bryan shook his head. "Today's nothing. We had a riot in the waiting room the other Saturday night."

"A riot? In a hospital waiting room?"

"Well… more of a fight. Two rival gangs from the council estates found themselves in A & E together, and they didn't take kindly to it."

"I bet they didn't."

"This missing bloke you're after… what's he done?"

"He was poisoned yesterday along with three others."

Bryan's eyebrows rose in shock. "Oh, the mass murder on the moor? Horrible business, that was."

"Yes, it is indeed." Henry recalled the back garden at Cragg Hall littered with bodies, and the dining table on the patio covered in deadly food and drink. The plates of burgers and sausages and the mounds of lettuce and freshly cut tomatoes, all dripping in the poisonous vinaigrette. "We think Mark Hardy knows why they were poisoned," Henry said.

"Right… bloody hell."

Static erupted from Bryan's walkie-talkie.

"Come in," he said into it. More static masked a voice that Henry couldn't interpret. "I got that." Bryan looked past Henry and down the corridor behind him. "They think they know where he went."

* * *

Henry followed Bryan past the front reception, through a foyer, and into the Emergency Department. They were in a far corner of the brightly lit ward, with four cubicles surrounding them. The privacy curtains were drawn, and inside, Henry could hear the patients moaning and writhing in pain. Bryan's walkie-talkie issued more static, and he gestured to Henry to keep following.

They walked down a corridor, went through a door marked 'Hospital Staff Only' and crossed a small office where a young doctor was fast asleep on a camp bed with his white coat still on.

Bryan opened another door, and they found themselves in a stairwell. A security guard standing next to an open fire exit called them over. Weak daylight poured through the gaps around the opened door.

"I noticed the alarm on this one went off a few minutes ago. I just got here to find it like this," said the security guard.

Bryan stuck his head out the door and turned back to Henry. "This leads to the staff car park. We'll have him on CCTV if he's walking around there."

Henry followed Bryan through the door and found himself outside. They were standing between two rows of parked vehicles in a small, unsheltered car park, lit by the fading early evening sun. The area was pressed in by the walls of the hospital on one side and a multi-storey car park on the other. Henry noticed signs on the walls in front of each parking bay, declaring the name of the doctor who had the right to use it.

The only exit was through the larger car park on the left.

"Are any cars missing?" Henry asked Bryan.

Bryan shrugged and spoke into his walkie-talkie. A response came back in static. "They're checking the CCTV now."

Henry surveyed the row of cars in front of him. Of the ten parking bays, two were empty.

Had Mark stolen a vehicle, and if so, how? Was he well adept at hot-wiring cars or was he hiding somewhere close?

"Here," Bryan said. "They've spotted him near an exit in the main car park."

Henry bounded up the entry ramp and into the multi-storey car park, with Bryan following behind.

At the far corner of the ground floor, behind a row of stationary cars, a fire exit hung wide open. A whiff of urine assaulted Henry's nostrils, and he covered his nose while stepping over litter and smashed glass on the floor.

"The homeless sometimes sleep here," Bryan explained.

Henry looked up at the reinforced concrete ceiling. "Are there any cameras watching this door?"

"I'm afraid not."

Henry stepped through the open fire exit and onto a strip of grass littered with cigarette butts. The area was walled in by other parts of the hospital.

It was a dead end.

"There's no way he escaped through here," Henry said.

"Agreed." Bryan kicked a can of pop and lifted his walkie-talkie. "He's not here. Are you sure he came this way?"

A burst of static responded to him.

"Right." Bryan tapped the antenna against his bald head. "My man in the control room saw someone heading in this direction and assumed he came out through here."

"Well, doesn't your man know there's nowhere to go?" Henry asked. He looked up at the high walls surrounding him. "This isn't much of a fire escape plan, is it? You're completely stuck here; you'd have to be helicoptered out."

Bryan didn't argue with him.

"Let's go back inside," Henry said.

They re-entered through the fire door and walked over crisp packets and shattered bottles. Something caught Henry's attention underneath the nearest parked vehicle.

Minding the broken glass and puddles of suspicious liquid, he got down on all fours and peeked underneath the car. From his perspective, he could see underneath all the vehicles on the row.

Nobody was hiding under any of them.

"Good idea. I'll go check the other side." Bryan marched over and got down on one knee alongside the car parked at the end of the opposite row.

Just as Bryan bent over, a shadow flitted out from behind a white Transit van. The figure darted towards the exit ramp.

"He's over there!" Henry shouted. He scrambled up, cutting himself on some glass, and chased after the figure.

Henry's hips burnt immediately, the false one oddly less painful than the other, and he was quickly out of breath.

But he kept pushing forwards.

Bryan caught up with him and bellowed to the security officer who'd remained near the hospital door. "Get him!"

The lithe figure cut through the centre of the car park, but was tackled by the security officer, a few decades younger than both Henry and Bryan.

Henry tramped the rest of the way, struggling to catch his breath, and came to stand over Mark, who lay on his back on the ground.

Mark's eyes rolled upwards until only the whites could be seen.

"He needs help," said the security guard, getting off him.

"Fetch… a bloody… doctor…" Henry managed to say. "I need… this bugger… to talk."

Chapter Twenty-Eight

Mark Hardy was given a private room back on the third floor, and a security guard was stationed at the door. He was back in a hospital gown, lying in his bed, and in a stable condition despite his overexertion in the car park. The tubes and wires that he had hastily ripped out of himself had been replaced, and the monitor next to him displayed his vital signs, which the doctors had regarded with concern before they left the room.

Henry and Hargreaves were seated in chairs at the foot of Mark's bed. A golden glare from the setting sun came in through the only window.

"Can you tell us why you tried to escape from hospital?" Hargreaves asked, her pink mobile phone in hand. Henry had watched her start the recording just beforehand. "You nearly died yesterday of cyanide poisoning. So, you really shouldn't be running around like that."

Mark didn't answer. His half-closed eyes stared past them, as if they weren't in the room with him.

"We've talked to quite a few people since we spoke earlier today," Hargreaves continued. "Haven't we, Henry?"

Henry nodded. "Aye, we've spoken to Curtis Quaker, who was very talkative, wasn't he?"

"He was," she replied. "He told us all about the financial issues Sales Expedited has been having. He explained to us it's about to close down, which isn't good for you, is it?"

"It's not," Henry concurred, as Mark hadn't answered. "Curtis was very upset about losing his money. Over a million pounds he's lost. But he's even more upset about some business associate of yours… some mysterious, Australian fella."

Mark's eyes flickered.

"So, what can you tell us about this Aussie?" Henry leant forwards.

No reply came.

"Maybe his escape act has worn him out too much?" Hargreaves asked, shifting in her chair.

Henry shook his head. A spark of annoyance caused him to reject the idea. "Listen, Mark, we know you tried to flee from this hospital for a reason. If you were perfectly innocent, you wouldn't have taken such a risk."

Mark's glazed-over eyes focused on Henry.

"So do yourself – and us – a favour and tell us what is going on. Who is this Australian fella we've heard about, and what does he want with you?"

Mark closed his eyes.

Hargreaves exhaled and stopped the recording on her phone. "Alright, it was worth a shot, I suppose. But nothing's going to happen here, he's not talking. We might as well head onto our next stop."

Henry kept his eyes on Mark, who was visibly paler and sicker than earlier.

"Mark," he said. "Last chance to talk to us before we go. The next time we come here, we won't be as kind or forgiving. And we will already know more about Sales Expedited than you'll ever want us to. So, you might as well save us the time and hassle. We might go easier on you if you do."

Mark wheezed.

"What was that?"

He gave a hacking cough and closed his eyes.

"Sod this!" Hargreaves jumped out of her chair and dialled a number on her phone. "Can you get me the home number for the senior investigator at the Serious Fraud Office who's looking into a company called Sales…"

After she stepped out, the door slowly closed behind her, cutting off the rest of the chatter from the corridor.

Henry remained in the small room with the sleeping Mark. He wondered what kind of fear could drive a man out of his hospital bed like that. Was it all so he could avoid answering questions about this Australian?

What was this Aussie capable of? Mark clearly knew the answer to that. Only a real monster with a heart as cold as stone could kill three innocent people by hiding cyanide in their salad dressing.

Henry got out of his chair, with the clear intent to find this Australian and bring him to justice.

* * *

Hargreaves was standing near the busy nurses' station, leaning on its wooden counter. She was oblivious to the two nurses on the other side who were giving her funny looks. She was in full conversation when Henry approached. Her pink phone was pressed against her ear.

"Yes, Sales Expedited. So, you have been looking into it?" She gave Henry an excited look. "Right. Listen, I need to put you on loudspeaker, but first…" She pulled her mobile away and addressed the two nurses. "Are there any quiet rooms available?"

One of the nurses scoffed. "In ICU? We've got beds lining the corridors."

Hargreaves pulled a face and then pointed at the fire door that Mark had used in his escape attempt earlier. Henry followed her into the empty stairwell, and she explained to Simon Edwards that she was putting their call on loudspeaker.

"–be careful who listens in on this," Simon was saying. His tinny voice echoed on the concrete walls. "This is highly confidential."

"It's alright," Hargreaves said. She introduced Henry as a police consultant. "So, can you summarise your suspicions about Sales Expedited?"

Simon cleared his throat. "Well… I received a tip-off three months ago."

"From whom?" Henry asked.

"Anonymous. Still unknown. The email told the SFO to look into the company as its finances didn't make any sense."

"Who could've known that?" Henry asked.

"Anyone involved with it, I guess. But that's not the point."

Henry and Hargreaves shared a confused look.

"Do you get a lot of similar tip-offs?" she asked.

"We do sometimes. However, this one was very vague, so it sat on a list for a while before it was assigned to me last month."

"What did you find out?" Hargreaves asked.

"Sales Expedited is a shell company. None of its imports or exports are real."

"How do you know?"

"Well, their apparent warehouse, where they receive and hold their goods, is a derelict building on the outskirts of Bradford. After asking to look at their records, which I did two weeks ago, I quickly realised the whole business was faked – and obviously so."

Hargreaves peered down at her mobile. "Does the company have much money coming in?"

"Oh yes, it receives hundreds of thousands a month in its bank accounts. Who knows where it all comes from?"

"Isn't it your job to find that out?" Henry asked.

"The investigation is still ongoing. I do know, however, that the company only has three major clients. All three pay similar amounts to the business every month – almost on a subscription basis."

"Does it have any staff?" she asked.

"Yes. I found three names…"

They heard the sound of paper being shifted on a wooden desk.

"Mark Hardy, Peter Blackburn, and Justin Nabwood."

"Peter Blackburn?" Henry furrowed his brow. "What details do you have on them?"

"Well, Mark Hardy, I understand you know. He's registered as the sole company director. Peter Blackburn is–"

"We know him, too," Henry said. "And who's this Justin Nabwood?"

"Ah, well… He turned up on the records only four months ago, and he's getting paid quite a lot for his job description, an 'Administration Manager'. He receives five thousand pounds a month before taxes." More paper being shuffled. "He's Australian. His visa seems above board. There's a photocopy of his passport–"

"Can you send all that to us immediately?" Hargreaves said.

"I will do…" Simon said, slightly perturbed by her urgency.

"Who do you think's paying them all this money?" Henry asked.

"As I've mentioned, that hasn't been cracked yet. In fact, I've been preparing a report to send to the Organised Crime division. It appears these three clients of theirs could be criminal entities of some kind. I tried tracking their accounts, but it quickly got very complicated. I hazard it'll take a financial investigator a long while to untangle it all."

Henry nodded grimly. "Are you aware, by any chance, of any links to chemicals, or anything like that?"

"Erm…" Simon paused as he considered the question. "Well… I'm not sure. I suppose it's not impossible."

"Alright, thanks for your answers, Mr Edwards."

Hargreaves also thanked him before hanging up. "What now?" she asked Henry.

"Is it worth having another crack at Mark Hardy to see what he's willing to tell us?" Henry asked.

"Nah, let him rest. I don't want him to conk out on us." She gestured at the steps heading downstairs. "Let's go over to Pete Blackburn's and find out why his name's on Sales Expedited's records."

Henry nodded and then stared at the steep flight of steps before him. "Alright, but I'm getting the lift. I've already run down these steps today, and my hips won't let me do that again."

Hargreaves rolled her eyes but relented, and they headed back through the fire exit and onto the ward.

Chapter Twenty-Nine

The sun set over the moors surrounding Pete Blackburn's cottage, and brilliant orange and pink rays streaked the sky. Two cars were parked on the narrow driveway next to Pete's old house, and Henry assumed they belonged to DS Forrester and the doctor. Hargreaves grumbled as she was forced to park her Audi with its rear sticking out onto the road.

"Are you sure you can leave it like this?" Henry asked, after getting out of her car.

Hargreaves shrugged. "Why? What's wrong? It's not like there's tons of traffic on this road." She pointed at the narrow, quiet country lane behind them, and Henry acquiesced. "Come on," she said, "let's go focus on Pete. We've got a number of things to ask him."

"Aye," Henry agreed.

They knocked on the door, and DS Forrester answered. Her red hair was tied in a long ponytail, and she wore a blue blouse underneath her charcoal suit jacket. She smiled at them, crinkling her pixie-like nose, and let them into Pete's hallway.

She spoke softly. "The doctor is still with Pete."

"How's he doing?" Henry asked.

"He's fine… calmer than before. The doctor gave him a sedative, which knocked him out a little, but he's coming round."

"Do you think he'll talk?" asked Hargreaves.

"Aye," Henry grunted. "We've just left one unconscious person of interest in ICU."

"It's fine. He's talking," Forrester said. "Is Pete a person of interest?"

Henry raised an eyebrow. "Possibly. Why?"

"Well, he's completely devastated about his wife. He doesn't strike me as a killer."

"I might agree with you there, but he knows a few things that we need clarifying." Henry nodded towards the living room. "Is he in there?"

"Yes, come through. Do you want some tea?"

Henry said yes while Hargreaves said no, but she quickly relented, and Forrester went off to make it. They stepped into the living room. Pete Blackburn was sitting in the same chair he had been in earlier. Both his hands had been bandaged up. His eyes didn't move from a spot on the far wall. He stared intently at it, as if he was in the middle of an eye test.

A man in his late thirties with dark, curly hair was seated in the armchair. He wore a shirt and tie and was typing on a tablet resting in his lap. He stood up when he saw the two detectives enter.

"Hello." He stepped towards them to shake their hands. "I'm Dr Blackfoot. Clinical psychologist."

Hargreaves introduced herself and Henry. "Is he alright?" she asked, looking at Pete who was still staring at the wall seemingly unaware they were in the room with him.

"He's… better than before." Dr Blackfoot spoke while wearing a slight wince. "Unfortunately, I can't get him into a facility for tonight. I'm able to stay another hour or so, but then I really do have to go." He looked towards the kitchen. "Your fellow detective said she can stay until around 9 p.m."

"It's okay. We'll find someone for him," Hargreaves said. Although Henry didn't think she believed the words herself.

"Does he really need to be in a facility?" Henry asked.

Dr Blackfoot turned to study his patient. "He might come round in an hour or so. Who knows. I'd prefer to remain cautious, considering the trauma he's been through."

"Can we talk to him?"

"You can try, but I wouldn't put too much weight on what he says. He's still confused."

Henry had an idea. "Doctor, what do you think could have caused him to have this reaction?"

The doctor scratched his scalp between two long, black curls. "Well, having his wife and friends murdered on the same day can definitely cause a reaction like this."

"Could he also be feeling guilty?"

The doctor scrunched up his face. "Possibly, but I really wouldn't like to speculate. Not in circumstances such as these."

Henry nodded his understanding before Hargreaves tapped his shoulder, giving him a look that said, 'let's get on with it'. They took a seat on the sofa opposite Pete, while the doctor remained near the door, his eyes on his tablet; evidently, he planned to pay attention to their conversation.

Hargreaves took her pink mobile from her bag, started the recording, and then told Dr Blackfoot everything they were about to discuss was privileged information and could not be repeated.

The doctor nodded his agreement, and Hargreaves looked at Pete Blackburn.

"How are you feeling?" she asked.

Pete lowered his eyes from the spot on the far wall. "Better." Then, he turned to focus on Henry and Hargreaves. "Why are you here?"

"We need to ask you a few questions," she said. "We've been looking into what you told us… about Sarah's ex-husband being in the country."

Pete's eyes widened. His fingers scratched the fresh bandage on his hand.

"What can you tell us about him?"

"Like what? I've never really met him."

"What's he called?" Henry asked.

"I'm not sure?"

"Is he Justin Nabwood?"

Pete turned away from them.

Hargreaves got the scanned passport image of Justin on her phone. She got up off the sofa to show it to Pete. He cautiously glanced at it before turning away.

"Is that him?" Hargreaves asked.

"Maybe…"

"Is that a yes or a no?" Henry asked. "Remember, Mr Blackwood. You wanted me to promise I'd find Louanne's killer. I can only do that if you're straight with us."

Pete let out a long sigh.

"When did you last see him?" Henry asked.

"Two months ago. I only met him once. At Mark's house."

"Was Sarah there?" Hargreaves asked.

Pete shook his head. "She was out."

"Did she know Justin was there?"

He continued shaking his head. "She wouldn't want to know."

"How did Sarah's ex-husband end up at her house in Addingham?" Henry asked, frowning.

"I think he contacted Mark first. He seemed to know something…"

"What?"

"Something about Sales Expedited. He…" He bit his lower lip. "He knew what was going on."

Hargreaves raised her head. "Can you clarify what you mean?"

He groaned. "He… I don't know. He knew a lot about it. Sarah must have told him."

"She knew her ex-husband was back in the country?"

Pete looked lost. "Ex-husband?"

"Yes, you said he was her ex, Pete," Henry clarified.

Pete fell silent.

"That leads me onto my second question," Hargreaves said. "What's your job?"

"What do you mean? I'm an academic."

"And if I had HMRC check your National Insurance contributions, would I see anything from Sales Expedited on there?"

Pete's fingers scratched the dressing on the back of his hand.

"Mr Blackburn, please answer the question," Henry said in as soothing a voice as he could manage.

Pete nodded. "I believe I am a registered employee there."

"And do you work for that company?"

He shook his head. "I'm not even paid by them."

Hargreaves read the report that Simon Edwards had sent her on her phone. "It says here you're paid three thousand pounds a month, which isn't that bad."

"I don't receive a penny of it."

"Where does it all go?"

"I don't know. You'll have to ask Mark. He used my National Insurance number."

"Why would he do that?"

"Because he wanted to set me up as a fake employee."

Hargreaves gave Henry a dissatisfied look. "Did you conspire to commit fraud with Mark Hardy?"

Pete scowled. "Mark needed an NI number, so I gave him mine."

"Why did you do that?" Henry asked. His eyes had narrowed, and his tone of voice was less soft than before.

"Because… well, he asked me." Pete's fingernails had done a good job of scratching through the top of the bandage and had now reached the bloody scabs underneath.

"Why would you let Mark Hardy use your National Insurance number and set you up as a false employee?" Henry asked.

"Well…" Pete scratched the back of his hand. "He needed a number, and I had one…"

"Do you always do whatever Mark Hardy asks you to do?"

Pete blinked, as if something was caught in his eye. "If… if he needs something, I try to give it to him."

"And why?" Henry furrowed his brows. He turned to Hargreaves and saw she was doing the same. "Why help him commit a crime?"

"Why?" Pete sounded unnerved by the question, as if a fundamental part of his psyche had been challenged. "I'd do anything for Mark… absolutely anything."

As Henry watched the wretched man, he wondered if 'anything' could include committing murder.

Chapter Thirty

DS Forrester came into the living room with cups of tea on a tray which she passed around. While she handed Pete his, she gently chided him for destroying his bandages and told him she would return to apply fresh ones.

Henry sipped his tea and glanced at Dr Blackfoot, who remained standing in the doorway. The doctor's eyes were on his tablet, and he sipped a cup of tea that Forrester had given him.

The day was ending through the windows, and twilight inched across the sky over the horizon. The few cars passing on the country lane outside had their headlights on and were forced to slow down as they manoeuvred around Hargreaves' badly parked Audi.

Henry peered over her shoulder as she read another document on her large pink phone. He didn't recognise it at first, but its antiquated typing and browned paper made him realise it was the scanned copy of the police case notes from the St George's school investigation. Hargreaves pointed at Pete's typewritten name on the document.

Henry sipped more tea and looked at Pete over his steaming cup. "So, what can you tell us about St George's school?"

Pete was peering down at the cup of tea in his hand, and, mercifully, was no longer scratching his hands. "It's a school we went to."

"Did you enjoy going there?" Henry asked.

Pete shrugged. "I didn't dislike it."

"Were you friends with Mark, Allister, and Ralph at the school?"

"Yes. We were close friends."

"Were you involved with any groups or clubs while you were there?"

Pete licked his lips. "Not that I recall."

"Okay," Henry said, nodding. He glanced at Hargreaves' phone. "In October 1995, you made a complaint against the school. What can you tell us about that?"

Pete blinked wildly. "I can't recall any complaint, especially not one to the police."

Henry grunted in surprise. He leant to the side to get a better look at Hargreaves' phone. "Yes, Peter Blackburn, aged fifteen, September 1995, 'ten lashes found on victim's back, several wounds had become infected and needed minor surgery'." Henry straightened up and addressed Pete. "Was that not you?"

Pete shook his head, his front teeth biting his lower lip.

"Are you sure?" Henry asked. "Was there another student there with the same name?"

Pete continued shaking his head. His right leg had begun to shake so violently, he spilt tea down his black khakis.

"Pete," Hargreaves said. "Are you alright?"

His head shook erratically and morphed into a spasm.

"Pete?"

The cup of tea fell from his hand, spilling hot liquid down his leg, and rolled along the carpet. "It wasn't me," Pete said, his head still shaking. "It wasn't me."

Dr Blackfoot stepped forwards and placed a hand on Pete's shoulder. He knelt down beside him and gently brought his head to face his. He spoke soothing words, and persuaded Pete to take deep, calming breaths.

Pete didn't comply at first but then followed the doctor's orders and breathed deeply.

As Henry watched this unfold, he felt Hargreaves prodding his arm. She nodded towards the door, and they got off the settee and filed into the hallway, where they found Forrester.

"Shit," Forrester said, looking sadly at Pete. "I've not seen him that bad."

"Aye," Hargreaves said. "He's not looking good, is he?"

"What's all this about his school?" Forrester asked.

Henry explained the historical investigation into St George's school and their suspicion that an old grudge could be behind the poisoning.

"Well, that might make a strong motive to kill them… if thirty years hadn't passed between then and now." Forrester cocked an eyebrow.

Henry grunted. "It's just one angle we're looking at. One of many. Unfortunately for Pete, he's linked to the other lines of inquiry as well, the poor sod."

"I heard the stuff about the company. What else did he know?" Forrester asked.

"He knows something about Sarah's ex-husband." Henry sipped the lukewarm cup of tea that he was still holding. "When he's calmer, could you start asking him about that?"

Forrester winced slightly. "I don't know. I can try, but… I think he's going to be sent to a facility. That's probably what's best for him."

"Didn't the doctor say there weren't any beds available?" Hargreaves asked.

Forrester furrowed her brows. "That's the first I've heard of it. Are you saying he's got nowhere to go?"

"Yeah, that's what it sounded like."

"You're kidding me?" She huffed and then walked into the living room to have a quiet word with the doctor, who had succeeded in calming Pete down.

Henry sipped more tea and looked at Hargreaves. "Where to next?"

She hadn't touched her own drink but was still holding it as if she might. She then put it down on a side table opposite the front door. "Let's head back to HQ. Try to note down everything we've learnt, and then you can call it a day."

Henry agreed. He had been on the go since early that morning and felt like he had done enough for today. Besides, if he left now, he could still get in a quick walk with Tessa, who would be pining at his front door, waiting for his return.

Forrester came out of the living room, huffing and shaking her head. "The state of the mental health services in this country…"

Hargreaves turned to her. "We'll have to leave you with Pete."

"Alright, but I really need to get off in an hour or so and see the kids, and he can't be left alone in that state. Christ knows what he could do to himself."

Hargreaves nodded. "I'll see if I can get a uniform to check on him overnight."

"I'm not sure a police officer turning up on his doorstep at three in the morning will help."

"Well, do you want to sleep here overnight?"

Forrester shook her head.

"Then it's the best I can do. Unless we ask the doctor to turf someone else out of their bed, but I don't think that'd help anyone."

Forrester relented with a sigh.

"Come on, then," Henry said. "Let's head back to HQ and see what we've learnt." He checked his watch, and saw it was nearly 8 p.m. That made it thirteen hours of continuous work, and he wouldn't be paid for any of it. "I'm getting too old and retired for such long days."

Hargreaves scoffed. "You're barely in your late sixties."

Henry was about to retort and say he doubted she would want to work like him when she reached his age. However, looking at the way things were going, she would be lucky to retire at seventy.

"Alright, point taken," he said, forcing a smile. "Let's head back to HQ."

Chapter Thirty-One

They arrived back at Leeds Central police station, and the street lights in the near-empty car park were on. The glass and concrete building was lit up with spots, and the usually busy road running alongside the station was calm. Henry stepped out of Hargreaves' car and took a lungful of the pleasant evening air. He could hear birds gently tweeting in the rafters of the nearby warehouses, and the occasional vehicle driving down the street unsettled the stillness.

Hargreaves locked her Audi and said they had better hurry up to see Barnes before Henry signed off for the night. He spotted his lonely Skoda Octavia stationed opposite. It occupied the only bay in an entire row, and Henry longed to get in it and drive off home. He was running low on energy and felt tired enough to consider telling Hargreaves to speak with Barnes by herself. But images from the previous day – of the Hardys' garden and the shrouded bodies lying within it – forced him to muster the energy and follow Hargreaves into the building.

Barnes was sitting in the meeting room. Pictures of the victims Henry had just thought about were mounted on the whiteboard walls. Facts detailing each one had been handwritten underneath in green marker pen. Barnes was slumped over a laptop at the table, wearing round glasses that reflected the laptop's blue light.

"What did you find?" she asked.

Hargreaves gave her a summary of their fruitless conversations with Mark and Pete, while Henry helped himself to some coffee from a pot on the table. He poured some into a paper cup and drank it without milk.

Barnes's face expressed her disappointment. "Ah… So, nothing else?"

Hargreaves shook her head and pulled a seat out from under the table. "Pete admitted to giving Mark his NI number, and he identified Justin Nabwood as Sarah's ex-husband."

Henry found a question mark within a square on the whiteboard labelled 'Ex-Hus'. At least they now had a face and a name to put in there.

"We didn't get as much as we'd hoped from Mark," he said, blowing on his coffee. "But we've found out a fair bit about Sales Expedited. Firstly, it has been committing fraud on a massive scale, and Mark seems to be managing it all. And secondly, Sarah's ex-husband contacted him four months ago, apparently knowing all about it. He and Mark must have struck up a deal, as Justin became an employee for the company quickly afterwards."

Barnes stared into the distance. "And he's called Justin Nabwood?" she asked, refocusing on the room. She turned to type into her computer. "I'll start doing some research on him. Hopefully, we can find out where his salary is being paid into and if he's been spending it. But we won't know that until the banks reopen on Tuesday."

"Why would Mark let him into his scam?" Hargreaves asked, leaning back in her chair. "He'd have to be scared of him, wouldn't he?"

"I suppose," Henry said. "Or maybe – if there is a criminal gang involved – Justin went higher up the food chain and sorted it out with its boss. The boss then could have forced Mark into abiding by his request."

Barnes nodded. "And if you think about it, five grand a month isn't that much, all things considered."

"I wouldn't mind a salary like that," Hargreaves said, huffing. "Especially when it's free money, as he doesn't have to do anything in return."

"Perhaps Justin *is* doing something in return," Henry said. "He could be working for them in a criminal capacity, or he might just be paid to keep his mouth shut about it."

"Well, why did they keep him alive, then?" Hargreaves asked.

"Maybe he had a lot of clout, and they were too worried of the consequences of killing him. Or perhaps it wasn't in the gang's interest to get rid of him at all, and they agreed sixty grand a year was worth his silence."

Barnes squinted through her round glasses at her laptop's screen. She pinched her forehead and took a sip from her coffee. "Justin Nabwood?" she repeated.

After typing on her keyboard again, she leant back on her chair and shook her head. "I can't find anything on him. He hasn't got any criminal records with us."

"Well, we'd have to get on the phone to Australia, wouldn't we?" Henry said. He looked at his watch and did the mental arithmetic. "It'll be 6 a.m. in Canberra, so you'll have to wait a few hours before ringing them."

"Canberra?" Hargreaves said. "Don't we need to speak to Sydney?"

Henry rolled his eyes. "I know Sarah Hardy's originally from New South Wales, so was Justin – probably – but we'll have to speak to Australia's capital first or they won't be very happy with us."

Hargreaves was still confused. "But isn't Sydney the capital?"

Barnes interrupted them. "It'll need to go through the UK National Crime Agency anyway. I can't call up some Aussie copper and just ask him about it. I must go through the official channels."

"And how long will that take?" Henry asked, raising an eyebrow.

Barnes exhaled. "A few days, at the very least."

"And Murphy wants a suspect by tomorrow afternoon?"

Barnes scrunched up her face.

"We could tell Murphy that Justin is our suspect," Hargreaves suggested.

Barnes shook her head. "On what grounds? All we have is that he's involved in this Sales Expedited company.

We don't have him obtaining or handling the poison. We don't have him at the house on the day of the barbecue–"

"But we do have him at the house two months earlier," Henry said.

"Do we?" Barnes tilted her head to the side.

Henry nodded slowly, a smile spreading on his lips. "Pete saw him at Cragg Hall. Justin was with Mark, but Sarah was out. What if…" He held his finger in the air. "Justin planted the poison before the barbecue?"

"He poisoned the salad dressing two months beforehand. Why would he do that?"

Henry furrowed his brow. "I don't know… maybe he wished to kill Sarah."

"But we don't know if he even wanted to kill her," Barnes said.

"Well, Pete did mention Sarah had an 'odd' background in Sydney," Henry added.

Barnes winced and shook her head. "I don't think that works."

"However, we haven't thought about that yet, have we?" Hargreaves said. "That the poison was brought into the house before the barbecue."

"And was put in the salad dressing weeks or months ago?" Barnes asked, her tone of voice verging on incredulous. "Why hadn't someone already been killed by it, then?"

"Alright. Point taken. But what do we know about this vinaigrette?" Henry asked. "Was it homemade or bought from the supermarket? If it was homemade, perhaps one of the ingredients had contained the cyanide."

Barnes's unsatisfied expression remained. "I don't know…"

Henry approached the whiteboard and took out his phone. He snapped some photos of the key players and victims, and then took pictures of Barnes's notes. He then spotted the circles he had drawn earlier. The words 'poison', 'school', and 'Mark's company' were still written in the middle of each.

"We've made progress on the school and Mark's company," he said. "But we're still unsure about the poison, who obtained it, and who put it in their food."

Barnes leant her elbow on the table and peered at the whiteboard. "I suppose, you're right."

Henry looked at Sarah's picture on the board. He suspected it was a recent photograph of her. Her blonde hair, glossy in the sun, fell around her face, and she beamed at the camera. Her teeth shone bright against her tanned skin and a sunny aura surrounded her, as if she would have been a barrel of laughs to be around.

"Any more information on Sarah Hardy's cause of death?" he asked.

"Nothing as yet. Dr Anderson said he needed another few days to work it out."

"A few days?" Henry asked. "Well, Murphy's deadline isn't going to be met, is it?"

Barnes huffed in reply.

"I'm sure we'll find something," Hargreaves said. Her eyes were fixed on her mobile phone's screen. "There can't have been that many people with access to the Hardys' house. Besides, you can't just buy cyanide from any old place."

Henry nodded in agreement and finished his coffee. Scrunching up his cup, he strolled over to the wastebasket. He caught a glimpse of Ralph's photo on the wall. "Here, doesn't he have access to chemicals?"

Hargreaves concurred. "He works for a chemical company. But he works in marketing, remember. It's like saying a receptionist in a hospital has access to morphine, which isn't necessarily the case, as they'll never be allowed anywhere near it."

Henry gave in with a grunt. "Still might be worth following up."

"I'll add it to the low-priority to-do list," Hargreaves said.

He checked his watch. If he didn't set off now, he wouldn't get back home before 10 p.m., and he imagined Tessa howling at his front door in desperate need of a walk. "Alright, then. That's me for the day. I'm clocking off."

Barnes mumbled an acknowledgment while Hargreaves said 'bye' without looking up from her phone.

"Oh, great," Henry said. "It's been a joy working with you two all day, as well."

They made another attempt to sound more appreciative, but Henry shook his head and left the room. What a pair, he said to himself, as he traipsed down the steps.

Chapter Thirty-Two

Henry parked outside his cottage on Addingham Main Street. The road was quiet, and the trees around him swayed in the gentle breeze, rustling their leaves. The street lights were lit as night had fully descended, and when Henry approached his front door, he heard his dog howling on the other side.

After he opened the door, she encircled is feet, barking. Henry knew he would have to take her for a walk and grabbed the lead hanging on the coat hooks and re-locked his front door.

He took her up to the top of Addingham Park so she could burn off her pent-up energy by running around the football pitch. She fled away from him as soon as he unhooked her leash and disappeared into the gloom that shrouded the other side. Henry then took himself for a walk, following the boundary line, so that he could think through everything that had happened that day.

His mind was tired, and trying to formulate complete thoughts was difficult. The one thing he could easily conclude was that he didn't like this case. It was too much for him. Even if they were making some minor progress, it felt too vast. He tried to recall ever working on similar cases throughout his career but couldn't remember any. There had been serial killings and murders that involved multiple victims, but nothing like this. Not a mass poisoning.

He then corrected himself when the memory of a case involving a faulty boiler came to mind. A household of six had died of carbon monoxide poisoning in their sleep. The safety features on their boiler had been tampered with in an attempt to reduce their gas bill. The few hundred pounds they had saved that year had come at a great cost.

Other than that, he didn't have any other recollection of similar cases. Three had been murdered by cyanide poisoning at Cragg Hall, though one, Sarah, might have been killed by something else. He squinted into the gloom ahead of him and spotted Tessa's white and brown form flitting through it.

He took out his mobile from his pocket and searched for Dr Anderson's number. It was 10.30 p.m., but something told him his old colleague would still be up. And indeed, he was. Dr Anderson cleared his throat as he answered the phone.

"Ward?"

"Dr Anderson. I hear you're having problems with one of the bodies we found yesterday."

Dr Anderson huffed. "You could say that. I've been doing research on it all bloody evening." He sipped some liquid from a glass. "I don't like not confirming the cause of death, Henry. It's the only thing that people pay much attention to, and when they don't get it from me, they start wondering."

"Wondering if you're too old to still be hanging around?" Henry said, smirking.

"No, heavens. You can hang on in this position for as long as you want. No, failure to pronounce the cause of death causes people to wonder how the process really works, and then they start with their bloody awful questions."

Henry chuckled. "I suppose you don't want to show people what's really behind the curtain."

"Of course not. Neither them nor me. They don't really want to know how I decide on a cause of death, especially when it's not clear-cut. It's a fine art, you see, and thus, by its very nature, can be challenged quite easily."

"Well, God forbid anyone challenging you."

Dr Anderson sipped more of his drink. "What is it you want? Why are you ringing me after ten in the evening?"

"Just to get some facts." Tessa burst out of the nearby darkness and ran full pelt across the field as if chasing imagined game. "What can you tell me about Sarah Hardy?"

"She's different from the others. I believe she died earlier, and as I mentioned, she doesn't have the telltale signs of cyanide poisoning, such as the cherry-red skin, almond breath… heavily congested internal organs."

"Congested?"

"Yes. The hearts and lungs of the other victims were engorged with blood. Cyanide attacks the cells' ability to break oxygen down into energy, you see. So, the body pumps around bright red, highly oxygenated blood, but the organs can't process it, so they quickly begin to drown in it."

"And the victim dies quickly?"

"Within minutes."

"And you think Sarah Hardy died by other means?"

Dr Anderson grumbled. "Toxicology samples have been taken from her, so let's see what the lab comes back with. But for me, she didn't die from cyanide poisoning."

"What could she have died from?"

Dr Anderson sipped more of whatever he was drinking. "If I knew that, Ward, I wouldn't be speaking to you past my normal bedtime."

"Was it natural causes?"

"It could be…" Dr Anderson didn't sound convinced by the idea. "It could also be poisoning. Her heart had failed. Which could have been caused by cyanide or another compound."

"Like what?"

"I don't know, Ward. It could be anything."

Henry focused on the darkness ahead of him. He had almost done a full circle of the boundary line and was about to begin another. He kicked a stick that lay in the field and bent over to pick it up. He tossed it for Tessa to chase, and she sprinted after it.

"Well, I shall leave you to your research, then," he said.

"Yes… you can, Ward. By the way, why do you want to know so urgently?"

"I have a feeling that this case hinges on Sarah Hardy. I don't know why. Let's put it down to a retired detective's intuition."

Dr Anderson chuckled. "I don't believe there is such a thing. And, by the looks of it, you're not fully retired."

"I am in terms of pay. You can trust me on that," he said, chuckling in return. He bent down to pick up the stick and threw it across the field again for Tessa to chase.

"You strike me as the type who'll never fully retire," Dr Anderson said. "You know the ones, they keep their ear to the ground, or they sit by their police radios every evening – not that we have those scanners anymore."

"We certainly do not." Henry laughed.

"You'll never be able to get yourself out of the game."

"And is that such a bad thing?"

Dr Anderson paused. "I don't know. I'll never fully retire from this, but that's because it's been my life's work. My entire adulthood, nearly fifty years of it, has been spent researching, learning, working, writing about my work… It's been my whole life, and I'm proud of that."

"Well, can't I be proud of the career I had? Of all the police work I've done, all the cases I've solved, the lives I've improved by putting terrible people away."

"Of course you can, Ward. But your career ended over ten years ago." Dr Anderson took a breath. "I just thought you might have moved on by now."

Henry nodded at his words, despite feeling wounded by them. "You think I should've moved on in the meantime?"

"Well, yes. Over ten years have gone by, and it's like you've been stuck in stasis. Now that they've brought you back to life, you're acting as if nothing happened. Can't you remember how badly they treated you just before they kicked you out?"

Henry gritted his teeth as the memories of his fall from grace and forced retirement flashed through his mind. He collected the stick from the grass where it had landed and tossed it again for Tessa. She was panting heavily now, lolling out her tongue, but she still sprinted after that stick as if her life depended on catching it.

"Well, Doctor. Thanks for your unvarnished and *unwanted* opinion."

Dr Anderson scoffed. "It's not my professional one, Ward. Don't take it to heart. I've just had one too many fingers of Scotch."

"All the same." Henry hesitated, then asked, "What would you have done if it had happened to you?"

"If they'd kicked me out ten years ago?" Dr Anderson exhaled. "I don't know, I probably would have packed it in and headed off to warmer climes."

"Really?"

"Well, I suppose not. I would've sniffed around them, like you are now, and would probably have ended up in academia." He sipped his drink. "Thank the Lord that didn't happen, as I bloody can't stand academics."

Henry grunted his agreement. "Have a nice evening, Doctor."

"You too, Ward."

Chapter Thirty-Three

Henry woke up early the next morning and, after showering and changing, had breakfast in his backyard. Sitting in his comfy foldable chair, he enjoyed the morning sun on his face. He ate his butter and marmalade on toast and had a cup of hot coffee resting on the wrought-iron table next to him. The air was warm but damp with the remnants of passing morning dew. He wore a fleece over his white-and-blue striped shirt to keep away the chill.

Tessa came into the backyard, carrying a squeeze toy shaped as a large goldfish, and plopped it down on the damp flagstones by his shoes. She quietly chewed the toy, as Henry had long removed the squeaking mechanism inside.

It was barely past 7 a.m. and Henry made the most of this quiet time. He finished the last slice of toast and put the plate on the table next to his cup, which he then picked up and held in both hands. He peered up at the blue sky and spotted three magpies flying overhead. He would give a lot to stay in his backyard and out of the way for the rest of the day, which was odd for him, as he was normally raring to solve cases. Perhaps his conversation with Dr Anderson the previous night had hit a nerve. Why should he be helping the police after what they had done to him? They made up false corruption claims, all to get rid of him. All because he was either too good for them, making the ambitious ones look bad, or because he was too focused on solving crimes instead of playing politics.

Henry sipped his coffee, considering which was the more likely reason, and concluded it was a mixture of both.

The plants around him were dripping wet, and waves of humidity oozed off them. The heat from the sun made him feel like unzipping his fleece.

Drinking more coffee, he wondered if he ever would forgive the police for what they did to him. The 'corruption' investigation they had conducted on him was clearly nonsense, any copper in West Yorkshire Police could have seen that. However, despite the false claims, it didn't help Henry's conscience to know that he had broken some rules over his career. Despite these infractions, he knew full well that the corruption investigation hadn't been based on anything Henry had really done. It had been instigated to create a stink around him strong enough to dislodge him from his position and out of the force. And it had worked. And who had been the one who had gained most from Henry's departure?

Murphy.

And who had Henry spent the past few days working for free for?

Murphy.

And why was Henry facing legal action from Curtis Quaker that could potentially bankrupt him – if it ever went to court?

To help Murphy.

Henry drained his coffee and then exhaled. That was why he wasn't enthused with this case. It wasn't the crime and its victims that upset him. It was the fact he was being used by the same man who pushed him out of his career over a decade ago. But could he put his personal animosity aside and help solve this case for the sake of the victims and their families?

Henry patted his jeans pockets, searching for his phone, but couldn't find it. He hauled himself out of the chair and padded inside. He found it on the kitchen table and searched for Jean's number. As he rang it, he stepped back into his yard.

"Hello?" Jean asked, sounding concerned. "Are you alright?"

"I'm fine."

"Is my house alright?"

Henry glanced above the garden wall at the upper floor of her cottage. "It's fine." He frowned.

"Then why the bloody hell are you ringing me at seven in the morning?"

Henry hadn't factored that into his calculations. "Well, does it matter? You're up, aren't you?"

"Aye, I am now. Well, you know me, I rarely sleep past six."

"How's Cambridge?"

"Fine."

Henry heard an internal door close on Jean's side of the line.

"Chris is doing his best to keep me entertained," Jean said, "but it's not quite working."

"How do you mean?"

"Well, I like museums as much as the next person, but seeing three in one day…"

"Ah. Right. Can't you tell him?"

She exhaled. "He's just like his father. Once he's got an idea in his head, if you go against it, you become public enemy number one." She tutted. "Even his poor kids are sick of the museums. Little Harry was crying as we walked around the contemporary art gallery. He's only six, he can't take it."

Henry chuckled at her minor crises, wishing his own had the same level of importance.

"Anyway… what is it you want?" she asked.

"The other day, I mentioned I wanted to talk to the Taylors."

"Oh yes."

"I think I'll go see them this morning."

"Oh, good. They've been waiting for you to call by. I told them you'd go up there yesterday." She paused. "How's the investigation going?"

"Okay…" he said. "I can't say too much, as I don't want a journalist repeating my words back to me later."

"What's that?" She sounded alarmed.

"Yesterday. I had a call from Roy Parker, remember him?"

"The journalist you helped out. What did he say?"

"He said he'd heard that I was involved in the investigation." He cleared his throat and took a breath; his indignation was rising. "Now, I'm not suggesting you told–"

"I definitely bloody didn't tell anyone anything!"

"I know, I know! But I just want you to be careful who you speak–"

"I only told the Taylors you wished to speak to them, which is what you asked me to do." She took a breath. "Are you accusing me of leaking something to the press?"

"No, Jean. I'm not. I'm just telling you what happened yesterday."

Jean didn't say anything.

Henry imagined her glaring into the distance – most likely northwest, in West Yorkshire's direction. "Now," he said, "I think it was the Taylors who spoke to this journalist, and I'm not blaming them either. They probably thought he was a nice chap."

"Right."

"Anyway, would you kindly tell the Taylors that I'll be over in the next hour."

"Well, rather than me being your secretary, why don't I send you their numbers so you can do it?" Her tone suggested she'd had enough of Henry for the day.

"Okay, that'll be fine." He paused. "And remember, Jean, this is nothing against you–"

"Well, it certainly sounds like it. You're accusing me of–"

Henry sighed. "Oh, I shouldn't have bloody said anything. Listen, Jean, I'm dealing with the murders of three people up here."

"Well, nobody's bloody asking you to deal with them, are they?!"

Henry bit his lip.

"If it's so much bloody hassle then just pack it in and do something else. Put your feet up and enjoy your Bank Holiday. There's no need to be so bloody ratty about everything."

Henry's shoulders slumped as Jean's words sunk in. His dog's brown eyes peered up at him. She had stopped chewing the squeaky toy, which remained between her jaws. Henry patted her on the head and then went back to his outdoor chair and sat down. "Alright, Jean," he said into the phone. "I'll consider what you've said."

"No, you bloody won't. Here, go speak to the Taylors."

Henry grunted a reply.

"And enjoy your day… if you can." She hung up.

Henry let the hand holding his phone flop down over the armrest. Did she have a point? It wasn't his case, and why should he do anyone favours, especially bloody Murphy. His phone buzzed in his hand, and he looked at its screen, expecting to see Jean's message containing the Taylors' contact details.

Instead, it was a message from Hargreaves.

You're in deep shit.

He clicked on the link in her message, which went to the *Yorkshire Gazette* newspaper. The lead image, above a report on another sighting of the kookaburra, was a photo of Henry standing next to Hargreaves. They were in the empty car park of Leeds Central police station, and the photo must have been taken by a long-lens camera yesterday afternoon. Henry read the article's headline, which sent streaks of doom running through his mind.

Corrupt Ex-Cop Working Shock Poison Case

"Oh, shit," Henry said, shaking his head.

Chapter Thirty-Four

Henry called Hargreaves. When she answered, she sounded as though she was in her car, driving fast.

"You've seen my text then?" she asked.

Henry remained in his outdoor chair with the morning sun beaming down on him and a gentle breeze blowing through his hair. He leant forwards. "Yes, I've seen it."

"You mentioned Roy Parker ringing you yesterday, and I didn't think… I forgot all about it."

"Me, too," Henry said. "Well, I've just spoken to Jean, which reminded me of it–"

"Why? What have you told her now?" Hargreaves' voice was thick with suspicion.

"Nothing of any import," he said. "Anyway, this isn't about her. After what I did to help Roy… I never would have thought he'd stab me in the back like this."

"Well, well, what did I tell you? Never expect favours from a journalist. Even if you have saved his life, they would sell their grandparents' organs for the chance to have their name in the byline of a national newspaper." Hargreaves mumbled something which quickly turned into a loud swear word. "Sodding learn to drive!" she shouted.

"Are you heading to HQ already?"

"Yep. I was woken up at six by Murphy, who's on the warpath, by the way."

Henry exhaled. His chest was rising and falling as if he'd sprinted up the stairs. "So, Murphy's seen the news?"

"Of course he has. He's fuelled by good publicity. He was the one who sent me your story. I don't read the news if I can help it."

"What about Barnes?"

"I've not heard from her yet. Though, I've not tried–" she swore at another car "–bloody bank-holiday drivers!"

"Where are you?"

"Driving down Elland Road."

"So, you're nearly at Leeds Central?"

"Aye. I've got my blue light on. Murphy ordered an 8 a.m. meeting with me and Barnes. There's talk that DCI Acton will be brought in."

"Oh," Henry said. His mouth was dry, so he picked up his cup of coffee but found it empty. "I've not been called about this meeting."

"That's probably because you're as welcome as foot-and-mouth at a cow market." She tutted at another vehicle.

"I'm out in the cold, then?"

"What do you think, Henry? Your face is plastered on the front page of the region's most-read newspaper, along with mine, for Christ's sake. A salacious article is claiming that we're relying on a dodgy old detective to solve our cases for us. If Murphy could, he'd have you sent off to Siberia… or wherever it was they kept those Gulags."

"Aye, it was Siberia." He squinted at the morning sun. "So, can I take it that I'm off the case?"

"You were never officially on it, so you won't be taken off it. But let's just say, don't expect to be back inside Leeds Central police station ever again, unless you've been detained for something."

Henry ground his teeth. "But what about all the work I've put in these past two days?"

"Well, you know I'm grateful."

Henry didn't hear much gratitude in her voice.

"But Murphy doesn't want you anywhere near this or us ever again. Or at least," she added, "until he's calmed down and some other story has come along to piss him off."

Henry bit a fingernail. "Do you know if he's recanting on our deal?"

"Listen, I don't know anything about deals or arrangements struck up between you two. That's between him and you."

Tessa was looking up at Henry, her eyes wide open and filled with concern. She squeezed the squeaky toy in her mouth, got up, and dropped it by his shoes. Henry acknowledged her gift by patting her head. Perhaps this was what he should have expected? Being booted off the case when it became inconvenient for Murphy.

He shook his head. "What about the case? What about the victims, and Sarah Hardy?"

"We'll have to battle on without you, Henry. Acton's likely to take over Barnes as lead, and he will want to re-evaluate everything, which means Murphy's deadline will be delayed until tomorrow – or hopefully later, because even tomorrow will be damn-near impossible."

Henry exhaled. "Well, it sounds like everything's been tied up, and I'm left to my own devices."

"Yeah, well. Just be careful you don't stick your nose into this again."

"Why?"

"From what I heard from Murphy; it sounds like Curtis Quaker is very serious about pressing charges against us for his arrest yesterday."

"But it was above board."

Hargreaves groaned uncertainly. "Yeah… I can argue my part, and I'll have the police force protecting me. But you…"

"He can't really be thinking of suing me–"

"It's not completely confirmed, but Murphy said Curtis is still wittering on about it. And Murphy said that if legal action is taken against you, the force couldn't intervene to help. You'd have to fight it by yourself."

Henry held his head in his hand. "So, he really is going to sue me?"

"Possibly. Let's see how he feels when he's released later today."

He heard her pull up her handbrake and cut the engine.

"Can you keep me in the loop?"

She scoffed. "Are you kidding? Murphy would go ballistic if he found out I was still contacting you."

"Well, at least update me on Quaker's civil claim, as a courtesy."

"Alright," she said. "I have to go. Look after yourself."

She hung up.

Henry stared at the mobile in his hand. It took him a moment to realise his hand was shaking, and he placed the phone on the wrought-iron table next to him. He felt as if he was being watched, and scanned the top of his garden walls, expecting to see a cameraman with a long-range lens snapping photos of his despair. He then came to realise it was Tessa who was staring up at him. She barked and wagged her tail. Henry picked up the squeaky toy and tossed it across the yard. The saliva-slicked rubber slipped horribly out of his hand.

He leant back in his chair, still feeling shell-shocked. One day, you were with the in-crowd, the next, you're back on your own. All over a silly article written by someone who should have shown more respect. Henry ground his molars together and grabbed his phone. He had not read the article yet and quickly scanned it.

'Corrupt detective', 'forced to resign twelve years ago', 'no reasons given for his unofficial return'. Henry scrunched up his face and couldn't stomach any more of it.

It wasn't even 8 a.m., and he hoped Roy Parker would be just waking up to face his habitual hangover. Henry dialled the journalist's number but didn't get through, so he left a blunt message asking Roy to call him 'as soon as possible'. However, he doubted the journalist would have the courage to face the music and planned to call him again later that morning. He could even head over to his home and bang on his front door.

Laying back in his chair, he closed his eyes as the sun shone in his face. What would he do that day? He could just remain in his chair and hope that the newspaper story would blow over. As the saying goes, 'today's news, tomorrow's fish-and-chip paper'. And there was also hope that Curtis Quaker would calm down once he was released. He seemed the type to get distracted easily. However, his lawyer might be keen to pursue a civil claim against the police and Henry, just to collect the fees.

The uncertainty caused Henry's stomach to cramp and gurgle, and he gnawed on his lower lip. What could he do? He doubted he could sit there all day and not take action. He would surely go mad. His phone vibrated on the wrought-iron table, and he reluctantly glanced at its screen. The message was from Jean, and it contained the Taylors' contact details. She also had added:

The Taylors said you were in the paper? Is that true?

Henry grumbled and got out of his chair. He wouldn't solve any of these messes sitting here. He gestured to Tessa to get back in the house, and she just peered at him with wide eyes, as if asking why he didn't just relax and spend the day with her in their garden.

"Because I've got a case to solve and a killer to find," he said to her. Then, giving into Tessa's stare, he added, "And you can come along with me if you promise to behave."

Chapter Thirty-Five

Henry arrived at the Taylors' house shortly before 9 a.m. Tessa was in the back seat, staring out the window at the open fields beyond the crumbling drystone walls. She barked and yapped with excitement. Henry parked up on the country lane and got out the car. He put Tessa on the lead and walked her down the lane towards the Taylors' cottage.

The wind was stronger up here on the moor, and it blew forcefully between the barn conversions, farmhouses, and old cottages that had been up here for hundreds of years. This small hamlet, known as Addingham Moorside, was south of the larger village in the valley below. Apart from sharing names, the two were largely disconnected.

Henry strolled down the country lane that ran through the hamlet, which ended abruptly just beyond the final house. Tessa walked ahead of him, pulling on her lead as she sniffed the weeds and plants growing at the bottom of the walls beside them.

Soft cloud cover hid the sun, and Henry recalled the wonderful sunset he'd witnessed over Cragg Hall and the valley below when he'd last been there. He paused for a moment outside the Hardys' barn conversion, which was now devoid of life. Its windows were dark, and the front door was locked and covered in police tape. The wind shook the surrounding trees and plants violently. A sense that something bad had happened within its walls had settled around it, and Henry doubted that feeling would ever be lifted.

The Taylors' cottage was directly opposite. Its outer walls were whitewashed, and the stone windowsills were painted black. Pansies and red roses grew in the front garden, which was fenced off from the lane. Henry opened the squeaky gate and knocked on the front door.

He planned to leave Tessa tied up in the garden, but when the elderly Mr Taylor saw her, he insisted she be brought inside. An unused dog lead hung on a coat hook in the hallway, but there were no other signs that a dog currently lived there.

Arthur Taylor ushered Henry and Tessa through the hallway and into the living room on the left. The house smelt of floral air-freshener. Ellie Taylor entered the living room carrying a tray complete with a pot of tea, cups, and a plate of digestive biscuits. Henry introduced himself, but she, like her husband, was visibly more interested in Tessa. Ellie snapped a biscuit in half and offered it to her, which Tessa ate quickly. Henry spotted a framed photo of a Labrador on the mantelpiece and rolled his eyes as the Taylors fawned over his own dog. Tessa was enjoying every moment of it.

He turned to the front window which overlooked the valley below and, more importantly, Cragg Hall opposite. He could feel the eerie dark shadow surrounding the property from his position at the window and noticed that a lot of the house could be seen from here.

Henry took the offered cup of tea and called Tessa away from the plate of biscuits. She had positioned herself so close, her wet nose was pressed against the edge of the coffee table, slowly inching towards the plate.

"Heard all this about the kookaburra?" Arthur asked.

"Aye, I have." Henry seated himself in a rocking chair by the window.

"It's exciting, isn't it?" Ellie said. "Imagine if it makes an appearance in Addingham."

"That'd make a welcome change," Arthur added.

Henry nodded an agreement and sipped his strong Yorkshire Tea. Both Mr and Mrs were in their mid-seventies. Arthur had on a light-blue shirt and jeans, while his wife wore a bright-pink apron over a white blouse and black trousers.

"Some good news is definitely what is needed around here," Henry said. "Unfortunately, it's the bad news that has called me here to see you."

"It's terrible, isn't it?" Ellie took a seat on the settee next to her husband. She shook her head in dismay, and then husband and wife shared a look.

"Well, we only know what we've read in the papers," Arthur said, glancing at the coffee table.

Henry noticed the folded copy of today's *Yorkshire Gazette* under the tray. The headline, which had been seared into Henry's mind, was half visible over the crease:

Corrupt Ex-Cop Working Shock Poison Case

"You can't go believing everything you read in the papers," Henry said.

Husband and wife shared another look.

"What is it?" Henry asked.

"We'd just like to know if we should be talking to the police, instead," Arthur said.

"I've been in contact with them," Henry said, "and I've been assisting them with their investigation."

"Yes," Ellie said, "it's just that… We're not sure what we should tell you."

Henry glanced at the word 'Corrupt' in the newspaper's headline and shook his head. "Listen, if you don't want to talk to me, then why didn't you say so when I phoned earlier? It would have saved me the bother of coming up."

He plonked his cup of tea on the coffee table and clicked his tongue to get Tessa's attention.

"Oh, don't go," Ellie said. "We're just not sure what to think."

"What about?" Henry rested back into the rocking chair, which moved back and forth.

"Well…" Arthur's eyes went to the folded newspaper. "We read stories about you being…"

"I am not, and never have been, a bent copper. What isn't in that hack-job article is the fact that no evidence was ever found suggesting I was corrupt, and the internal police investigation cleared me."

"But didn't you have to resign?" he asked.

"I was forced into early retirement. But if I had been so corrupt, would the police let me work with them now?"

Ellie tilted her head as she reflected on Henry's words.

"I suppose that could make us feel better?" Arthur said. He glanced at his wife, waiting for her reaction. She clearly had the say-so around here.

She gave a curt nod and then sipped her tea.

Arthur lowered his head. His eyes misted over, and they stayed like that for a moment. Henry was about to ask what was wrong with him, when Arthur started his story.

"It's been an odd few years, living opposite them – the Hardys. They moved in three years ago, and at first, we were glad to have them living opposite, weren't we?"

Ellie concurred with a nod.

"The house had been empty beforehand for a while. It'd been bought over ten years ago and gutted by another couple, the Smiths, but they separated after a while and left the building work unfinished. It stayed empty until the Hardys bought it."

"He's local," Ellie said. "Mark Hardy."

"Aye," Arthur said. "I knew his parents. His dad was a doctor, and they lived down by the river in a big house. They had three sons, didn't they?"

He looked at Ellie for confirmation, which she quickly gave.

"And the other two went off down south. The eldest was a barrister, the middle one–"

"He's an architect in Chelmsford," Ellie said.

"Yes. And Mark, well… he didn't amount to much, did he?"

Ellie shook her head.

"He was always the spoilt one," Arthur said. "The one who stayed at home too long, the one who got into bother all the time."

"I don't think he went away to university in the end, did he?" Ellie asked her husband.

Arthur shook his head. "He did some business course at the local college, and he barely got through that."

"He wasn't that good at sport, either?" Ellie asked, already knowing the answer.

"He was terrible. He couldn't do much of anything. It drove his dad to despair."

"And Mark didn't take his lack of talent very well too," she said.

"He didn't. He wasn't just a little toerag, but he was nasty with it."

"Oh, yes. He was a nasty little boy, wasn't he?"

Henry knitted his brows as he sipped some tea. "Did you know Mark when he was growing up?"

Husband and wife enjoyed the moment of light relief.

Arthur raised his eyebrows. "Oh, we knew him, yes, didn't we?"

"We worked at his school," Ellie said, smiling. "We knew all the Hardy boys."

"Which school was this? St George's?" Henry asked.

They both nodded.

"Ellie was a dinner lady, and I taught history for twenty-five years," said Arthur.

Henry tilted his head to the side. "Well, that's very fortunate, as I've been looking for someone from that school to talk to."

"Oh?" Arthur asked. "Why's that?"

Henry narrowed his eyes. "What can you tell me about the apparent child abuse that was reported between 1993 and 1995?"

Arthur winced as if he'd just been struck by something. He turned to his wife, who gave him a worried look. "I'm not sure we can talk about any of that," he said.

Henry leant closer to them, rocking his chair forwards. "Of course, you can. Why don't you start at the beginning?"

Chapter Thirty-Six

Henry caught Tessa's collar and pulled her away from the biscuits on the coffee table. She sat back on her haunches and breathed heavily through her open mouth, staring at the snacks and then at Ellie Taylor.

Mr and Mrs Taylors didn't seem to notice Tessa's behaviour, however, as both appeared lost in uncomfortable memories. Ellie nursed her cup of tea while Arthur clasped his hands together. Both were staring into the distance in silence.

Henry sipped more tea, which remained hot and strong. He got their attention by clearing his throat.

Arthur Taylor spoke first. "It's been a long while since I've thought about all that." He squeezed the lumpy knuckle of his index finger. "Yes… all that was very unpleasant."

"Apologies for awakening old ghosts, but I would like you to tell me what you know about it," Henry said, raising an eyebrow expectantly.

The Taylors looked at each other.

"Well, we don't know much, really," Arthur said.

"Tell me what you do know, then."

Arthur sighed. "The first I heard of it was when the police got involved."

Henry nodded. "Aye, I remember that. I was involved in the initial investigation."

Arthur's eyes widened. "Right, well" – he turned to his wife – "you might know more about it than me, love. You heard more about what happened than us teachers did."

Henry looked at Ellie.

She scrunched up her eyes. "Yes, we heard a lot of things before it was made official." She sipped some tea and rallied herself. "While serving the children in the dining hall, there was all sorts of gossip. Especially from the pupils who'd hang around us. Usually a few of the quieter, lonelier children would latch onto us. One of them in particular, Tyler Jones, from the year bellow Mark Hardy's… Well, he always hung around us at lunchtimes. He'd help us tidy up, despite us telling him not to."

"What was this Tyler Jones saying to you?" Henry asked.

"One day – I forget when exactly – we were cleaning up the dining hall and, as usual, Tyler was with us, chatting away. He had verbal diarrhoea, that boy. He could go on all day. I think he liked the attention he got from us. Plus, it kept him away from the other boys. He was bullied rotten, I think, though he never fully admitted it. We tried to do something about it when we saw him with a black eye once, but the headmaster, Mr Jessop, he was very…" She paused to let her husband answer for her.

Arthur turned to Henry. "He was very laissez-faire. He wanted the children to learn independence and personal responsibility. He rarely intervened, not unless a boy had obviously been badly beaten up. And he only did it then for child safety reasons."

"And we didn't have many child safety rules back then," Ellie said, her arms crossed over her bright-pink apron.

"So, getting back to Tyler," Henry said.

"Yes… so he was talking to us about this 'Dragon's Blood Club' group, and that they were looking for members from year ten."

"Dragon's Blood?" Henry asked, furrowing his brow.

"It was some club the pupils had created. I think they'd been inspired by the school's coat of arms. You know, George's dragon. They were just being silly boys," Ellie said, shrugging. "Anyway, Tyler said he'd like to join this club, and that it'd make his life easier, as boys in the Dragon's Blood Club were treated with more respect. But

Tyler wasn't sure he would pass the challenge to enter. So, I asked him, 'What's this challenge?' And he said, fairly brazenly, that they had to pass an initiation if they wanted to join the club. I asked him, 'What kind of initiation is that?' And he said, 'It depends, no one knows for certain, but it's supposed to be painful and demeaning.'"

"He said 'painful' and 'demeaning'?" Henry clarified.

She nodded. "I asked him what he meant by that, and he said it ranged from 'truth or dare' to something worse… He then laughed and joked about 'torture'."

Henry leant further forward in his rocking chair.

"So I asked him to describe what he meant by 'torture', but he seemed to have realised he'd said too much and went off on his way." She drank more tea and swallowed hard. "A few weeks later, we started to see a lot of the kids in year ten looking out of sorts."

"Why only year-ten pupils?"

"This secret club was run by the students in year eleven, the oldest ones, and they were about to leave the school. Apparently, they had to select another group from the year below."

"How long had this Dragon's Blood Club existed?"

Ellie shrugged. "It was the first I'd heard of it." She turned to her husband, who also didn't appear to have the answer.

"So, what did you see when the year-ten students came in? Were they visibly injured?"

Ellie narrowed her eyes as she recalled. "Not quite. Some were, they were bent over and looked pale and visibly in pain. The others just looked haunted. They had dark rings under their eyes and appeared lost and shaken. Even chatty Tyler didn't talk to us much. He was off sick for a few days and then didn't talk to anyone on his lunch breaks for a while. When he looked more like himself, I asked him if he'd tried to join that club, and he said yes. I asked him, 'What was it you had to do in this challenge?' Well, his eyes teared up, and he said he'd promised never to talk about it, and then he ran off. He literally ran away. The next time I saw him, I knew better than to ask again."

"What do you think happened to him?" Henry asked.

She shook her head. "It could have been anything. The boys in that year eleven were pretty vicious."

"And you say Mark Hardy was in that year?"

Ellie and Arthur looked at each other again.

"He was," Arthur said. "And he failed his GCSEs and retook the year. So, he was in year eleven in 1994 and again in 1995."

Henry considered the dates in his mind. "Did all this happen again the following year? Children getting abused to join the same club?"

Ellie nodded. "Yes, it happened the following year, but then it stopped after the police got involved."

"The headmaster was minded to put an end to this club and the bad behaviour when the authorities intervened," Arthur said.

Henry grunted. "At the time, the headmaster told us nothing was going on. Yet you're telling me he was aware of this club but decided to lie to the police about it?"

Arthur looked down at the carpet, while Ellie stared at the cup of tea in her hands.

"I suppose Mark Hardy left the school in 1995, so maybe his leaving ended all of this?" Henry asked.

Ellie nodded. "I believe you might be onto something there."

Henry pursed his lips. "So, how did you feel when you saw Mark Hardy and his wife move into Cragg Hall three years ago?"

Going off their looks, Henry could guess their answer.

Chapter Thirty-Seven

Tessa's eyes were transfixed on the plate of biscuits, and she began to whine and lick her lips. Henry hushed her with a look and silence descended over the Taylors' living room. Only the faint birdsong in the hamlet outside could be heard.

Henry repeated his question. "So, how *did* you feel when Mark Hardy moved in?"

"Well," Arthur Taylor said. "I couldn't say I was happy about it when we saw it was Mark Hardy moving in." He turned to his wife who groaned an agreement.

"She was very nice, Sarah," Ellie said, her face beaming. "She was full of it and a joy to be around."

"Oh, yes," Arthur said, smiling. He looked at his wife as she wiped a tear from her eye and patted her hand. "She'll be missed, Sarah will be. She did all sorts for this hamlet. Ran little baking competitions, jam stalls, and helped organise the street party for the king's coronation."

"Yes," said Ellie. "She was a great help. She was very patriotic, which was odd if you think about it, considering she was Australian."

"Well, they are still a part of the Commonwealth, and we share the same king."

Ellie nodded.

Henry sipped some tea. He was still leaning forwards in the rocking chair, with Tessa beside him, curled up on the floor. Her ears were cocked towards the table, listening for any mention of biscuits.

"What about Mark?" Henry asked.

"Well," Arthur said, turning to his wife again. "He was less easy to deal with, wasn't he?"

"He's a bloody prig!" Ellie said. "He complained about us parking outside our cottage on the lane. He said he needed the space free so he could turn his huge great big BMW more easily." She shook her head in pure disdain. "And he made a huge fuss about our exterior walls."

"He asked us not to paint the outside of our house white," Arthur explained.

"Not only that, but he also wanted us to remove the paint, have it all taken off, because he thought 'natural stone walls' were more in keeping with the area. This cottage has been painted white for over two hundred years!" Ellie's indignation was so strong, the cup of tea in her hands shook.

Arthur patted her thigh. "We got very worked up about it all. He's not a pleasant person to live opposite."

"He complains about where we put the wheelie bins when they come to collect them. He also says we need to tidy up our front garden." Ellie shook her head. Her face and neck had become bright red.

"He does sound unpleasant," Henry said. "And how did Sarah deal with him?"

"Well, she apologised when I told her about what he'd said. She thought he was out of line, and she said she'd talk to him and tell him to get off our backs. But he wouldn't take any notice of her. He did as he pleased, as always." She took a sip of tea. "He was the same at school. A petulant little sod."

Henry placed his empty cup on the coffee table. Tessa lifted her head and gave him a sidewards glance as he stretched his arm towards the biscuits. But Henry didn't give her one, as she'd already had too many.

"Have you seen people go into Cragg Hall recently? People you hadn't seen before?" he asked.

They both shook their heads.

"Considering all the cake competitions and jam stalls they had, they rarely had people over," Arthur said.

"Oh really? I thought Sarah was a social butterfly."

"She was one," Ellie answered, "but he wasn't. I don't think he liked people coming into the house. When she did the competitions, he'd be away on business. I don't know if that was on purpose."

"And you never saw unfamiliar people around the house?" Henry asked.

Arthur shook his head. "As we told the police constable who knocked on the door yesterday, we haven't seen anyone sneaking around the house or anything like that. In fact, that barbecue was the first time we've seen them have guests for a while, wasn't it?"

Ellie nodded, and then her face creased up, and she a wiped tear from her eyes. "I just can't believe something as awful as that could happen just over the road."

Arthur gripped her hand.

Henry let the moment pass.

Ellie pulled a handkerchief from the front pocket on her pink apron and padded her eyes and cheeks.

Henry felt sorry for them living out their retirement in this cottage opposite a house that had so clearly been marked by death. When Ellie had calmed herself down, he asked, "What do you know about Mark's job?"

"He runs a business, doesn't he?" Arthur said, still gripping his wife's hand.

"Yes," Henry said, "and what do you know of it?"

"Very little," said Arthur. "As you can probably understand, we don't talk to him if we can help it. Sarah, though, we talked to her a lot."

"I chatted with her every day," Ellie said, sniffing.

"And she didn't tell you what her husband did?"

Ellie swallowed the lump in her throat and shook her head.

"And what did she do?"

"She didn't do much," Ellie said. "I think she was involved in some marketing thing, but I couldn't tell you what it was. She didn't seem that busy with it."

"Okay," Henry said. He had gone through the questions he wanted to ask, and now he felt like there was little left to say. "I'd like to thank you for your time."

"Wait…" Arthur raised his hand. He turned to his wife, whose head was lowered. She continued wiping her eyes with her sodden handkerchief. "When the police constable came yesterday, we'd already heard that a detective was coming to talk to us, so we didn't tell him about…"

Henry narrowed his eyes. "Didn't tell him about… what?"

Arthur looked at his wife, and this time, she patted his arm. "The police constable didn't ask, so we didn't say. We thought it might not be relevant," Arthur said. "But there were a few occasions, on an evening, when we heard shouting outside the house."

"Outside Cragg Hall?"

"On the front step," he said. "Late, around eleven. Even Ellie heard it from upstairs in the bedroom."

"The window faces their house," she explained.

"I stay up to watch *Newsnight*," said Arthur. "Although, I won't be doing that for much longer… considering they've shrunk it down beyond recognition."

"What did you hear outside?" Henry asked, looking at them both in turn.

Ellie was now fidgeting with the handkerchief, her cheeks puffy and red, while Arthur held his chin in his hands and stared out the front window at Cragg Hall and the valley below.

"The last time was a few weeks ago," Arthur said, "and she was shouting at him. They were arguing in their front garden. It seemed to me as though they'd been going at it for a while inside. The walls of that house are so thick, they could have a party in there and no one would know."

"Could you hear what they were arguing about?"

Arthur shook his head. "I couldn't as I had the TV on…" He looked at his wife.

"I was upstairs, it gets hot up there and the bedroom window was open. I heard them arguing about a lot of things… Australia, her feeling isolated, and him not wanting children."

"Right?" Henry said.

"And then… he must have grabbed her hand. It must have been painful, as I heard her shout at him to get off her."

"Okay."

"And then he must have tried to pull her inside the house, I think, as I heard them wrestling. Then, I heard him cry out… I think she'd cut him with something, as he complained about a 'knife' and said he was bleeding."

"What did you see?" Henry asked.

"I couldn't see anything, I was lying in bed, listening through the window." She looked at Arthur.

"I got up off this settee and went to the window to check," he said, "but they'd already gone back inside."

Henry tapped his chin, lost in thought. "And had that happened before?"

They both nodded.

"It was usually him having a go at her," Arthur said, "and then her ending it somehow."

"By attacking him?"

Ellie scrunched up her face. "I wouldn't say she attacked him–"

"It sounds like she did," Henry said. "If she cut him with a knife."

"She knew how to handle herself and didn't take any nonsense from him, which I don't think he liked."

"How long had this been going on for?"

"Not long, really. It started fairly recently," Ellie said.

Arthur nodded in agreement.

"I'd say it started…" She looked at her husband to answer.

"I'd say since March," Arthur said, considering his words carefully.

"March this year?"

Husband and wife nodded, and Henry realised that coincided with Justin Nabwood's arrival in the country. "Have you heard any discussion between them about an ex-husband being on the scene?"

They both shook their heads; Ellie wore a mystified expression. "Ex-husband? She was never married before, I don't think?"

"And have you seen this man anywhere near the house recently?" Henry pulled his mobile phone from his pocket. He got the passport picture of Justin Nabwood on its screen, which he had snapped a photo of the previous day.

Arthur took Henry's phone with one hand and patted the chest pocket on his blue shirt with the other. He took out some glasses and put them on. He then squinted at the image and frowned at his wife, handing her the phone.

"Don't you think it looks a bit like Ben?" he said.

"Ben?" Henry asked.

Ellie nodded, while Arthur returned Henry's phone back to him. "Yes, Ben? Sarah's brother."

Henry double-checked the image he had shown them was the right one. "He was introduced to you as Ben?"

Ellie nodded. "Yes, Sarah said he'd come over from Australia a few months ago, but I don't think he was staying at the house. In fact, I've no idea where he stayed."

"Menston, I heard," Arthur said, his face fixed with a grimace. "I didn't like him. I thought he looked like trouble."

"I suppose," his wife said. "Sarah thought a lot of him, though."

"So, Sarah introduced you to him?"

Ellie nodded. "Oh yes, she seemed quite happy he was here. Apparently, things weren't going well in Sydney for him, and he decided to visit her here. I don't know, I got the impression she liked having him around as a counterweight to Mark."

Arthur cleared his throat. "I don't think we can say that, can we? That's taking a leap."

"Well, I don't know. It's just the impression I got."

Henry narrowed his eyes as he considered what they had just said. "When did you last see Ben at Cragg Hall?"

"Oh, that was the other day," Ellie said. "Thursday, I think."

"Was he by himself?"

She shook her head. "He was with Sarah. He was mostly at the house alone with her, but sometimes Mark was there as well."

"Was he ever there alone with Mark?" Henry asked.

Arthur eyed his wife. "We couldn't say for certain, could we, love?"

She pursed her lips and then shook her head.

Henry ground his teeth. Of course, he thought, a couple of days before the barbecue. The perfect time to get close and plant the poison.

Suspicion clouded Ellie's eyes. "Why? Is it important?" She turned to her husband. "He can't think Ben's involved in this. He was her brother!"

"I don't know, love," Arthur said, looking at Henry.

"I'm not sure what happened at the barbecue yet," Henry said, "but yes, the more I hear about this Justin Nabwood, or Ben character, the more I'm sure he's involved somehow."

Chapter Thirty-Eight

Henry walked down the Taylors' garden path, squinting at the bright sun that had broken through the cloud. It was now mid-morning, and the curtains of the neighbouring cottages around him were open. A car drove down the lane and slowed as it passed Cragg Hall. Its driver peered at the

Hardys' home, at its police tape and the dark aura that hung over it. The car then sped up and went on its way.

Henry stared at the Hardys' house opposite him. Would it be worth having a snoop around while he was here? Part of him wanted to get in his car and be on his way. But the other wanted to see if there was anything to find in that house and its grounds. He had never done a thorough check of it himself, not that he doubted Forensics' abilities.

He pulled Tessa away from the Taylors' front door. She appeared unwilling to leave the nice couple who were very generous with biscuits.

"Come on," Henry said to her, gently pulling her lead. "You've had enough for the time being. If you eat any more, I'll have to put you on a diet."

Tessa reluctantly came away, giving Henry sad eyes. Henry ignored her and refocused on Cragg Hall. The blue police tape around the door rustled in a breeze that carried scents of fresh grass and spring flowers.

"Come on," Henry said, bounding down the path. "Let's have a quick look before we set off. We might as well, seeing as we're here."

His explanation didn't calm the frightened part of him, which wanted to get away.

Henry went through the front gate just as another car slowed down on the lane so its driver could gawp at the now infamous house. Henry gave the driver a scowl before she sped up and went down the lane.

When Henry reached the front door, he recalled what the Taylors had told him about Sarah attacking Mark on this very doorstep not so long ago. He looked around the frame and then the front step and the old stone wall. Why would a woman like Sarah attack her husband with a knife?

His hand went to the door handle, but then he remembered he'd be breaking protocol as he wasn't dressed to enter the property. He had some latex gloves in his car, but he would need shoe covers, which he didn't have.

Besides, he couldn't bring Tessa in with him.

She stood beside him on the doorstep, sniffing the basil in a plant pot.

Henry pulled her behind him as he walked along the gravel path that circled the house. He reached the row of hedges, which marked the Hardys' property line, and saw a narrow path between the vibrant green spruce and the pale stone walls.

He had to turn sideways to fit down it. Sprigs from the hedge stabbed his gut as he shuffled past. Tessa toddled along after him, giving him curious looks.

He stepped out into the back garden, and Tessa came to heel as if she knew they shouldn't be there. Henry headed to the patio and looked over the railings at the lawn down below. He studied the wall at the foot of the garden, where Sarah Hardy had been found.

He turned to the outdoor table and chairs beside him. All the food and drink had been cleared away, and the chairs pushed underneath. It looked as a luxurious garden should.

He peered through the windows into the house's dark interior. He saw nothing out of the ordinary but plastic bags and yellow tags left by Forensics. An oppressive feeling hung in the air.

He went to the head of the outdoor table where Mark Hardy had sat and pulled out the chair. He lowered himself into it and surveyed the long table.

He imagined where the guests had been seated at the barbecue. Tom and Lee had been at the far end while Allister, Ralph, Pete and their wives had been closer to Mark. The table was so long, Henry doubted Mark could have heard what Lee and Tom were saying at the other end, especially if the people around him were in full conversation.

Henry turned to look at the railings that ran along the side of the patio area. There was a steep slope to the wall at the bottom of the garden; that was why the stone steps at the side had been put in.

From this position at the head of the table, Henry couldn't see much of the drystone wall, as the wrought-iron railings blocked his view. That meant Mark probably hadn't seen Sarah lying down there from his seat. Tom and Lee must have told him that his wife had fallen ill.

Surely that wasn't the first lie Mark had told.

Tessa barked and suddenly became aggressive.

Henry looked about to see if someone was coming.

Then Tessa sprinted towards the spruce hedge behind him. He grabbed her lead, but it was pulled out of his grip.

The wire fox terrier rushed towards a crow nestled in the hedge. The crow leapt into the air and spread its wings. It then careened over Henry's head and soared into the sky.

Tessa growled, circled herself, and then spotted more prey in the hedge. She barked again.

"Oi!" Henry said, hauling himself out of Mark Hardy's chair. "Stop that racket!"

Henry rushed over to pick up the lead on the flagstone, but it was pulled out of his reach as Tess jumped headfirst into the hedge. Her back legs kicked out, and then she disappeared into the neighbours' garden.

"Jesus wept!" Henry said. He lost his balance and tumbled forwards onto the ground.

He got off the grass and looked at the new hole through the fence, knowing full well he wouldn't be able to fit through.

Tessa mauled something angrily in the neighbours' back garden, and Henry couldn't see what kind of poor animal it was.

"Tessa! Calm the bloody hell down!" he shouted through the hedge. He then rushed down the side of the house, which was even tighter than the side he'd entered through.

He arrived at the neighbouring house's front door and saw its sides were fenced off. He knocked loudly and brushed a large sprig of leaves off his shirt.

The door opened, and a rattled old man stood in the doorway.

Henry recognised him but was too distressed to place his name. "It's my–"

"Dog! I've just seen it."

"She's harmless… usually." Henry coughed. His asthma was flaring up. "Can I come through? I need to sort her out."

The old man looked frightened for an instant but nodded.

Henry stepped inside as the man closed the door behind him.

The air in the hallway was dusty and damp. Henry paid no notice of it and followed the man down the landing and into a kitchen, which lead to a conservatory. Henry brushed past the old man and stepped out onto the decking.

Tessa rolled over the freshly cut lawn down below; her teeth clamped down on some unfortunate animal.

Henry was stunned for a moment. He'd never seen his little Tessa behave like this before. She flicked off speckles of saliva as she savaged the small creature. Oddly, there wasn't any blood.

He descended the wooden steps and grabbed her lead from off the grass. He yanked her towards him.

"Drop it, Tessa! Let go!"

She eyed him and growled, the small dead beast still in her teeth.

"Drop it!" he repeated, giving her the glare he reserved for startling suspects. "Do it, now!"

She whimpered and spat out the dead animal. It landed on the grass. Its black fur was white with slime.

The poor thing looked to have been a small mammal. A mole or a beaver. Which was odd. Why would a mole or beaver be hiding in a hedge?

The lack of blood and the cable sticking out of its back end answered his question. He recognised the wet, black fur was actually a microphone cover.

Henry glanced at the old man standing next to him. "Has she been mauling a mic?" He noticed the cables leading out of the hedge and into the old man's house through an open basement window.

"Have you been recording your neighbours?" Henry asked.

The old man swallowed guiltily. He then stared at Tessa, as if wanting to change the subject.

And then Henry realised who the old man was.

"Oh, I know who you are."

He peered down at the broken microphone, and it all made sense.

Chapter Thirty-Nine

Henry lowered himself into a wicker chair in the old man's conservatory. The doors to the garden were open, and a gentle breeze came into the stuffy room, blowing the shabby net curtains.

Tessa's whimpers could be heard outside along with the distant twitter of birds. Henry watched her through a smudged windowpane. She tried to move away from the outdoor tap to which Henry had tied her lead. She gave up trying to pull herself free, and her black eyes pleaded at Henry through the glass.

"Nope!" said Henry. "You should've thought about the consequences before you mauled that microphone."

Tessa snapped her head away from him in annoyance and continued her sulk.

Henry chuckled to himself. His eyes took in the conservatory, which, going by the yellowing white PVC framing, he guessed had been built in the mid-1980s. The cane armchairs had floral cream cushions that reminded Henry of a sitcom he used to watch with his wife a long time ago.

The conservatory was just as unkempt as the rest of the house. Dusty birdwatching magazines were piled high on the wicker coffee table, some of which Henry recognised from his own collection.

A tinkle of crockery preceded Victor Quail as he came through the doorway from the kitchen carrying a tray laden with tea and biscuits. He placed it on top of two magazine piles and then went about pouring tea from a chipped teapot.

The garden was a similar size to the Hardys' next door, but it had higher hedges at the bottom, blocking off the view of the valley below.

Victor sat back in the wicker chair beside Henry, which creaked and cracked, and sipped his tea.

"Well, thanks for the drink," Henry said, raising his own cup.

"No bother."

"And apologies again for the dog. We were over in the garden next door. The atmosphere must've got to her."

"Aye. It's horrid what happened. I've avoided thinking about it. I've barely stepped out the door since I heard the news."

"Did you know them well?"

Victor sighed regretfully. "I said hello to them every now and then." He raised an eyebrow. "What were *you* doing over there, Henry?"

"Oh." Henry cleared his throat. "I'm helping the official police investigation with its inquiries."

"Ah. I heard you used to be with the police. I didn't know you were still involved with them."

"When they need a hand, I help them out."

"And I suppose, what with this happening in Addingham, it makes sense…"

"They thought I might be of some use to them. Besides, I think they find it useful to have someone with a wiser mind hanging around to point out things they've missed." He shook his head. "These young'uns, they know everything there is to know about computers and that digital stuff, but they do struggle with common sense."

Victor chuckled. "Aye. You're right. My son, he knows a lot…" He trailed off slightly. "Well, let's just say, those microphones, I needed his help to put them up."

"Right? You were listening out for the kookaburra's distinctive laugh, I suppose?"

"That among others." Victor's eyes smiled at Henry. "You've heard the reports from Malham, I suspect? It's been reported there, the kookaburra. That's less than twenty miles away." He gazed out through the open doors. "It apparently likes high climes, so I might be in with a chance."

"I'm sure the other members of the birdwatching committee would be jealous if you spotted it first."

Victor gave a fox-like grin. "Old Lowercroft would be spitting feathers." He chuckled with glee.

Henry joined in with a mischievous laugh. The bitter rivalry between Victor Quail and Patrick Lowercroft was well known in Addingham's birdwatching community.

"So, how long have you lived here, Victor?"

"Addingham all my life. But we moved up the Moorside just after the millennium."

Henry's eyes took in the conservatory; with its layers of dust and the dead flies decaying on the floorboards, he surmised that Victor now lived alone.

"You said your son set up the mics, plural?" he asked.

Victor raised an eyebrow.

"How many do you have?"

When Victor didn't answer, Henry fixed his eyes on the garden. Several cables ran around the sides of the lawn and into the hedges. Some of them were wrapped around plant pots and stones in an attempt to conceal them. Henry counted five cables in all.

"Bloody hell, Victor. Do your neighbours know you've been recording their gardens?"

Victor chewed his bottom lip. "Well, it's farmland at the bottom."

"Aye, but you've got neighbours on both sides."

Victor scrunched up his nose. "I don't think I've ever…" He coughed. "I've never explicitly told them."

"And have you ever recorded their conversations? Because, if you have, you'd be on shaky ground, legally speaking."

Victor's face dropped. "Not as far as I know. My son deals with it all. He checks the computer."

"Right…" Henry frowned. "How long have they been up?"

Victor's thumbnail scraped the lip of his cup. "Well… A couple of months."

"Crikey. And you don't know if you've ever recorded anything beyond the birds tweeting?"

He nodded. "As I said, my son handles it all. He wipes out all the 'background noise', as he calls it. I tried to do it once myself, but I got into a right mess, so now I let him do it. It's all his gear, you see. He's job's live music, concerts and gigs and things."

A stronger current of air blew into the conservatory, flicking the pages of an open birdwatching magazine on the coffee table.

"What did your son say when you asked him to set up five mics in your garden?"

"He warned me… but I'm up here on the moor. I barely hear anything apart from the birds, the wind, and a few cars."

"So, if I were to listen to your recordings, once we got them out of the computer–"

Victor rose a hand in fear. "It's an Apple one. I've no idea what the hell to do with it."

"Don't worry. I can find someone to handle that. If I got the recordings out, would I be able to hear any eavesdropped conversations from your neighbours?"

Victor shook his head, but his bulging eyes suggested the opposite.

"And you've never heard stuff before?"

"I told you. My son handles it all. But it was me who told him to do it. I should take the blame if there's any to be doled out."

"Your son will be fine. When was he last here?"

"A couple of weeks ago. He's due up in a few days to go through all I've recorded since. If it's been working."

"What do you mean?"

"Well, there's been a light flashing on the computer. I don't know what that means. It might still be recording but I've not got a clue. That's why I called him over. I wanted him to sort it out in case the kookaburra's been calling."

Henry drained his cup. "Well, I suggest you get your son over here pronto to check what you've recorded. Otherwise, the police–"

"Police!" Victor rose out of his wicker chair.

"Don't worry," Henry said, also standing up. "I'll not get you or your son into trouble. But you'll have to make it worth my while. I want you both to listen to those recordings and tell me what you heard from Saturday."

"To see what happened next door at that barbecue?"

"No, to see if the kookaburra's been." Henry rolled his eyes. "Aye, to see what that mic picked up–"

"I don't know if it's been recording. As I've said, the computer's been flashing. And it's one of those Apple ones. I've no idea–"

"Don't worry. Just see what you've got recorded. If there's anything of note, you have my mobile number." Henry bent down and rested his teacup on the tray. He glanced at the magazine open on the coffee table. "And here, if the kookaburra's call is on there, please let me know."

Victor's disgruntled look didn't shift.

Something hovered over the valley beyond the fence. Henry squinted at it. It was only a blackbird.

"Anyway, I must be getting off."

"Don't forget that bloody dog of yours!"

"Aye, I suppose you won't be wanting her to stay."

"No, I bloody wouldn't."

Henry chuckled to himself as he went to collect Tessa.

Chapter Forty

The light cloud cover remained over the valley as Henry drove down the hill towards Addingham. Tessa was in the back seat and stared out the window with her tongue lolling. Despite being happy with her new-found freedom, she hadn't forgiven Henry for chaining her up and was subjecting him to the silent treatment.

After Henry had made some progress down the hill, he pulled into a lay-by, which was actually a gate entrance to a field, and picked up his mobile phone.

His thumb hovered over Hargreaves' number. He had to tell her about the recordings Victor Quail had, plus he had some information from the Taylors which might prove interesting. But he wasn't prepared for the barrage of insults she would release on him. She'd prefer it if he was trapped in his back garden, chained up like Tessa had been, until the stink from the newspaper article had blown away.

But needs must. Three people had been killed, and Henry wasn't going to let a clue go amiss just to avoid a bollocking. He pressed Hargreaves' number, and it rang and rang. The voicemail greeting finished and the beep came, but Henry lost his nerve and hung up.

He refocused on the country lanes ahead. It was stupid, this, feeling worried about talking to Hargreaves. If it hadn't been for that bloody article, he would be able to go about his business unhindered.

He started his engine and continued down the hill. When he reached the roundabout at the top of Addingham, he saw the sign to Skipton, where Roy Parker lived with his wife. It was just past 11 a.m., and Henry suspected the journalist would be at home this time on a Bank Holiday Monday. Henry took the first exit at the roundabout and turned off towards Skipton. He put his foot down as he joined the dual carriageway and told Tessa they weren't heading home just yet.

Roy Parker lived in a recently built cottage in a quiet, leafy cul-de-sac off Skipton High Street. His house was at the far end of the low curve of properties, with small English yews planted between each drive. The road was filled with parked cars, so Henry left his Skoda a short distance from Roy's house and strolled over.

The cottage's stone walls were the dark colour of caramel, and the external woodwork was painted a dark forest green. Henry walked up the drive and knocked on the door. He heard Tessa barking from his vehicle behind him. The back window had been left open two inches, and she poked her snout through the gap. He waved at her and then rang the doorbell a second time.

A short, middle-aged woman answered. She had bronze-coloured hair, which was cut short, and she peered at Henry with concern.

"Yes?" she asked, matter-of-factly.

"I'm looking for Roy Parker," Henry said, lifting up his chin. "I want to speak to him."

"He's not available."

"Is he in?"

She didn't answer.

Henry had prepared for this and held out his phone. He dialled Roy's mobile number. The responding ringtone came from inside the property's front hallway. "Did he leave his mobile at home?" he asked Roy's wife.

She winced, and her eyes searched the doorstep for an adequate response.

Henry shouted through the open front door, "Come out here, Roy! Don't let your bloody wife fight your battles for you!"

Roy's wife shrunk backwards as Roy Parker stepped into view. He held his large phone in his hand, and it took a moment for Henry to realise he was being filmed.

"What do you want?" Roy asked.

"Don't record this," Henry said.

"I'll do as I please," Roy said. "This is my property." Then, he turned to his wife. "It's alright, love. I'll handle it from here."

"Very chivalrous of you," Henry grunted, as Roy's wife disappeared inside.

"What is it you want?" Roy asked, standing at the threshold. His large black phone covered his face, and his long dark hair was dank and greasy. He wore a burgundy-coloured T-shirt that almost failed to cover his protruding stomach and a pair of jeans.

"Why did you write that hack job article in the *Yorkshire Gazette*? Why do you want to ruin my reputation?"

"You're doing a good enough job of that yourself," Roy said. His mobile's camera flickered in the daylight.

"All I'm doing is assisting the police with their inquiries. Yes, I was suspected of something a few years ago–"

"You were investigated for being a bent copper–"

"But I was cleared, which is something you failed to report in your article."

"Well, why don't you write to the Independent Press Standards Organisation instead of turning up on my doorstep in a rage?"

"A lot of good that'd do me. It'll take them months to write back with a measly response. Meanwhile, the damage would have been done."

Roy waved aside his argument. "I think the readers in Yorkshire have a right to know who the police are working with."

"Are you saying they didn't have that right to know a while ago? When I was helping them find out where you were being held hostage?"

Roy's phone shook in his hand. "Look, I appreciate what you did there, but as I've said before, this is just a story and I'm a journalist. I'm paid to write articles like these and get them to readers."

"No matter who you destroy in the process?"

"Listen, I didn't particularly want to take the angle we finally went with."

Henry shook his head in confusion. "Come again? 'We'?"

Roy sighed with exasperation. "I… Look…"

"Did someone force you to go after me?" Henry asked, stepping closer to Roy. "To write that hit piece?"

"They…" He paused and then lowered his phone and stopped filming. "I was asked to go hard on you."

"By whom?"

Roy's eyes scanned the cul-de-sac. "You'd better come in so we can talk." He looked back down his hallway. "If you promise to behave."

"What do you take me for? Some kind of thug? I'm a retired DCI, for Christ's sake."

Roy mulled over Henry's words and then gave a curt nod. "Come in, then. And be quick, I've got to get over to Leeds Central for 12 p.m."

"Why's that?"

"Detective Superintendent Murphy's giving another press conference. There's been some developments in the poisoning case."

Henry arched both eyebrows. "Already?"

He swallowed his bitterness. Neither Hargreaves nor Barnes had bothered to call him. They hadn't even sent him a text message. He cleared his throat, hoping that would expel his disappointment.

"Alright, let's discuss who had you write that article."

Roy nodded. "Alright, but you won't be happy when you find out who it was."

As he crossed the threshold and entered the house, Henry said, "Aye, I suspect I bloody won't."

Chapter Forty-One

Henry took a seat at the breakfast table in Roy's kitchen. His wife offered to make them coffee, but Roy said he would do it. She left them and went into the living room, closing the door behind her. Pale daylight came through the French doors that opened up onto a back lawn and patio. Eight-foot-high fir trees surrounded the garden, making it private and cosy. Which was needed, as the Leeds & Liverpool Canal ran along the other side, and had dozens of walkers travelling its towpath every day.

Roy placed two cups of instant coffee on the varnished breakfast table, and asked Henry if he took milk. He accepted a dash and noticed Roy didn't take any. He, instead, added four sugars into his cup.

"So?" Henry asked. He heard late-morning TV coming from the room next door.

Roy raised his eyebrows. "You want a name, then?"

Henry nodded.

"Of the one who put me onto you?"

"That's why I'm sitting here, yes."

Roy slurped his black coffee. He had bags under his eyes, and his wide, wrinkled cheeks were red with what Henry suspected was hypertension. "I heard about the poisoning Saturday afternoon." Roy sniffed. "What's the latest on that?"

Henry remained silent on the case. "Oh, by the way," he said instead, "everything I say here is off the record, not that I'll mention anything worth printing."

Roy rolled his eyes. "Don't get your knickers in a twist. I'm not going to publish anything you say."

"Good, and you'd better not put that video of me on your doorstep online."

Roy scrunched up his lips before nodding. "Fine. I'll delete it."

"Good. Now, getting back to this article."

Roy blew steam off his coffee and drank some. "Look, as I said, the article didn't go the way I wanted it."

"Aye, because someone forced you to write it like that?"

Roy nodded.

"And who was that?"

He heaved a sigh. "I never reveal my sources."

"This isn't a source, though, is it? It's a meddler. Someone who pushed you to do this. Who was it?" Henry set his jaw. "Was it Murphy?"

"The detective superintendent?" Roy scoffed and shook his head. "God no, he wouldn't ask me to do him a favour. He bloody hates me."

"Was it someone in the police?"

"It was, yes."

Henry tilted his head to the side. "It couldn't have been DS Hargreaves?"

"Who?" Roy frowned. "No. It was a detective inspector."

"Barnes!?"

Roy nodded. "She approached me with the story and then gave me the low-down on all the dirt she has on you."

"No… It couldn't…"

Could Barnes have been responsible for the hit piece? For a moment, Henry tuned out of the kitchen, his ears buzzing as if a bomb had gone off right next him. He felt dizzy and slightly sick.

"Barnes…? She told you to write it?"

Roy had been watching him. "I met her after the kidnapping. She took my statement, and we ended up chatting. I gave her my card." He gave Henry a half-charming smile. "I'm always on the lookout for police intel, as you well know."

"It was Barnes who pushed you into writing that hit piece on me?" Henry repeated, his mouth agape.

Roy frowned as he studied the hurt on Henry's face. "You shouldn't take it personally. I think she was doing it for the 'bigger picture', rather than just to attack you."

"She gave you – a journalist – loads of dirt so you could destroy my reputation in the press. How am I not supposed to take that personally?"

Roy conceded his point with a nod. He slurped more coffee. "You need to look beyond yourself and at the police force," he said.

Henry grunted. "What is this 'bigger picture' that I'm missing?"

Roy wiped his lips. "Listen, why is Murphy letting you work on these cases? Because both you and I know he shouldn't be letting you anywhere near them."

"Because he wants them solved."

"And why does he need a retired detective to help him solve these crimes?"

"Because he doesn't have the staff. The police force has been cut to the bone. They don't have the resources. It's either he lets me help them clear these cases or they sit there, untouched, and fester."

"Yes," Roy said. "All very true. But what's recently changed? Everyone is expecting a new government after the election. There's talk that they will be increasing police funding to help them solve all these murders and crimes."

"Right?"

"Well, Barnes, she's worried that if you're picking up the slack, the government won't think there's a problem at West Yorkshire Police."

"So… she helped you write a hit piece so that her department could get more funding?" Henry shook his head. "Pull the other one."

"It's the truth… I think." He bit his lower lip. "Well, there was something else. She doesn't want you involved in cases anymore. She says it's too risky."

Henry grunted. "I suppose she did say words to that effect yesterday… That by helping the police, I am putting them – and me – at legal risk… and all that." He recalled Curtis Quaker's civil claim looming over his head and shook the thought out of his mind. "But that can't be why she did it, can it? There must be another reason."

Roy shrugged. "I didn't ask her. Well, I did at first, and that's when she explained her reasoning about police funding, which sounded fair enough. She did say she thinks you mean well and usually do a good job when you help out. But I see her point. By picking up too much slack, the government won't think there's a funding problem. I mean, if the police can solve all these cases with the money they've got, why give 'em more?"

Henry picked up his cup of coffee and took a tiny sip. It was bitter and acidic. "I don't know. It seems very out of character for Barnes to do something like this."

"Is it? Do you think she's always happy to see you on these cases, when you've illegally involved yourself?"

Henry scrunched up his nose and turned to face the French doors.

He spotted two sparrows fluttering across the back lawn.

"No comment," he said.

It couldn't have been Barnes who had stuck the knife in, could it? He recalled the times he had worked with her over the past few years. He couldn't say that she had always been enthusiastic about his involvement, except for when she wasn't in a fit state to handle the cases herself.

It was a great shame, as he always thought they worked well together. How had she come to do something like this? He couldn't even blame Murphy for it, as Barnes and the superintendent weren't close, and she would never follow an order like this from him. If Hargreaves had been the one to bring Henry down, he would have seen Murphy's hand somewhere in the background, as she and him were as thick as thieves. But Barnes? No, Henry realised, she must have done this on her own volition.

"I can't believe it…" Henry said, staring wistfully ahead.

Roy checked his watch and pushed his chair back across the floor. "I really need to be getting off now. There's that press conference, remember?"

Henry nodded absent-mindedly. "Aye. You get off then." An idea came to him. "Here, are you any good with computers?"

Roy tidied away the coffee cups. "I'm not an expert, but I'm not bad. Why?"

"Well, it's just that I might have some stuff that needs checking. Some recordings."

Roy stopped mid-stride. "What recordings?"

Henry narrowed his lips. "I can't say."

Roy tilted his head to the side. "I can hire someone to go through them if you like, as I don't have time myself. But only if I can print whatever I hear on them."

Henry guffawed. "Bloody forget it!" He hauled himself out of the chair. "You know, I used to respect you as a journalist, but now I fear you're just a hack."

Roy laughed coldly as he placed the cups in the dishwasher. "You have to move with the times, Henry. You may not have noticed, but local news is dead. If you want to earn a living these days, you have to make the news, not just report it."

"Is that why the world's going to hell in a handcart?"

Roy's eyes cleared for moment. "Aye, one of hundreds of reasons."

Chapter Forty-Two

Henry got back into his car, where he found Tessa whimpering on the back seat. The sun was beating on the windscreen and the car's interior was heating up, despite the open windows. "Apologies, little one." He started the engine. "Let's get you back home."

Tessa barked in reply.

As Henry was about to drive off, he saw Roy Parker jump into his red Ford estate. The vehicle reversed out of its parking space, spun around, and then headed out of the cul-de-sac.

Henry's engine ticked over while he mulled over his next steps. What was Murphy planning to announce in that press conference this afternoon? Whatever it was could be serious. An unwelcome twinge in his gut suggested he was onto something.

If he entered the police station on the same day as that article had been published, he would be as welcome as a leper at a pool party. Although, while he was there, he could make sure Hargreaves had someone go through Arthur Quail's bird recordings – if there was anything of interest on them.

And there might be more links between Sales Expedited and Mark Hardy's circle of friends to be found in their private correspondence. Perhaps Barnes could–

Barnes!

Henry gripped the steering wheel and ground his molars together.

Barnes. That bloody snake. She'd stabbed him in the back. Reporting to a gutter journalist? And for what? So the police could ask for more funding from a new government? Hadn't they been friends, Henry and her? Partners? Allies, even?

Tessa barked with impatience, and Henry spun round – ready to snap back. But he caught himself before he did.

He relaxed his grip on the steering wheel and exhaled.

"You're right. Let's get you home and then go and do what's needed in Leeds. Those idiots won't solve this case without a swift kick up the backside from yours truly."

* * *

The glass walls of the police station reflected the bright sun. Henry squinted as he rushed towards the entrance, moving between the lines of cars in the nearly full car park. Three men wearing creased shirts and smoking cigarettes stood around the automatic doors. They looked like journalists, going by their unshaven faces and the bags under their eyes. Unless the standards in the police these days really had slipped.

Henry entered the foyer and saw more journalists milling around the waiting area. Some gawped at the rolling news on the large TV while others were seated on sofas typing on laptops. Henry spotted Roy Parker among them, talking excitedly into his phone. Probably planning his next reputational assassination.

"Got your badge?" The police officer at the front desk stared at Henry.

Henry patted his jean pockets as a show. "I must have forgotten it. You remember me, though, don't you?"

The young officer narrowed his eyes as if trying to recall Henry. "Sorry. No badge, no entry."

Henry heaved a sigh. "Call DS Hargreaves, she'll set you straight."

The officer reluctantly picked up the desk phone and dialled a number.

The chatter in the foyer grew louder. The voices, echoing off the tiles and glass like they did in a swimming pool, built up to a clamour. Murphy was about to make a big announcement. The journos buzzed around like excited wasps trapped inside a sweet shop.

"She's not answering her phone," the officer at the front desk said. "You'll have to come back later."

"Can't I take a seat?"

The officer frowned. "Not today. As you can see, we're busy."

"Expecting a big announcement?"

The officer turned to his computer screen. "I couldn't say."

Henry tapped the varnished countertop while his brain came up with a better plan.

His eyes travelled around the busy foyer and settled on some movement at the top of the staircase. Hargreaves walked down the steps behind Murphy, who was wearing his full uniform and a Cheshire-cat grin.

Henry left the front desk and passed between the clusters of journalists until he reached the bottom of the stairs.

Murphy's smarmy smile soured when he spotted Henry. He turned over his shoulder to Hargreaves and said something Henry couldn't pick up over the noise.

Her eyes widened in panic when she noticed him.

Henry's gut twinged again. This wouldn't be good.

When they reached the foot of the stairs, the journalists swarmed around them, shouting out questions that Henry couldn't decipher.

Murphy raised his hands and gave a good-humoured nod. "All will be revealed shortly."

A young journalist pushed Henry to the side and shouted, "Have you found a suspect?!"

Murphy nodded. "A suspect has been identified." A deafening buzz filled the foyer. "But I kindly ask you to wait for the press briefing, which will begin shortly."

Two uniformed officers shepherded the journalists into the briefing room at the side. They all went in gladly, some pushing to the front to get the best seats.

Henry was left standing alone before Murphy and Hargreaves.

Murphy's dress shoes clacked on the tiles as he approached him. "What the shit are you doing here?"

"What's all this about finding a suspect?" Henry asked.

"Hush!" Murphy's eyes searched the room for any idling journos. "I can't talk here."

"The last I knew, we didn't have a suspect and not much hope of finding one."

"Would you shut it!"

Hargreaves stepped forwards. "Henry, we're going to announce Sarah–"

"Sarah Hardy?" Henry frowned at Murphy. "You can't say it was her. We've no idea–"

"I'm announcing her as our suspect and that we're closing our inquiries," Murphy said under his breath.

"What if it wasn't her? In fact, I very much doubt–"

"Henry!" Murphy raised his finger. "She prepared the food, she told them all to eat it, and she didn't touch any herself. Add that to the fact she was the first to fall ill. It all looks like she poisoned the food, wanted them to eat it, and had poisoned herself beforehand. We put this down to a nasty case of murder-suicide committed by an unstable woman."

"But why would she do it?"

Murphy scrunched up his lips.

"Okay, I agree, it looks bad from her perspective," Henry started, "but we don't know why–"

"We've found her phone," Murphy said.

"And what was on it?"

Hargreaves gave Murphy a sidewards look. "The techies are just getting into it now. As yet, nothing has been found."

"Where did they find it?"

"In her en suite. In a hidden compartment," Murphy said.

Henry scrunched up his eyebrows.

"See, there was more to 'sweet Sarah' than people realised," Murphy continued.

"Henry, maybe she'd had enough of Mark," Hargreaves said, "and decided to take herself out and him along with her."

Henry was about to argue back but recalled what the Taylors had told him about Sarah attacking Mark with a knife. Could murder have been the natural progression?

He shook his head. "I'm not buying it, and I'm surprised that you are." He eyeballed Hargreaves.

"Henry, we've no other leads. It's a messy case. If we say it was Sarah…" She ran out of enthusiasm and couldn't finish her point.

Henry turned on Murphy. "Even *she*'s struggling to repeat your script," he said. "So, you go and destroy an innocent woman's reputation to close a messy case. What then?"

"We move on with other police work. It's not like we're lacking any," said Murphy.

"What if her family sues for defamation?"

"They're in Australia, who cares? Besides, I'd be more worried about legal action closer to home, if I were you. That Quaker lad is still threatening to drag you through the courts."

"Well, that's a load of bollocks, isn't it?"

"Is it?" Murphy turned to Hargreaves, who offered a weak shrug. "Well, let's see what the judge says in a year or two, after Quaker's bled your assets dry." Murphy pulled his chin in. "Now, if you'd excuse me, I need to announce this case is closed and move on."

Henry grabbed Murphy by the lapels and pushed him backwards. A few startled yelps came from uniformed officers who'd been watching.

Murphy raised his hands to them. "Henry, don't scruff up my suit. I'm due on telly in a minute."

"Give me twenty-four hours."

"You what?"

"Henry?!" Hargreaves said, sounding upset.

"Twenty-four hours to solve this."

"Why the bloody hell should I?" Murphy growled.

"Because if you don't, I'll do my upmost to undermine you. I'll keep digging and prove that you unfairly pinned a mass murder on an innocent woman. The victim of a coercive and nightmarish husband."

Murphy snarled.

"Don't bet against me," Henry said. "You know I'll crack this one. I just need one more day."

Murphy sucked his lips together. His face was growing redder and redder.

"Besides, there's still the fact we don't know how she died. What if it turns out it was natural causes, completely unrelated to the poisoning?"

"Unlikely."

"Well, we don't know yet, do we? Plus, have you heard back from the Aussie police? What if they say something that exonerates her? I'm sure the pen-pushers at Police Complaints will be very interested to learn you've framed an innocent victim."

Murphy squared his jaw and surveyed the foyer. Henry couldn't tell if he was going to call a uniformed officer to arrest him or not.

Barnes then appeared at the top of the stairs. Her face paled as she noticed the scene playing out at the bottom.

Murphy clicked his fingers at her. "Barnes! Have we heard back from Anderson on the cause of death?"

Barnes shook her head as she rushed down the steps.

"And the Aussies?"

"Just an acknowledgement. There'll get back to us tomorrow."

Murphy seethed.

"Sir…" Hargreaves said, "maybe just give it one more day."

Murphy spun towards Henry. "You think you can solve this?" He jabbed his finger into Henry's chest. "In twenty-four hours?"

"Aye." Henry knocked his hand away. "And if I do, I'd like some compensation–"

Murphy hooted. "Jesus wept! If you do it in twenty-four hours, you can have whatever you like. Here, I'll give you a bloody badge."

"What's going on?" Barnes eyed Murphy and Henry.

"The boss is giving Henry twenty-four hours," Hargreaves answered.

Barnes shook her head violently. "No! That's insane, you can't let him–"

"Oh, and what are you going to do about it?" Henry asked. "Brief against me to the press again?"

Murphy turned on her in flash, his pent-up rage about to blow.

"Aye," Henry continued. "Barnes here decided to sacrifice my reputation in order to get more funding."

Murphy towered over Barnes, whose posture crumbled. "What's this?" he demanded. "Roy Parker! You briefed Roy Parker about him?" Murphy tossed his head in Henry's direction. "Do you know how much shit that caused? I've been dealing with the consequences all sodding day!"

"Sir–"

"Get to my office!"

Barnes froze to the spot. She eventually nodded at Murphy and disappeared through a door at the other end of the foyer. Silence descended on the remaining three while Murphy strutted up and down, his fingers pulling on his lower lip.

Eventually, Hargreaves said, "Sir, we're late for the briefing now."

Murphy clicked his heels together. "Right. Let's get this over with."

"Murphy." Henry smirked. "How much better would it be if you had a suspect to parade in front of them? And then imagine the buzz when you get a conviction a year down the line?"

Murphy's cheek twitched.

"And more importantly, you'll be able to explain why someone poisoned four people. You can't do that yet. What will you do when the press start asking about Sarah's motivation? I mean, what are you actually going to say to them?"

Murphy snapped. "Fine! For God's sake! Have it. Have your twenty-four hours! If you manage to do it, you can have whatever you bloody want in return."

"Good, I'll be sending you a list."

Murphy smirked back. "Go ahead. But if you don't, I'll be announcing Sarah Hardy as our suspect regardless, and I'll be requesting a restraining order to keep you away from this building. And then, I'll sit back and watch Curtis Quaker and his posh lawyer drown you in a legal quagmire."

Henry raised his head higher. "Deal." He held out his hand, which Murphy gawped at, before reluctantly shaking.

"Hargreaves," Murphy started, "tell the press to be back here tomorrow evening. We'll make the announcement then."

"Best call it 7 p.m.," Henry said.

"Fine, 7 p.m. it is." Murphy spun round and headed across the foyer to his office, where he would no doubt give Barnes both barrels.

"You'd better solve this, Henry," Hargreaves said before jetting into the briefing room.

Henry nodded. "I will," he said. "I've got no bloody choice."

Chapter Forty-Three

Henry made his way back to Addingham. The tension dissipated little by little with each passing mile, but he was still a wreck. He'd gone and thrown himself in the deep end of a very dark and dangerous body of water, and now he had to sink or swim.

He couldn't bear to let his thoughts wander towards the 'what if' scenario that Murphy had painted for him.

No. He had to solve this and not let Murphy get to his head.

Tessa yapped angrily at the door when Henry entered his cottage, and he agreed that a brisk walk would do them both good. He attached a lead to her collar and led her along the pavement towards the park.

"Don't go attacking other people's property again," he warned her as she sniffed a bush.

They went back to the football pitch and he let her run free. The sun was out, and the sky was a deep blue. Three lads played football around the goalposts at one end of the field. Tessa went to join in with them, but Henry knew she could play nasty and whistled at her to leave the lads alone.

She ran off in the other direction, and Henry let his mind wander as he trekked around the field's touchlines. He kicked up the grass and threw glances at Tessa, who was busying herself in the hedges nearby.

Henry lost himself in his thoughts. So, he had just over twenty-four hours to solve an almost impossible case or face reputational and financial ruin. He heaved a breath to calm his shuddering nerves and decided to focus on the positives. There were the recordings from Victor Quail that could be useful, and then there was Sarah's phone now. If the police found something on there, it could help solve the case.

Or so he hoped.

Why did he always put himself in these impossible situations? He would have thought he'd learnt his lesson by now.

His phone buzzed in his pocket. It was Hargreaves.

"Murphy's okayed everything on your list," she said.

Henry had scribbled down his demands on a scrap of paper before leaving the station. One of them was legal assistance for the private case Curtis Quaker was mounting.

"Murphy wasn't very happy about some of the items, mind you," Hargreaves continued. "But he did say you've got as much chance of solving this as Leeds United do of winning the Premier League."

"That's a bit harsh," Henry grunted. "So he's agreed to get me access to the National Crime Agency files."

"Yes, I'm sending PC Smith over with the printed case files you've requested. Murphy insisted I tell you that you're not allowed to take pictures of them, scan them, or copy anything written down. By pain of death."

"Fine. But I'll have to scribble notes on them. If that's a capital offence, please let me know now."

"That might be alright. PC Smith will pick up the files from you the day after tomorrow, when we've finished with this case. All the pages are numbered and attached, so you'll know if you've lost any." She huffed. "Do you really think you can do it? Solve this case in just over twenty-four hours?"

"I hope so."

"Henry, we need more than bloody 'hope'."

He chuckled. "Isn't that all we really have in the end?"

"Don't be getting philosophical, we don't have time."

"Understood."

"I'll arrange the meeting with the witnesses and victims for tomorrow afternoon," she said. "I'll have to rack my brain to see how I get Mark Hardy there. He's still unconscious in hospital."

"I'm sure you'll find a way. Getting him there will be vitally important."

"Do you think it was him?"

Henry grumbled a non-committal noise. "He's definitely involved, somehow."

"Okay. I'll see what I can do."

"You'd better make the meeting start as late as you can. Around six."

"Why so late?" she asked.

"To give us as much time as possible to make sure we're on the right track."

"And why do they have to be at Cragg Hall, again? Forensics are having kittens about it as they still need access to the property. And isn't it a bit harsh to make the victims go back so soon?"

"Well, firstly, have Forensics finished with the crime scene?"

"They've been there two days but want more time with it."

"Well, now they've got a hard deadline for tomorrow afternoon, which can only be a good thing, as it gives them something to work towards."

Hargreaves mumbled her disagreement. "What about the victims? Won't it be traumatising to go back so soon?"

Henry took a breath. "Aye, it probably will be. But returning to the scene of the crime might reignite memories that could be useful to us."

"Alright," she said, utterly unenthused. "I'll organise all that and start working through this massive to-do list you've given me."

"Right you are. Just before you go, can you confirm if anyone ever double-checked the relationship between Ralph Gaskin and his chemical company?"

"I don't think so. I thought it was ruled out."

Henry nibbled at his lower lip. "As a rule, it's often better to go and check hunches before ruling them out. Can you send me his company's address?"

"It's in Wakefield, I think. Why?"

"It'll be one of two stops for the road trip I'm planning tomorrow."

"Bloody heck. Don't go getting stuck in traffic. You know my neck's on the line for showing you a tiny bit of support?"

"And I appreciate that, Hargreaves. I really do. But if you wouldn't mind? Ralph's company address, please."

She groaned. "Just don't mess this up."

"I don't intend to."

He hung up and scanned the football pitch for Tessa. She was trying to play football with the three lads again, so Henry called her back to him. He found a stick on the ground and threw it for her. As she sprinted after it, Henry had another thought. He took out his phone again and called Dr Anderson.

"Ward, are you spamming me?" the doctor asked upon answering. Heavy metallic sounds in the background suggested he was busy at work.

"I don't think you can spam a phone, Doctor," he replied. "But I might be wrong. Any further updates on Sarah Hardy?"

"Not yet. Why, am I reporting to you now? Is that how things are going?"

"If you could keep me in the loop, I'd appreciate it."

"The results should come back tomorrow morning. Those poor technicians are doing the tests as we speak, on a Bank Holiday." A drill whirred in the background.

"Aren't you working today?"

"Of course, there was a body found in a canal in Halifax." He sighed. "No rest for the wicked."

Henry frowned. "I know what you mean." He bent down to pick up the stick and threw it again for Tessa, who galloped after it.

"I saw your face on the local paper today, not that I read the article. I don't waste my time with that nonsense."

"You do right, if only thousands of other people thought the same."

"Are you alright, then? You sound like you've done something reckless."

"How do you know I've done something 'reckless'?"

"I don't know… your voice goes a bit higher. Tighter. Your Yorkshire accent comes through more."

"Oh…" Henry cleared his throat.

"Why? What is it you've done?"

Henry wrestled the stick from Tessa's jaws and threw it again. "I've made a deal with Murphy to keep me on the case, but by doing so, I might've signed my own death warrant."

"How so?"

Henry gave him a curt explanation.

"Well, good luck solving this one any time soon." Dr Anderson spoke to someone in the background, then came back on the phone. "You know, I really do try my best not to get in-between you two. You were always knocking heads together. I never understood why you couldn't just get along."

"We're too different."

Dr Anderson paused. "You know, I don't believe that's true. You're both obsessive megalomaniacs, just in your own separate ways."

Henry reeled from his comment.

A circular saw roared in the background, causing Henry to hold his phone at a distance. When he placed it back to his ear, he heard Dr Anderson say he had to go and wished Henry luck.

Tessa padded along beside Henry with the stick between her teeth. Despite panting heavily, her expectant eyes peered up at him.

"Nope, we'd best get off and start doing our homework. It'll be a long night and an even longer day tomorrow."

She glanced at the field and then back at him, as if to say, 'but wouldn't playing here be a better idea?'

Henry struggled to argue with her, so he didn't make a comment.

Chapter Forty-Four

Parked vehicles lined the narrow lane that ran alongside Cragg Hall. The weather had turned for the worse that morning, and dark-grey clouds hung over Addingham Moorside, lashing it with wind and rain. Henry was forced to park a distance away, as he had arrived late for the meeting. He checked his watch and saw it was 6.30 p.m., and then cursed the weather outside his car.

Quickening his pace, he rushed towards the barn conversion with rain hitting his face and splashing his anorak. Before he entered, he spotted the Taylors' white cottage opposite. He was sure he saw someone watching him through the front window but gave up trying to figure out if it was Mr or Mrs. He sought shelter from the rain in Cragg Hall.

The atmosphere inside was just as bad. The lack of sunlight made the house's interior gloomy and moody. Henry found Hargreaves standing in the hallway, staring at her phone. She was biting her fingernail and jumped when she saw him.

"Finally! You're bloody here!" she shouted.

He took off his dripping anorak. The hooks by the door were already overloaded with wet coats, so he held his own under his arm. "Have we got everything?" he asked Hargreaves.

A message pinged on her phone which she checked. "We've got almost everything. The Aussies were surprisingly helpful, as you've probably seen."

"Aye, I have. I didn't think they'd keep such accurate records. It puts us to shame. Still no word from Dr Anderson about Sarah?"

She shook her head.

Henry swore under his breath. "Where is everybody?"

"Around the dining table, as you asked. They're all here. Even Mark. He arrived in an ambulance. His doctors kicked up a fuss, but Murphy twisted their arms – almost literally."

"Good."

Henry nodded to himself. It was now or never. He had spent the last twenty-four hours going over all the papers and details he had in his possession, and then he had gone on his little road trip to corroborate his hunches. He had managed to get four hours' sleep but had otherwise kept himself going on adrenaline, Yorkshire Tea, and chocolate biscuits.

He thought his apprehension might be showing, so he said loudly, "Right. Let's go see them, shall we?"

"Henry," Hargreaves asked, "are you sure you can do this?"

Henry noted the panic in her eyes. "Well, let's go see if I can."

"It's just that… we need a name now. And me and Murphy have pulled in a lot of favours… possibly too many. If you don't deliver…" Her shoulders shuddered feverishly. Her eyes were wide with panic.

"I think I know what happened here. I just need a few more things to fall into place."

"Like what?" she asked.

Henry didn't answer her. Instead, he strolled along the hallway towards the living room.

"A quick chat with the victims will clear everything up," he said.

He heard Hargreaves moan in disbelief behind him but kept on going. His heart was beating in his chest, and he took a deep breath. It really was now or never.

He entered the living room. The glass bifold doors were closed, and the long table outside had been cleared. Rain spilling from the gutters splattered the glass doors. More rain buffeted the patio and the furniture on it, causing the large parasol to swing from side to side. Henry scanned the kitchen cabinets, which hadn't been cleaned since Saturday. The worktops were marked with red and yellow labels left by the forensics team.

Turning round, he saw seven people sitting at the long dining table underneath a dimly lit chandelier, which was artistically made from antlers. They studied him with varying degrees of contempt. None of them said a word.

"Sorry I've made you wait," Henry said.

He placed his wet anorak on the chair at the end of the table that was closest to him. He took a seat. Mark Hardy, looking deathly pale, was sitting opposite him at the other end, slumped back in his chair. An untouched glass of water rested in front of him.

Next to Henry, Noura Emery wept softly. She wore a tight-fitting black top. A pile of scrunched-up tissues was on the table before her. Sitting next to her were the Gaskins. Claire wore a baby-blue sweater that was stained with rain, and Ralph sported a bright-red hoodie. Ralph had his arm around his wife and was seated on Mark's right.

To the left of Mark, on the other side of the table, was Pete Blackburn. He had on a thin, grey jumper. His elbows were on the table, his head in his bandaged hands, and his short hair was ruffled. He was the only one who wasn't staring at Henry; instead, he contemplated the tabletop.

Tom Dixon and Lee Combes, the rugby players, were positioned next to Pete. They were both dressed in blue-and-yellow Leeds Rugby Club shirts and shorts. The mud on their legs suggested they had been on a pitch before being called away.

"Well," Henry said, smiling. "I'm very glad you all could make it."

"We didn't have a choice," Ralph said, shaking his head. "We had to find a sitter for our little William."

"I'm sorry for the inconvenience… but three people were murdered here on Saturday."

"I know," Noura sobbed. "Why did we have to come back here?"

Henry looked into her red eyes. "I know this is distressing for you. However, I believe having you here will help me determine who killed your husband."

Noura burst into tears. Tutting, Claire released herself from Ralph's embrace and hugged the other woman, while staring daggers at Henry.

Henry gazed at the rest of the table. "Now, I have several questions to ask you individually, and then I'll let some of you go."

"Do you know we've been sitting here for half an hour waiting for you?" Claire shook her head in outrage. "Making us come back here like this… it's awful. That woman detective wouldn't let us leave. Are we prisoners or what?"

Henry simpered at her. "Visiting the crime scene and participating in re-enactments is a standard police procedure in other countries."

"Yeah, but not in England!" Ralph shouted.

"Well, admittedly, we're not in Spain, but it's not such a bad idea, is it? Coming back here, seeing the place and smelling it. All that can stir memories you might have forgotten." Henry nodded in agreement with himself. "Let's crack on, then. I don't wish to keep you here any longer than I have to." He turned to Noura. "Now, Mrs Emery. If you could, please can you tell me what time you arrived here on Saturday?"

Noura couldn't speak through her tears.

Everyone else regarded Henry with utter contempt. "Please, Mrs Emery," he said. "I understand you're very distressed. I really do, but once you've answered my questions, I'll have a police officer escort you home as quickly as I can. Alright?"

She sniffed and wiped her eyes. "I'll do it for Allister." Claire, beside her, squeezed her hand. "We arrived here around 4 p.m. on Saturday."

"And who was already here?" Henry asked.

"Erm…" The strength in Noura's dark eyes faltered. She turned to Ralph and Claire. "I think you were here… and baby William." She sobbed, letting out a long whimper, but soon regained control of her emotions. Sniffing, she looked at the two rugby players. "And you two arrived later."

"And Pete and Louanne?" Henry asked.

Noura tilted her head as she regarded Pete. "I think they were already here, too."

"From reading the reports," Henry said, "I understand you helped Sarah Hardy in the kitchen?"

Noura nodded, daring to look at the worktops at the other end of the room.

"What did you do?"

"I helped prepare the food, and I made the potato salad with Sarah."

"Who else was in the kitchen?"

She turned to Claire. "We both gave Sarah a hand."

"Where was Louanne?"

"She was outside, I think. On the terrace."

Henry nodded. "Alright, so you're in the kitchen on Saturday afternoon, cutting up potatoes, spring onions, and what-have-you; and you're with Sarah and Claire…" Henry pinched his lips. "Who brought the salad dressing?"

Noura frowned. "The what?"

Tom, the rugby player, spoke up. "Is that what it was? Is that what had the poison in it?"

Henry held up his hand to silence him and then returned to focusing on Noura. "Did someone bring the salad dressing or was it made here?"

Noura stared at Tom, and then her eyes travelled back to Henry. "Was it really in the salad dressing?"

"It was," Henry said.

She covered her mouth and gasped.

Henry glanced at the others around the table before leaning closer to her. "Are you alright?"

"But… it was me. I made that salad dressing."

Chapter Forty-Five

Shock and surprise rippled round the table. Claire leant away from Noura as if she had somehow become dangerous. Ralph put his arm around his wife's shoulder, pulling her close to him. Mark Hardy brought himself out of his malaise to give Noura a look of spite. The two rugby lads moved their chairs back and stretched out their legs, as if preparing to jump up from the table. Even Pete Blackburn managed to raise his head from his bandaged hands before lowering it again.

Noura had seen all their reactions, and her tears returned, now tinted with shame as well as sadness.

Henry patted her arm. "It's alright. I don't think you poisoned anyone, Mrs Emery."

She wiped her eyes with a tissue. "But… I made the vinaigrette, didn't I?" She heaved more tears. "How did the poison get in it? I used a recipe I found online years ago." She shook her head as if struggling to comprehend.

"What was in this recipe?" Henry asked.

"It's… olive oil, balsamic vinegar, mustard, ground pepper… salt…" She paused. "And then I added a secret ingredient. A teaspoon of sugar."

Henry smiled. "It sounds lovely. How much dressing did you make?"

"I don't know… Enough for ten people. I used an old jam jar, and it was less than half full. Sarah said she had a sauce boat to serve it in, but she never had time to find it."

"So, the jar containing the salad dressing was placed on the table outside after you made it?"

Noura started to nod but then shook her head. "No. It was placed on here, first."

"On this dining table?" Henry looked down at the tabletop.

Noura again glanced at the kitchen worktops across the room. "There's not much space to put things over there, and Sarah said we couldn't leave the food outside as the flies would get to it."

"Who would have had access to the food, then?"

Noura blinked. "Well…" She scanned the faces around the table. "We all did."

"Was some of the food covered in cling film?"

"Most of it was."

"What about the salad dressing?"

She shook her head. "I just left it in the jam jar. I didn't even put a lid on it, I don't think…" She stared at the tabletop. "Maybe if I had done…"

Henry shook his head. "Don't think like that. I suspect even if you had put a lid on it, the killer would have still laced it with poison."

Tom frowned. His huge, thick legs shook. "Was the poison already in the house, then; or was it in the olive oil or something?"

Henry acknowledged his question with a nod, before smiling at Noura. "That's all I needed to ask you, Noura. You may leave if you want."

She studied the doorway where Hargreaves was standing and then shook her head. "I'll stay… I want to know what happened."

Henry nodded his understanding and then focused his attention on Tom, who was still waiting for a reply. "That's a very interesting question you asked." Henry then turned to scrutinise Ralph. "How would you answer him?"

Ralph itched his nose. "You what?"

"Was the poison already in the house or did the killer bring it?" Henry paused before answering himself. "We've received the report from the forensics team. They didn't find any other trace of cyanide in the house. So, naturally, we believe it must have been brought here by the killer." Henry clicked his fingers as if remembering something. "That reminds me, you arrived here with all sorts of things, didn't you?"

Ralph furrowed his brows. "What do you mean?"

"You told us you brought your own beer and non-alcoholic drinks, and I assume you must've needed lots of things for baby William, including baby milk."

Claire gawped in outrage, her head still resting on her husband's shoulder. "We wouldn't keep deadly poison in our baby carrier, you idiot. We're not monsters."

Henry held up his hand. "I'm not suggesting *you* did, Mrs Gaskin. I'm saying Ralph might have done."

Claire's face scrunched up with confusion. "What are you saying about my husband?"

"Ralph works for a chemical company, doesn't he? I went to visit his office earlier today." Henry paused for effect. "Ralph's manager confirmed that the company holds cyanide on its production sites."

"But Ralph works in marketing," Claire said.

"I know, but he works in the same building as quality control, which tests dozens of chemical samples every day. And his manager told me that Ralph recently became friends with a man named Paul who works in that department."

Henry tilted his head and peered at Ralph, who wouldn't meet his gaze.

"Your boss mentioned it was odd for someone in marketing to mingle with a lab rat. And I'm wondering if that's how you procured the poison."

"What?" Claire said. "Ralph would never do that."

"Well, luckily Paul was available for me to speak to, and he almost became hysterical when I said I was with the police. He admitted everything before I'd even asked a question." Henry eyeballed Ralph. "In exchange for the chemical samples, which you claimed were to control a pest infestation at a friend's farm, you offered to help Paul get the personal email address of a female colleague he was enamoured with."

Claire freed herself from her husband's embrace and spun round to challenge him. "Tell him it's not true."

Henry continued, "According to Paul, Ralph has a way of obtaining people's email addresses. He didn't know how you did it, but you got the woman's email address within a day."

Ralph sunk low in his chair; his hand spread across his brow.

"Ralph!" Claire hit his shoulder. "Tell him it's not true!"

Ralph's mouth drooped open, and he avoided her glare.

Henry continued, "Could you confirm if that's how you obtained the poison?"

When Ralph didn't answer a second time, his wife slapped his chest. "Speak! Tell him it's nonsense!"

"I…" Ralph's voice wavered. He looked at Mark, whose face was almost as white as his own.

"Oh well, we don't really need you to admit it as Paul was more than willing to tell me what I needed to know. And I'm sure the Serious Fraud Office will be interested to learn how you glean people's private information." Henry eyed Mark Hardy. "Oh, I've heard back from them, by the way. They've quickly managed to track down three empty offices in the south of England. These locations were the registered company addresses of Sales Expedited's only three clients. Each one is linked to organised crime in some shape or form."

Ralph's chin quivered. He gave Mark a panicked look, then Pete, and then his wife. "I'm sorry," he said to her.

"What's he on about?" Claire's eyes teared up. "He can't be telling the truth. What have you three been up to?"

Ralph turned away from her, his hand searching his jeans pocket.

"Ralph?! Please, tell me…"

Ralph held her shoulder with one hand, while his other was hidden under his red hoodie. "I'm sorry… I did it all for William. I wanted us to have a good life. One better than I thought I could give." He waved away her many other questions and stared daggers at Henry. He then jumped up from the table, knocking his chair to the stone floor. His eyes burned with fury.

He rushed round the table towards Henry, who remained in his seat, watching him approach. Before Ralph was within a metre of him, Tom and Lee had blocked his path. The two rugby players towered over him, and each man was nearly twice as wide. Peering up at them, nearly defeated, Ralph lashed out, striking Lee's bulky bicep.

Lee winced in pain, and the metallic flicker of a blade flashed in the chandelier's dim light.

Henry hadn't expected that and, for an instant, felt he was losing control of the situation. Tom, however, grabbed the hand that held the knife and twisted it unnaturally, until the weapon clattered on the floor.

Ralph, whimpering, fell to his knees while Tom twisted his wrist further.

Claire, who had been gawping at her husband, stood up. "Please! Don't hurt him."

"He just sodding stabbed me," Lee said. His hand covered a four-inch cut on his bicep.

Tom, incensed at his friend's injury, bent Ralph's wrist until it cracked.

Ralph yelped.

Hargreaves rushed forwards. "Oi, get off him or I'll get the two officers outside to cuff you!"

Tom eyeballed her.

"You'd best let him go, lad," Henry said. "Or you'll be sitting in a cell next to him."

Tom paid no attention to Henry. His eyes were still white-hot with fury, but when his friend put a hand on his shoulder, he eventually let go of Ralph, leaving him crumpled up on the floor. Hargreaves stepped over and kicked the blade away from Ralph, sending it skidding along the flagstones. She knelt down and handcuffed his hands behind his back while explaining he was under caution.

Ralph squealed when she handled his injured wrist.

"Sorry, it can't be helped," she explained, handling him with little care.

Ralph's face was now ashen, and he scowled at the two rugby players, who had returned to their seats. Noura had given Lee a clean tissue, which he used to wipe the cut on his arm. It didn't look that deep to Henry, but it would still require stitches.

"You should get that seen to," Henry said.

"Afterwards," Lee said, breathing heavily through the pain. "I want to know who did this."

"Well, it was him. Wasn't it?" Tom said to his friend, pointing at Ralph.

"No," Henry said. "I don't believe it was."

"But he brought the poison into the house," Tom said.

"He did, aye."

"It's not possible," Claire said, her hands covering her face. "Tell me he's lying, love."

Ralph appeared too dazed to answer.

Hargreaves, standing behind him, pushed his shoulder. "Answer her."

"I want a lawyer," Ralph said.

Claire jumped out of her chair. "Would you just stop this madness, Ralph! That package…" Her eyes bugged. "I remember seeing it…" She squeaked. "Last week… I asked him about it. I saw a small white box in the baby carrier on Saturday. He said it was something from work." She held her hand over her mouth. "He did bring it. I… I saw it stuffed next to the nappies. I didn't think…" She wore an expression of confusion and hatred. "I can't…" She then flung herself at Ralph, clutching his red hoodie and slapping his face. "How could you put poison in the baby carrier?! It was right next to William's formula!"

Hargreaves waited a few moments before intervening and pulling Claire away from her husband, who was now a snivelling wreck.

"Why did you do it?!" Claire screeched. "Why did you bring poison here?"

"Because there was a plot to murder someone, wasn't there?" Henry asked, looking directly at Mark Hardy.

Chapter Forty-Six

Mark Hardy shifted in his seat. His eyes took in everyone sitting around the table, and then he lifted up the glass of water in front of him. His shaking hand caused some to spill down his blue shirt as he drank from it. He wiped his mouth and then placed the glass back on the table.

"I don't know what you're talking about," he said, coolly.

"I said you were planning to commit murder here on Saturday," Henry said.

"Murder who?" Mark asked. He coughed. "Because, as you can see, I was severely injured by this poison attack. I barely survived it. So, I will not sit here and take this slander–"

"'A privileged boy who hadn't had to work for much in his life'," Henry said. "'But he quickly found he wasn't very good at anything, apart from committing petty crimes and manipulating his friends'. Do you know who said that?"

Mark's eyes were wide with panic, but then he put on a half-amused expression.

"It was your old headmaster, Mr Jessop."

Mark's face soured.

"Mr Jessop said that to me earlier today. That's why I arrived late. Not only did I drive over to Ralph's company, but I also drove down to Barnsley to visit him at his care home. He's in his late eighties now, but his mind's still sharp, and when I mentioned your name, those are the exact words he said. Do you know what his next words were?"

Mark sneered.

"No, they weren't 'Dragon's Blood Club'," Henry said, smirking. "They were 'poor Pete Blackburn'." Henry's eyes rested on Pete, who lifted his head out of his bandaged hands. "Mr Jessop said he wished he could have done more to intervene. He said that, back then, things were different. He wanted me to apologise to you, Pete, on his behalf."

Pete's eyes glistened.

"He said he was of a different generation, and when he'd been growing up, they'd had similar issues."

"Similar what?" Tom asked.

Mark's eyes were electric with hatred.

"Fagging, he called it. But this was more than just having Pete do your chores, wasn't it, Mark? It was more extreme. Let's call it bullying and manipulation, or just plain old child abuse."

Noura frowned. "I don't understand–"

"Mark ran a secret group at their school called the 'Dragon's Blood Club'. He and his friends selected pupils in the year below to do chores for them. Well, basically become their 'slaves'. The poor buggers had to go through humiliating initiations to gain that privilege."

When Noura turned to look at Mark, Henry added, "I'm sorry to say, your late husband was in that club too, Noura."

Her hand touched her shirt collar. "Allister?"

"So was Ralph. Mark was the club's leader. Pete was the poor so-and-so who was their 'servant' in 1995, weren't you?"

Pete sniffed, keeping his eyes on his bandaged hands.

"And that 'club' has pretty much continued up until the present, hasn't it? Although now, you just claim to be friends."

Mark remained silent. As did Pete.

"So, Mark planned to kill Pete with the poison?" Tom asked, his face creased up.

"No. They were planning to murder Justin Nabwood. The police have seen your message to him, where you invited him to the barbecue. But he didn't show, did he?"

"Who's Justin Nabwood?" Lee asked, still pressing the bloody tissue against the cut on his bicep.

"Good question," Henry said. "Who is Justin Nabwood, Mark?"

Mark sneered and looked out the window. Rain continued to splatter the glass. He took a breath. "It won't change anything, will it, if I tell you? It's immaterial who Justin Nabwood is now."

"I don't think so," said Henry. "I think it's very important. You planned to lace his glass of punch with poison, that's why Ralph brought the cyanide to the barbecue."

Mark's cool evaporated, and his eyebrows shot up in alarm. Then he seemed to understand something, and he slumped back in his chair with renewed assurance. "You can't prove a thing."

Henry lifted his chin in the air. He was out of ammunition. All his bullets had been fired, and now he had nothing but blanks.

"You don't know what I've got," he said.

Mark smirked. "Then show me."

Henry's chest pounded. Everyone was watching him. They were realising he didn't have a smoking gun.

"Come on," Mark said, enjoying this. "Tell me what messages you have that link me to anything."

Henry's cheeks burned.

Hargreaves stood by the table, glaring at him. She and Henry were about to find out how bad that what-if scenario would be.

"You don't have anything," Mark said. He scoffed.

Then Henry's phone pinged with a message.

"Excuse me," he said. His phone trembled in his hand. He saw the sender's name and nearly broke into hymn. A second message came, followed by a third that contained a digital recording.

Henry took his time reading the messages. Then a smile spread across his face. "Aye, if we'd only read through your digital communication, you'd be right. I wouldn't be able to prove a thing. As you've been using disappearing messages."

Mark's eyes flashed in the dim light. They bore into the phone in Henry's hand, which pinged again with another message.

"But unluckily for you," Henry continued, "the kookaburra has been spotted in the area."

Mark's face creased with incomprehension.

Noura peered around the table. "Sorry. The what?"

"The kookaburra," Henry said. "It's a rare Australian bird. It was brought over here and kept in captivity but escaped into the wild. Somehow, it's managed to thrive in our harsh conditions. It's a beautiful bird. Looks like a large kingfisher."

Everyone in the room stared at him in utter confusion.

"Anyway." Henry cleared his throat. "Your neighbour next door is a member of my birdwatching committee–"

Hargreaves snapped, "Get to the bloody point, Henry!"

"He had microphones in his garden, which were listening out for the kookaburra's distinctive call."

The implication showed on Mark's face. His cool calm dissolved into alarm.

"It seems," Henry continued, "you and your friends had a brief conversation near your neighbour's hedge on the day of the barbecue. Can you remember it?"

Mark's face drained of blood.

"I think I've gathered the gist of it, but let's all have a listen anyway, shall we?" He played the digital recording attached to the message and turned the speaker on his phone to maximum.

Wind muffled the microphone. Footsteps could be heard on gravel, then grass, followed by the chit-chat from a group of men.

Ralph's voice asked, "So, where the fuck is the Aussie?"

"Shh." The footsteps grew louder. "I don't know," Mark's voice said. "I think she figured it out and got word to him."

"Sarah?" a third man asked.

Henry didn't recognise the voice, but Noura's gasp confirmed it was Allister's.

"How did Sarah find out?" Allister asked.

"Fuck knows," Mark said.

"We've got to sort something out soon, or the gangs will–"

"Shut it!" Mark snapped.

Some more footsteps approached.

"So…?" Pete asked.

Real-life Pete was now slumped back in his chair. His fingertips stroked his bandaged hands.

"Is he coming?" Pete's voice asked in the recording.

"You're off the hook, little Petey," Mark said. "For now. But we need to move soon, or we'll all be in the shit."

"Okay… Erm… What do I do with this?"

A gust of wind blew the microphone.

"Put it away, dickhead!" Ralph growled. "I can't take it back with me."

"The Aussie will be back at some point. When he is, you'll do it then," Mark said.

Mark Hardy's blank eyes stared down at the table.

"I still have to do it?" Pete asked in the recording.

"Of course you do. That shithead is draining our funds and causing a stink."

Mark ran a hand over his pale face as he listened to his own voice.

"And our clients are paying top dollar to avoid bad smells, and currently we fucking reek," Allister added. "With the SFO sniffing around, we need to get as much out of this mess as we can. Then close the whole thing down and pray for the best. If we're lucky, we'll keep our cash and our lives…"

Some dry leaves brushed against the microphone.

"Do you understand, Pete?" Mark asked. "Do this for us, and I swear, your bond with us is cut. It's the one last thing I ask of you."

"Really? No more requests?"

"I swear, no more."

There was some laughter in the distance. "Come on," Mark said, "let's go back over. Sarah's about to put on a show."

The recording ended abruptly, and silence descended on the table.

Mark's empty stare was trained on Henry's phone, while Pete had crumpled further into himself.

Claire stirred herself out of her shock, slipped past Hargreaves and hit Ralph's shoulder. "Is that why you brought it? Poison! To murder someone? Are you mental?!"

Hargreaves pushed her away from him.

Ralph sobbed. "It was Ben. He kept wanting more and more from us! We couldn't carry on like that. We were having to get greedier. Our clients were unhappy. And they are not the kind of people you mess with–" he sucked in a breath "–we were becoming more visible. Making more mistakes. And then the SFO started looking into us. And it was his fault – Ben's."

"Who?" Claire turned to Henry for an answer. "What's he on about? Who's Ben?"

"Sarah Hardy's brother," Henry said, "Ben Lyles. I was falsely led to believe he was her ex-husband, but that didn't turn out to be true." Henry raised an eyebrow at Pete, who seemed oblivious. "Ben had several convictions for fraud and wouldn't get a visa into the UK otherwise, so he bought a stolen passport. It seems that Sarah was planning an exit strategy to get away from her hellish husband." Henry glared at Mark, who ignored him. "Sarah had signed a prenuptial, so if she left Mark, she would have nothing to show for the chunk of her life she'd wasted with him."

"So, why did she bring Ben over?" Claire asked.

"That was her exit strategy. She'd somehow learnt the truth behind Sales Expedited and decided to get her brother over to drain funds away from Mark and his pals through blackmail." Henry looked at Pete and Ralph. "I suspect Sarah and Ben planned to siphon off as much money as they could before returning to Sydney. But something went wrong. Sarah learnt of the plot to kill her brother–"

"Who from?" Hargreaves asked.

Henry looked at the faces around the table. "I don't know." His eyes rested on Pete. "Possibly the weakest link. Perhaps, you thought you wouldn't have to go through with it, Pete, if Ben didn't turn up?"

Pete sniffed.

"The Taylors saw Ben with Sarah here on Thursday. Ben then went off and booked a flight to Sydney, unbeknown to Mark and his pals. I suspect he took the money they'd saved with him. But then Sarah's second problem occurred. She'd put all her trust into a fairly incompetent con man. The stolen passport Ben used to enter the UK had been flagged as stolen, and he was arrested at Sydney Airport on Saturday morning: the day of the barbecue."

"Australian police confirmed Ben had a quarter of a million pounds in cryptocurrency on a laptop," Hargreaves said.

Henry set his eyes on Mark. "She risked everything and brought her brother over to get cash out of you, didn't she?"

Mark shook himself out of his stupor. He snarled. "Yes, Ben came here. Yes, he knew everything about the business. Yes, she was the one who told him everything." He took a breath. "And yes, she did want to leave me. She had done for years. Why do you think she ended up shagging that ape?" He jabbed a finger towards Tom, who jumped out of his seat, readying to fight again.

"Sit back down!" Henry barked at him.

Tom scratched his nose but then did as Henry ordered. "She couldn't stand you, mate," he said to Mark. "You treated her like shit. She was an amazing lass, but you just couldn't see it."

Mark scowled at him, crossing his arms, and didn't respond.

"That's right. She couldn't stand you, could she?" Henry asked, glaring at Mark.

He didn't speak.

Tom leant forwards in his chair. "So, if Ben wasn't here, who put the poison into the salad dressing?"

"Pete," Henry said. "Can you answer that?"

They all gasped.

All eyes turned on Pete, who didn't respond.

"Alright," Henry said, "I'll tell them. Pete did it."

Tom rose out of his chair and loomed over Pete, about to bash his brains in.

"Hold it!" Henry also stood up. "Pete, can you tell us why?"

"I…" Pete was weeping so hard, he couldn't breathe. "I…"

"Get a hold of yourself, man," Henry said.

Pete sucked in haggard breath. "I… I just couldn't take it anymore. The constant belittling… the orders… the manipulation." He glowered at Mark, who now appeared unsettled. "I only intended for you three to eat it. I never thought…" He blinked. "I just couldn't suffer another day. Thirty years… My whole life, nearly. And last week, enduring the days until Saturday, when they'd all been at me, forcing me to… murder someone? I just cracked. I had the poison in my hand. It was just a white powder. Like salt. I saw the jar of oil, and I just thought… 'Sod you all'." He covered his face with his hands. "I tried not to let Louanne touch any of it when we started eating. I told her it had nuts in. She was allergic to nuts. I just… wanted a quiet life. Me and her. I loved her. I just wanted peace and quiet. Walks in the countryside." His throat made a clicking noise, and then he descended into hysterics.

Hargreaves walked round the table, handcuffed Pete, and explained he was under caution. He offered no resistance and winced as she touched his bandaged hands. She then did the same to Mark Hardy, whom she was rougher with.

Lee and Tom remained standing, watching the scene. Claire stepped forwards. "I remember seeing him… acting odd near the table." Her eyes flickered. "I wondered what he was doing but thought nothing of it. I mean… what could he have done?"

Then everyone became aware of Noura's crying. She was howling at Pete. "It was me…" she whispered. "I talked Louanne into trying that vinaigrette. She mentioned the nuts, and I promised her there weren't any in it. I said I'd made it myself. I put loads of it on her plate." She gasped. "I didn't know. I'd no idea…"

Pete stared at her, his face red and puffy. He neither cried nor said anything.

"Why didn't you touch any of it?" Henry asked Noura.

"I'm on a diet. I'm avoiding olive oil. Otherwise…" She burst into tears again.

A moment passed between them. A police radio beeped in the hallway, where PCs Watkins and Smith were ready to take the three men away.

Stirring himself out of his thoughts, Tom asked, "Wait a minute? What happened to Sarah? She never touched the salad dressing. She didn't eat anything."

Henry turned to the glass doors. The rain pelted the patio, and – through the railings – Henry could just make out the top of the drystone wall at the bottom of the garden. "Unfortunately, that still remains a mystery."

Chapter Forty-Seven

The following day was a sunny one, making up for the washout they'd had the day before. Henry was sitting in his foldable outdoor armchair. His head was nestled against the cushion, and the birdwatching book was open on his lap. Tessa was curled up next to his feet, fast asleep. That morning, they had been for a long hike along the River Wharfe between Addingham and Bolton Abbey, and now she was shattered.

As he had been strolling along the river that morning, watching the ripples on the surface of the water as brown trout sucked up mayflies, he'd kept an eye out for the kookaburra. There was an unverified report it'd been spotted in Skipton, but Henry hadn't seen it. Maybe the harsh climate in Wharfedale was too much for Antipodean creatures.

He imagined himself spending the rest of his day down by the river, sitting in his camping chair under the shade of a wilting willow tree. His plan had been to head back home, have a quick lunch, and then come back with his fishing rod.

Yet here he still was, in his backyard. Half-asleep. With one side of his face hotter than the other, and probably redder too. After lunch, he had seen the local newspaper on his doormat. He suspected Jean had posted it through his letter box, as he hadn't asked for it.

The front-page headline read:

Mystery at Cragg Hall Solved!

He hadn't read the article in full and instead had done his best to expel the details of the case from his mind. He didn't want to think about the secret club Mark Hardy had run, nor the fraudulent business he and his friends were managing. Nor did he want to think about Pete Blackburn who, after years of being forced to do things he didn't want to do, had finally snapped when ordered to murder Sarah's brother.

A faint wind blew across his face and turned the pages in the book on his lap. Tessa kicked out her back leg. Her eyes were closed, and she grumbled. Henry suspected she was chasing imaginary hares again.

"Well, good grief, look at you two!"

Henry started and raised his head. His eyes scanned his backyard, but nobody was there.

"You really do look a pair." It was Jean's voice.

Henry fixed his eyes on the fence between their two properties and saw her peeping through a hole.

"Oh, you're back from Cambridge," he said.

"Aye, only just got in."

Henry scratched the back of his neck. "Oh? You didn't drop by earlier with a newspaper?"

"A paper? Have you been daydreaming?"

Henry rubbed his eyes. "I don't think so."

"Are you coming over for a brew?" she asked, stepping away from the fence.

"Aye, I'll come right over," he said, getting out of his chair.

He left Tessa where she was and went into his kitchen. He picked up the newspaper that he had found on his doormat and skimmed the front-page article. His name wasn't mentioned, but DS Hargreaves and Detective Superintendent Murphy were quoted several times. There was even a picture of Murphy in his full uniform, standing at a lectern, giving a press conference.

"Well, I suppose I didn't do it for the glory," Henry said to himself. "But a thanks wouldn't go amiss."

He opened the paper to look inside. A handwritten note fell out between the pages, and Henry picked it up.

> *Maybe I spoke too soon, and Leeds United do have a chance. I've waved my magic wand, and your list of demands have been actioned. We've got you covered on this Curtis Quaker's legal case. The SFO have enough linking him to that dodgy business to put him inside, so winding you up will be the least of his worries. As for your third request, it'll take some doing, but most of the brass are now convinced, so it'll be confirmed next week.*
> *I'll be in touch with a cold case soon after.*
> *Murphy*

Henry grinned. He'd been certain his third request would be struck down. Murphy had probably been too elated at the positive press from the Cragg Hall case to see how it might cause him problems down the line. Typical Murphy.

So, Henry would be an official cold case investigator. He wondered if he'd get a badge. At least some ID. How else could he present himself to witnesses and suspects? He would also get a small salary, as other officers in the same boat did. Unless Murphy had stiffed him out of one.

The knock on the door stirred him out of his thoughts, and he rushed through his living room to answer. Jean couldn't be that desperate for a cup of tea, could she? DI Barnes was standing on his doorstep. She wasn't wearing her grey suit but a light red sweatshirt and jeans. Henry had never seen her in casual clothes before.

She cringed slightly upon making eye contact. "Hello, Henry."

"Hi," he replied. "Do you want to come–"

"No. I'm not staying." She rubbed her hands together despite it being warm. "I just wanted to apologise for what happened over the weekend, and to make it clear it was my decision to go to Roy Parker. It wasn't anyone else's."

"You mean like DCI Acton?"

"He didn't know a thing about it."

"Why did you do it? I still don't get it. I thought we got on, you and me."

"We did. It's just… I don't know. It seemed like the only good tactic at the time. I wanted to pressure Murphy into going… I thought that if he got enough negative press–"

"What's going to happen to you?" Henry asked.

"I struck a deal with Murphy."

"He really must be in a good mood this morning. What's this deal of his, then?"

"I'm heading back down south. I get to keep my job and everything, and he'll help me find a position near my hometown in Kent."

"That's merciful of him."

She glanced at the facade of Henry's cottage. "I'll miss Yorkshire, but it's time for me to move on."

Henry nodded. "Well… I'll miss 'working' with you if I can call it that."

She smiled. "Me too."

Henry offered her his hand to shake, but instead she stepped closer and hugged him. He froze awkwardly, as he hadn't been embraced for a while. Seemingly sensing his embarrassment, she stepped away, her face nearly as red as her jumper. "Well, take care, Henry."

"You too, Kate."

When she had reached the gate, Henry asked, "Hang on a minute."

She stopped and turned to him.

"Whatever did happen to Sarah Hardy?" he asked. "I've been racking my brains… and still haven't worked it out."

She squinted at him in the bright sunlight. "Didn't you hear?"

"No."

"Oh. We all thought you and Dr Anderson talked–"

"What is it?"

"The toxicology results came back this morning. She died from an overdose: a mixture of Xanax and Tramadol. Their effects on the body can be similar to cyanide poisoning, that's why Dr Anderson was confused. But we found three empty packets of pills under the sink in her bathroom. She must have taken them before the party started, knowing full well that she would collapse halfway through it."

"Christ." Henry took a moment to picture what could have happened if Sarah's plan hadn't been overshadowed by the other poisonings. "Remind me never to go to a barbecue again. Do we know why she did it?"

Barnes nodded. Her eyes took in Main Street, presumably to make sure nobody was in earshot. "I got access to the bank account in Justin Nabwood's name. It was emptied on the day of the barbecue, and we believe Sarah had access to it. She must have seen all the money had gone and that her brother had deserted her…"

Henry sighed.

Barnes gazed down the street. "I suppose, she felt like it was the only option available to her. To go out with a bang." She caught herself looking too wistful. "Bear in mind that I didn't tell you any of that."

"Of course not, Detective Inspector."

She glanced up at his cottage one last time. "I remember the first time I came here, back when you found that body at the top of Addingham. I threatened to lock you up for interfering back then." She half-laughed. "Nothing's changed much."

Henry chuckled. "It wouldn't have stopped me if you had arrested me. It would only have wound me up even more."

She smiled and was about to say something else, but stopped herself. "Well. Bye, Henry." She walked along the pavement and got into her car.

Henry watched her start the engine before considering what she had said about Sarah. So, that was the last piece of the puzzle. Sarah Hardy, a woman who felt like she was out of options, had done something reckless and destructive as a way of wrenching her fate out of the hands of others.

Jean's front door opened, and she poked her head round the corner. "Are you coming over? Your tea's stewing."

Henry nodded but failed to hide his sadness.

"Are you alright?" Jean asked. "You look like you've had bad news."

"No. It's not that. I'm just no good at goodbyes."

"What do you mean?"

Henry watched Barnes's car drive down Main Street and disappear round the corner.

"Anyway." Jean tapped his shoulder to get his attention. "Did you hear that strange bird in my back garden just now? It made an almighty racket."

Henry furrowed his brow. "No. It didn't sound like a cartoon character laughing by any chance?"

She nodded. "Aye, it did, come to think of it. I'm surprised you couldn't hear it out here. It was perched on top of our fence and then flew over your garden. It was a strange-looking bird. Any idea what it was?"

Henry struggled to get his words out. "You must be bloody joking!"

The End

If you enjoyed this book, please let others know by leaving a quick review on Amazon. Also, if you spot anything untoward in the paperback, get in touch. We strive for the best quality and appreciate reader feedback.

editor@thebookfolks.com

www.thebookfolks.com

Also in this series

MURDER ON A YORKSHIRE MOOR (Book 1)

Ex-detective Henry Ward is settling awkwardly into retirement in a quiet corner of Yorkshire when during a walk on the moor he stumbles upon the body of a young man. Suspecting foul play and somewhat relishing the return to a bit of detective work, he resolves to find out who killed him. But will the local force appreciate him sticking his nose in?

BUTCHER ON THE MOOR (Book 2)

Ex-DCI Henry Ward is woken in the middle of the night when a distressed woman calls him, demanding he arrest her son. After reluctantly heading over to her house, he makes a gruesome discovery before being attacked. With the police stretched, they reluctantly lean on Ward's local knowledge to track down a man with blood on his hands.

MISSING ON ILKLEY MOOR (Book 3)

Retired cop Henry Ward is taking a walk on the Yorkshire moors when he comes across a child's woolly hat. He quickly connects it with the apparent abduction of an eight-year-old girl from a local town. But when the child's mother acts like she doesn't care, he realises something is seriously wrong and takes it upon himself to investigate.

DETECTIVE ON THE MOOR (Book 4)

Henry Ward is considering rejoining the police when he is asked to investigate a lockdown party murder. A well-to-do local woman's son has been accused of the crime and she wants to clear the family's name. But when Henry starts private inquiries, he meets a wall of silence and will need to use all of his skills to get to the truth.

COLD CASE ON THE MOOR (Book 5)

An unusual spell of hot weather reveals a dark secret on the Yorkshire moors. A woman's body is found in a dried-up reservoir. When the police work out her identity, it brings the past flooding back for ex-detective Henry Ward. He was in charge of the investigation into her disappearance many years ago. Now he is more determined than ever to find her killer.

SHOOTER ON THE MOOR (Book 6)

A sleepy Yorkshire village has a rude awakening when a jogger is shot dead on the surrounding moorland. Local retired cop Henry Ward heads to the scene and meets some of his former colleagues, who agree to him doing some detective work on the side. Ward is soon on the trail of the murder gun, but is he ready to face down the person holding it?

All FREE with Kindle Unlimited and available in paperback!

THE MEEK SHALL INHERIT
by John Dean

Usually the police are called after a murder, rarely are they notified in advance. Yet an elderly couple are convinced that when their nephew is released from prison, he'll come after them again. Twenty years ago, he attacked them over his inheritance. This time, he'll want revenge. Can DCI John Blizzard stop the apparently inevitable?

FREE with Kindle Unlimited and available in paperback!

CRIMES OF THE FALLEN
by James Andrew

When DI John Belivat is called to the scene of a murdered woman, left naked on the seafront of a Scottish town, it brings back all his fears about the fate of his own missing daughter. He focuses on the victim, trying to establish her identity. But only after another body is found will the detective be able to piece together a motive and find a killer.

FREE with Kindle Unlimited and available in paperback!

Printed in Dunstable, United Kingdom

68488661R00153